· SHARON E. McKAY ·

THUNDER
over
KANDAHAR

Photographs by

RAFAL GERSZAK

annick press
toronto + new york + vancouver

We acknowledge the support of the Canada Council for the Arts, the Ontario
Arts Council, and the Government of Canada through the Canada Book Fund
(CBF) for our publishing activities.

ONTARIO ARTS COUNCIL
CONSEIL DES ARTS DE L'ONTARIO

Cataloging in Publication

McKay, Sharon E.
    Thunder over Kandahar / Sharon E. McKay ; photographs by Rafal Gerszak.

ISBN 978-1-55451-266-9 (pbk.). — ISBN 978-1-55451-267-6 (bound)

    1. Afghan War, 2001- —Juvenile fiction. I. Gerszak, Rafal II. Title.

PS8575.K2898T58 2010   jC813'.54   C2010-903311-6

Distributed in Canada by: Published in the U.S.A. by:
Firefly Books Ltd.   Annick Press (U.S.) Ltd.
66 Leek Crescent   Distributed in the U.S.A. by:
Richmond Hill, ON   Firefly Books (U.S.) Inc.
L4B 1H1   P.O. Box 1338
                                 Ellicott Station, Buffalo, NY 14205

The songs "Afghan People" and "The Book," both Dari songs, can be found
in the book edited by Louise M. Pascale, *Children's Songs from Afghanistan:
Qu Qu Qu Barg-e-Chinaar* (Washington, D.C.: National Geographic,
English edition, 2008).

The quote from Abdu'l-Baha'i cited in the epigraph is from *The Promulgation
of Universal Peace: Talks delivered by Abdu'l-Baha'i during his Visit to the United
States and Canada in 1919* (Wilmette, Ill.: Baha'i Pub. Trust, 1982).

Front cover: helicopters by Rafal Gerszak; woman in burka and smoke
© iStockphoto Inc./Lori Martin and ©iStockphoto Inc./Stephen Strathdee

Visit us at: www.annickpress.com
Visit Sharon E. McKay at: www.sharonmckay.ca
Visit Rafal Gerszak at: www.gerszak.com

To the women of Canadians in Support of
Afghan Women (CSAW).
Your commitment and ongoing tireless effort
to better the lives of women and girls in
Afghanistan will not be dismissed or forgotten.
Most especially, Liz Watson, Linda Middaugh,
Bev LeFrançois, and Christine Vasilaros.

The world of humanity is possessed of two wings:
the male and the female. So long as these two wings
are not equivalent in strength, the bird will not fly . . .

—Abdu'l-Baha'i

• • •

We are Afghan people
We are Afghans of the mountains

We have one stance and one way
We have one faith and one hope

We are Afghan people
We are Afghans of the mountains.

—Popular children's song,
originally in Dari

Yasmine

Herat, Afghanistan

"Come, put on your scarf. We will walk through the park to the university, meet your father, and buy ice cream—chocolate, your favorite."

Smiling, Mother held Yasmine's *hijab* between two pinched fingers and made it dance. It was gray and ugly. Well, maybe it wasn't actually ugly, maybe it was really quite nice, but Yasmine looked away anyway.

"I don't want to go out." Yasmine spoke softly. She meant no disrespect, it was just that going outside meant being careful about where she looked, whom she spoke to, what she said, what she wore. It was exhausting . . . and boring.

Yasmine sat on the floor on a big pillow with a book opened in front of her. Getting used to the furniture in this new place had been hard, too, although one low, brass-topped table and a bunch of pillows could hardly be called furniture. They had lived in Herat for almost a year now—ten months, to be really accurate—and Herat, Afghanistan, was a long way from Oxford, England. It was like living on Mars—assuming that there were camels on Mars, and goats, and land mines.

Mother put aside the headscarf and sat beside Yasmine. "I know these past months have been hard on you, but look at all you have accomplished. You speak Dari well now, and your teacher says that you are the best student in the class."

Yasmine shook her head. It was easy being head of the class. Half of the girls could barely read, and every week one or two left school to get married. Married! At fourteen!

"I want to go home," she whispered.

"Yasmine, *this* is our home."

Yasmine looked up past Mother's shoulder to the window—a window that looked nowhere. All the windows in the house Baba had rented either faced a wall or were covered up. Mother said that during Taliban times the windows in homes were blackened or covered to prevent strangers from seeing the women inside, and when the Taliban left the window coverings had stayed, *just in case*. In case of what? Baba said that the Taliban had been beaten by the United Nations forces, but at school they said that the Taliban had only retreated, they were never far away. Which was true? Really, how could this place ever be home? "You will come to love this country, you'll see. And you should be very proud of Baba for deciding to come back here to teach. Your father is an important man in the West, but here is where he can do the most good. And soon I will go to work, too. There are not many women lawyers in Afghanistan."

"But we were all happy at ho . . . in England. And I miss Grandfather," said Yasmine.

"Your grandfather understands why we are here. I was born in this city. Herat is a city of writers and poets. Come now, the flowers are in bloom and the cypress trees—they are so beautiful, emerald green. Wait until they turn as red as fire. Imagine, trees so brilliant that they almost light the way! We will be happy here, you'll see." Exasperation was creeping into Mother's voice. She handed Yasmine the headscarf and picked up her bag and house keys.

Yasmine tied the *hijab* under her chin, careful that it hid all her hair. She did not wear headscarves all the time in England. Thing was, she didn't mind wearing a *hijab* in England because she didn't have to. That made *all* the difference.

Trailing behind her mother, Yasmine walked from the back of the house, which was the family area, to the formal sitting room at the front, the one reserved for guests. The house had four rooms and a courtyard. It might have been nice, had the bricks on the outside walls facing the street not been damaged and repaired and then damaged all over again. Yasmine knew the history of Afghanistan, Baba had explained it over and over. First the Russians had invaded. *Mujahideen* guerrillas, Afghans, fought the Russians. Then the Russians left and the warlords fought each other. And then came the Taliban times, and now the United Nations forces were here to fight the Taliban. With so much war, it was sometimes amazing to think that any buildings still stood, or that any people were still alive!

Never mind the condition of the outside of the house, the inside was pretty rough too. There was no air conditioning or central heating inside. They had already lived through one freezing winter. Mother had bought lots of nice Afghan rugs, and they had plenty of blankets, but nothing could make this house as wonderful as home—and England was home, no matter what Mother said.

In Oxford their flat was cool in summer and warm in winter, and they had huge windows that looked out across a city crowded with church spires, brick chimneys, and stone buildings. Rain or shine (mostly rain) Yasmine would stare out the windows to the streets below. You couldn't actually see the pastry and flower shops, clothing stores, coffee houses, libraries, and movie theaters, but they were there! Inside, bookcases reached the ceiling. Some books were written in foreign script, Dari mostly, while others were writers she too was beginning to read; Twain, Waugh, Tolstoy, Kipling, Donne, Wiesel. Plump sofas and overstuffed chairs cozied up every corner, and Mother always put tall, fresh-cut flowers in a giant vase in Baba's study. Best of all, Yasmine had her own room, with a canopy bed, and her own television, too. Here in Herat she was supposed to sleep on a big mattress stuffed with cotton—on the floor!

Mother smiled again as she locked the courtyard door behind them. "I love the park."

Yasmine nodded half-heartedly. They had been to the park many times, and it wasn't that great, not like the parks in England. Why didn't Mother see it?

The sidewalk along Jada-e welayat was made of colorful tiles. It might have been amazing a long time ago, but now it was dirty, and the tiles were damaged and chipped. Mother said that the city of Herat was beautiful, but there was garbage in the streets, and lots of the nice old stone buildings were being replaced with great big ugly glass-and-metal ones. Many of the shops were boarded up or covered with corrugated tin or chain-link fence. Behind the main streets was a labyrinth of laneways and homes hidden behind mud walls. They passed *Toos*, Yasmine's favorite restaurant. At least they had pizza on the menu there.

Old men sat in groups, on blankets or in plastic chairs, many holding small children in their arms. Boys trailed women in *burkas*, their feet dragging in the dust. When the Taliban were in control of everything, a woman could not go out of the house without a *maharam*, a male to walk with her. It wasn't like that anymore, but still, most women on the street were accompanied by men or boys. And in Taliban times, all women had been forced to wear *burkas* outside the house. Many women still wore the long gown that covered every inch of them, even their faces. To Yasmine, it just looked ugly. And it was hard to imagine that there was a real woman under there. They looked like shadows that could be blown away by the wind. Seeing the way they moved, heads held unnaturally high and swiveling from side to side because they had no peripheral vision, made Yasmine shudder.

A woman in a *burka* was coming towards them. The lump under her *burka* wiggled. Yasmine guessed that she was holding a baby in one hand and her shopping bags in the other. The *burka* covered everything, like a tent, but her head was bent and she was shuffling.

"Why is she moving like that?" Yasmine whispered.

"It's best if the grille is pulled tight against the face. That way a woman wearing a *burka* can see more. But her hands are busy so she is looking down, trying to see the ground instead." Mother spoke in a low, controlled voice.

Yasmine turned away. It seemed rude to stare, even if the woman couldn't tell. One thing was for sure, she would never wear one, ever. The clothes she and her mother had to wear were bad enough—plain black skirts that fell below their knees, trousers underneath, and long jackets over white blouses that buttoned to the neck. It was hot out, and they were dressed for winter . . . well, fall, anyway.

"See, the sun is out. It's not really that bad, is it?" Mother looked at Yasmine and smiled. It was a thin, pleading smile. Even dressed in dull clothes, Mother was beautiful, with almond-shaped, jewel-green eyes like her own, a high forehead and cheekbones. To Yasmine, Mother was the most beautiful woman in the world. Daughters know such things about their mothers.

"Careful." Mother reached for Yasmine's hand at the corner of the street. Yasmine was fourteen years old, too old to hold her mother's hand. But then, crossing the street in Herat was different from crossing the street in Oxford. For one thing, the crossing lights here only occasionally worked, and anyway, the cars didn't always stop. Both of them looked right and left and right and left, and then made a run for it.

A balloon-seller stood a short distance from the giant iron gates of the park. The colors of the balloons reminded Yasmine of home: lemon-yellow like the daffodils that grew in Mrs. Asquith's garden, red like the pillar box on the corner of their street, cobalt-blue like the English sky after rain.

Mother reached into her purse and handed the balloon-seller a few Afghani.

"Mother, I am too old for balloons." In England she would have felt silly but in Afghanistan, it was worse. Here a fourteen-year-old was considered a grown woman. If anyone from her class saw her—not that that was likely—she would *really* look silly.

"One each, please. I'll take a green one, the color of a bride's dress." Mother, smiling now, whispered into Yasmine's ear, "Pick one. Perhaps we are his first sale of the day." Yasmine chose a yellow balloon and tried not to think of daffodils.

They stood at the gates of the park and looked in. The paths were covered with white and gray pebbles and bordered by pink, yellow, and white flowers. But some of the plants looked like scrub, as though they didn't get enough water. Up ahead was a pond.

"My cousins and I used to float little white paper boats in that pond. The water was so sparkly. One year my uncle brought remote-control boats from India and we raced them across the water. My cousin's boat sank. He was so upset he jumped into the pond to retrieve it." Mother laughed as her eyes misted up.

Yasmine glanced at Mother, then looked back at the pond, trying to see what her mother saw. Instead she thought of Christ Church Meadow and the boat races on the Thames during Oxford's university term.

"After, we would drink sweet tea sprinkled with sugar and cardamom," said Mother.

They walked on, Mother chatting on about people who were gone now, some to America, most killed by the Russians or the Taliban.

"Do you remember the song I sang to you when you were little? *I'm a friend of children. I am beautiful and eloquent. I have lots of words hidden in my heart.*" Mother whispered the words in her ear.

Yasmine tried not to shrug. To shrug here was considered very rude.

"You remember the words, Yasmine. *Open my heart, open my treasure house, so I can tell you my secrets. Tell you a hundred stories.*" Mother sang in a soft, lilting voice.

"Mother, I am too old to sing baby songs." Really, this was too silly.

"*Open my heart, open my treasure house, so I can tell you my secrets. Tell you a hundred stories,*" Mother sang again.

The corners of Yasmine's mouth turned up.

"Ah! Do I see a smile?" Mother asked.

Yasmine couldn't help herself, she grinned.

"There it is!" Mother was laughing, but Yasmine's grin

was really more of an embarrassed grimace. Maybe she could pretend that she was little again and they were at Oxford's Botanic Garden, just off the High Street. *"I'm a friend of children. I am beautiful and eloquent. I have lots of words hidden in my heart."* Mother's words were little more than whispers floating in the air, but still people turned their heads, some of them scowling.

"Shush, Mother!" This time Yasmine giggled.

They were coming to the tall, majestic gates at the other side of the park. As they passed through them and onto the road, Yasmine had to admit that perhaps once, a long time ago, they must have been really amazing. The two walked along the sidewalk, shaggy bushes to one side, a busy boulevard to the other.

"I'll tell you sweet stories, ancient wisdom. Tell you tales and—"

"Mother, stop!" This time Yasmine laughed out loud.

A truck pulled up beside them, its wheels squealing like little animals caught in a trap.

"I'm a friend of children. I am beautiful and eloquent. I have lots of words hidden in my heart . . ."

Feet pummeled the ground. Yasmine turned. Men in black turbans, with black *surma* smeared around their eyes, piled out of the back of a truck. They carried sticks, chains, and clubs, all raised up in the air. They were running towards them.

"Mother!" Yasmine cried as her hand slipped from Mother's grasp. No, her hand had not slipped away, Mother had pushed her away, pushed her so hard that she tumbled into the prickly sweetbriar shrubs along the sidewalk.

"Hide, hide!" Mother waved her off while running back into the park, as if to draw them away from Yasmine. She did not get far.

"Mother!" Yasmine screamed.

They had surrounded her. Mother fell to the ground and covered her head with her arms. The whacks on her back sounded like rice bags being dropped from a great height. *Thud, thud, thud.*

"You, the daughter of America, don't you know our laws? You dress with no respect. Don't you know that a woman cannot go out without a man?" they yelled.

"Mother, Mother! Stop! Don't hurt my mother! Stop!"

Yasmine scrambled out of the bushes. She lifted her fists and beat at a man wearing baggy pants. He hurled her back into the thorny bushes, as if she were nothing, a piece of paper, litter. Yasmine reeled backwards, smacking her head hard on the ground. She lay face up, surrounded by white and yellow flowers, in stunned silence. A green and a yellow balloon drifted up into a clear blue sky. Finally she heard the crunch and pings of spraying stones under tires as the truck pulled away.

Chapter 2

Home Again

"Wake up, Mother, wake up." Yasmine rolled over and crawled towards her mother on hands and knees. She whispered into her mother's ear. Mother, curled on the ground, lay still.

People came to help. They made calls on cell phones. A man wanted to lift Mother up into a car but he was afraid to touch a woman who was not his wife. "They are everywhere, the Taliban. The *khariji* soldiers, the foreigners, think that they have beaten the Taliban, but they return like waves in

11

the sea." Distraught, the man helped by flagging down a pickup truck. The driver agreed to take mother and daughter to the hospital. Three women lifted Mother up and into the back of the truck.

"Come, girl." A woman opened her arms and hoisted Yasmine into the truck. "Do not cry. Be brave."

Yasmine lay down beside her mother on the floor of the truck and whispered into her ear, "Mother, wake up. Wake up, Mother."

The truck stopped in front of a gray, cinder block structure. Bullets had strafed the building and the windows were either broken or boarded up. No, this wasn't right. This was not a hospital. Yasmine knew what a hospital was like. She had been to one back home, after hurting her wrist while playing field hockey. There were supposed to be attendants that helped people out of cars and ambulances, but here there were only dirty little boys standing by a door. They tried to pull Mother out of the truck as if she were a sack of apples. Mother slipped out of their grasp and slammed down onto the ground. Together they shifted Mother onto a gurney and then rolled her through swinging doors, only to lower her down onto a thin rug on the floor in a hallway.

Yasmine kissed Mother's cheeks while trying to straighten her own *hijab*. Where were the nurses with uniforms and clipboards, pushing little trolleys filled with medicines? And hospitals were supposed to be clean. This place smelled of cigarette smoke and dirt.

"Help my mother!" she cried to a woman in a *burka*.

The voice from under the veil said, "You must wait your turn."

"Please, I need to telephone my father."

The woman pointed to an old phone that hung on the wall. Yasmine called the university. The man who answered said that he would pass on the message, but really, the professor should not be disturbed.

"Please, please," Yasmine begged. "It's very important! Tell him that, that we were . . ." She dithered while wiping her face with the back of her hand. What to say? How to describe what happened? "Tell him that we are at the hospital. Please, please!"

Yasmine sat close to her mother and pulled her knees to her chest. Despite the heat of the day the building was humid, and the rug covering the cement floor did nothing to keep the damp away. "*Mother wake up, wake up. Baba come, Baba come, Baba come,*" she repeated over and over and over. What if Baba did not come? What if Mother died? What happened to girls who were left all alone?

"*Baba come, Baba come, Baba come.*" Yasmine closed her eyes.

There was no way to tell the time, but after a while she heard a sound, something familiar, that made her look up. "Baba!" Yasmine leaped to her feet. She saw her father running towards her along a cement walkway under stone arches. "Baba, Baba!" she screamed as she raced towards him, arms outstretched.

She could hear his labored breathing as he grew closer. "Are you hurt? What happened?" Baba asked while touching her arms, as if trying to reach in and feel her bones.

Yasmine shook her aching head. "Men came, in a truck, with clubs. They attacked Mother!"

He grabbed hold of her hand and she led him quickly back to where her mother lay.

Baba knelt down and whispered into Mother's ear, but still she did not wake up. As soon as he saw someone who looked like a doctor, he took paper money out of his pocket. "Help my wife," he said, trying to force it into the doctor's hands. The doctor just shook his head. He tried another doctor, but got the same response. Yasmine stood at his side. Baba was holding her hand too tightly. His face glistened with sweat. He was tall and strong, but now he looked different, he looked frightened!

Finally, one doctor, his face pale and gaunt, took Baba aside to a corner and spoke quietly, his head bent forward.

"Never mind who's running the government now, doctors are still being watched," he explained. "Male doctors do not want to take the chance of attending a woman, and the only woman doctor in Herat has been forbidden to work by her husband. By looking at your wife, I think that her back is not broken but her left leg is, in two places, maybe three. Take these. It is *mosaken*. It will reduce the pain." He slipped Baba some pain pills.

It was going to take days to have Mother's leg put in a cast, so instead a brace was found for her leg. The leg would at least be immobilized. And when Baba was sure the hospital had given Mother all the help she was going to receive, he hired a foreign car to take them home. Mother was awake when Baba lifted her into the car. She moaned in pain.

〜❦〜

As the automobile pulled up to the front of their house, they saw a small, nervous man pacing up and down the walkway. He looked at Baba and nodded. Baba carried Mother into the house and laid her on a mattress. He placed long pillows, *toshaks,* around her as bolsters.

"Stay with your mother, Yasmine." Baba left them.

Only then did Yasmine start to cry, and only then did Mother speak.

"Hush, Yasmine, my daughter. I am alive, and you and your father are safe. That's all that is important." But the sound that came out of Mother was not like her voice. It was low and rough, as if her words were dragged over stones. Yasmine lay beside her mother, buried her face in the pillow, and tried to muffle her sobs.

"Yasmine, I want to speak to you." Baba stood in the doorway now.

Again, Yasmine wiped her face with the back of her hand, tucked a loose strand of hair into her headscarf, and followed Baba out into the first room, the one that was reserved for guests.

"This is Professor Maywand," said Baba.

Yasmine nodded her head in acknowledgment.

"I hear that you speak English." The professor spoke gently to her.

At first Yasmine did not look up. She had learned a lot in a year. Do not meet a man's gaze. Do not be alone with a boy who is not a relative. Do not let any skin show. There were many *do nots.* Mother was teaching her what was *halal,* or correct for Muslims, and what was *haraam,* or unacceptable, but it was complicated. But inside she was still a

British girl, still the girl who could walk to school by herself, play sports, and draw and read whatever she wanted.

"Yes, I speak English." Yasmine deliberately raised her head and looked the man in the eye.

"Then I will speak English to you. It is good that I practice. I am very sad to hear that your mother was attacked." He spoke slowly, enunciating every word. "We want to know if the attack was deliberate or random. What were you doing just before it happened?"

Yasmine, shaking, throat dry, could not think of what to say, so she repeated the words of the song, "*I'm a friend of children. I am beautiful . . .*" The thought was sudden. Was it because they were singing? Were they at fault?

"You were singing?"

Yasmine nodded. Why did she feel ashamed? They had done nothing wrong.

The professor's expression changed as he ran his hands through his hair and looked up at the ceiling.

"Your wife should not have called attention to herself that way," he said to Baba. "Herat is not as dangerous as Kandahar City, but things happen. You should have warned her."

Startled, Yasmine looked at Baba. It wasn't his fault!

"Go back to your mother, Yasmine," said Baba with quiet resignation.

Yasmine dithered. At home she would have spoken up. She would have said something, defended her father, become angry . . . but here things were different. It was hard to know what to do. Silently, part angry and part frightened, she left the room, and returned to her mother.

The medication was working. Mother was asleep. Yasmine sat beside her and listened to the words of the men in the next room. It was hard not to hear. Wooden doors did not divide the rooms the way they did at home. Instead, beautiful curtains and long rugs hung in the doorways. Words drifted past unimpeded.

"If the attack was random," said Professor Maywand, "then perhaps there is no cause for real alarm. But there are other issues. There have been complaints at the university about the lectures you give in your World Religions course. Is it true that you have said in your classroom that Christians, Jews, and Muslims are all connected through Abraham?"

"Abraham is recognized as patriarch and prophet by all three religions," said Baba, with a hint of stubbornness.

"And did you say that one day, in the far future, this *fact*, as you call it, might unite us all?" The man sounded tired.

Yasmine went to the doorway and stood behind the curtain.

"Do we all not want universal peace? Is that not what we strive for? It is a university, a place for discussion." Baba sounded indignant now.

"Here, today, discussion can kill, my friend. We are living in a dark time. We suffered through many years of Russian occupation, and then came chaos and fighting between warlords, each with their private armies. But how could we know that the worst was yet to come? We thought the Taliban, ruling in the name of Allah, would bring us stability." The professor stopped talking for a moment. Yasmine crept closer to the curtain. "You and your wife have been very naive. Your naiveté puts you in danger, and it puts your colleagues at the university in danger, too. Please, take a leave of absence and let this settle."

Baba started to protest, but the professor began again.

"You have given up a great deal to come here—I understand and appreciate that—and your name brings great prestige to our university. Your intentions are good, but you are of no use to us if you are dead. They say that the Taliban have been defeated, but, as you have just discovered, they reemerge at will. I think this conflict is a long way from being over."

There was silence again. Perhaps Father was letting the advice sink in.

"Kam Air flies directly to Kabul," the professor went on. "From there you can take a commercial flight back to London. When the country is more stable, we will welcome your return. My friend," he said sadly, "dying is easy in this country, it is staying alive that is hard."

Yasmine crawled back beside her mother. "Mother, wake up. Mother, we are going home!" she whispered. Was it wrong to feel happy? She closed her eyes and slept.

Chapter 3

Call Back to the Land

Baba hired an old woman to come and nurse Mother. Over the next month Mother improved, but still she could only stand on wooden crutches for short periods.

Baba said that Yasmine should not go to school anymore. If the attack on Mother was not just random, then it would be best, he thought, if they were seen in public as little as possible. And so, the three of them were confined to their four rooms.

19

At first it was fine, but after three weeks it was not fine, it was lonely. And worse, a change had come over Baba. He was distracted and nervous, had stopped reading, and at night he paced the floor. Baba simply wasn't Baba. For one thing, he had grown a beard and wore baggy clothes and a turban. Mother teased him and said that he would never get on a plane dressed like that. "You look like a Talib," she said. Baba did not think that was very funny, but it was the first time Mother had laughed since the attack, so he laughed too. Yasmine did not laugh. If he could not get on a plane, how would they get home?

"What are you drawing?" he asked Yasmine one day.

She held up a picture of her best friend, Melissa. Her Third Form art teacher in Oxford had said that she had a gift for portraits.

Baba sighed. "My dear, if we are to survive we must make changes. You must not draw faces. It is frowned on," he said. He went through her sketchbooks and pulled out portraits. "I must keep you and your mother safe. And perhaps we should rethink some of these books." Baba pulled out all the copies of the *Children's Companion* magazines that they had brought from London. "They are too Christian," he explained. And so another reminder of Yasmine's old life was gone.

Weeks passed, and still there was no talk around the house about leaving Herat. Yasmine just had to know. The day came when her mother's leg was not so sore and she was feeling a bit better. Yasmine crouched down beside her and asked, in a shy whisper, "Mother, will we go home soon?"

Startled, Mother looked at her daughter. "What do you mean?"

"I thought . . ." Something inside her fell.

"Come. Sit." Mother patted the pillow beside her. "What happened was terrible, awful, but what would it say about us if we ran away?"

Yasmine couldn't believe her ears. Why would they stay where they could be attacked and beaten just for singing a children's song? How could staying possibly make sense?

"But the professor said . . ." Yasmine tried to keep her voice from breaking.

"Professor Maywand said that your father has made enemies, and that by staying at the university he is putting other people in danger, too." Mother paused. "Do you remember how it was that your father came to England?"

Yasmine nodded. "Baba's mother and older sisters were killed by a Russian bomb. Grandfather took Baba to England when he was ten years old. Grandfather sent Baba to a good school. Baba worked hard," said Yasmine. She had heard that story a million times.

Mother nodded. "We love England and we were happy there, but your father felt a *call back to the land*. It's a feeling many Afghans who live outside our country have. I feel it too. Do you remember the poem written by Khalili? '. . . But all the friends gather in the *khak*'s heart in the end / So in death as in life we are always in the company of friends,'" quoted Mother. "We belong here, Yasmine. To run away would be cowardly. If we want our country back we have to fight for it. The Westerners cannot do it for us. Do you understand?"

"Are we going to stay here?" Yasmine tried to keep her voice level.

"Grandfather has a house in Bazaar-E-Panjwayi, in Panjwayi District, Kandahar," said Mother.

"But the man, Professor Maywand, said that Kandahar was very dangerous." Yasmine could hardly believe what she was hearing.

"Kandahar City is dangerous, but we are going to a village in Kandahar Province. Your grandfather was born in the village, he is respected there. He paid money to rebuild the mosque. People in small villages sometimes do not accept strangers easily—it is the same around the world— but your father has made his pilgrimage to Mecca, so he is a *hajji*. He too will be respected. Your father has hired people to clean up the house for us. He will take a break from the university, and write his book. I will get better, and when all this is forgotten, we will return." Mother combed her fingers through Yasmine's long black hair.

"When do we leave?" She felt tired, but then doing nothing for weeks on end had been exhausting. And maybe it wasn't what she'd been hoping for, but there was no sense in crying. Anyway, at least in the country she could go outside.

༺☞❀☜༻

No one wanted to drive them to the village. There were bandits on the roads. They would have to cross territories controlled by warlords, and there was always the Taliban. "Too dangerous. Too dangerous," said one driver after another. Finally Baba found an old man who owned a car and a small truck big enough to carry a generator, desk, blankets, rugs, pillows, and even a proper bed so that Mother would be more comfortable. The man's son would follow behind in the truck.

Baba and Yasmine gently laid Mother out along the back seat of the car. Yasmine scrunched down on the floor beside a basket of fruit and naan to eat along the way.

"Where is your wife's *burka*?" the driver, a kindly man with a round face, asked.

"She does not own one," Baba said.

The driver pointed to a shop covered with chain-link fence. "Buy one for your wife and another for your daughter."

Yasmine was about to protest, but Mother squeezed her hand.

Baba returned with two silk, indigo-blue *burkas*, with crowns made of silver thread. The driver shook his head. "They are too beautiful and will draw attention. Never mind your daughter. She is young. Get another one for your wife, quickly." Baba tossed the new *burkas* into the car and looked around, his eyes searching the road.

A woman in a shabby, torn, saffron-colored *burka* sat against a wall at the end of the road. Her head was bent, an elbow rested on a knee, and her cupped hand was held up. Baba crouched down in front of the beggar and whispered a few words. The woman shook her head furiously. Baba stood then and ran into the shop. When he emerged, he held a new *burka*. Again he crouched before the beggar. This time she snatched the *burka* out of his hand and disappeared behind the shop.

When Baba returned to the car, he held the woman's ugly *burka* under his arm. Yasmine covered her nose. It stank like a goat's pen.

The city of Herat was soon almost behind them. Once past the timber-seller, where great logs pointing up into the air looked ready to tumble and squash pedestrians, men on bikes, and little rickshaws on the road below, they ventured out onto the highway. Land mines and scorching heat had turned the highway into a landscape of tiny blistered volcanoes. Often they had to pull over for a convoy of military trucks to pass.

It took days to reach the village. During the day they ate from the food basket, and at night the driver arranged for houses to sleep in along the way. Time passed in a blur.

⟨᠅⟩

"We are here," announced the driver.

Yasmine, asleep on folded arms, woke with a start, bolted up, and pushed her face against the dusty car window.

"Yasmine, no!" Mother reached over and yanked Yasmine's scarf up over her daughter's head. Yasmine fumbled a bit, then smoothed her *hijab* over her head with a flat palm.

The road was crowded with *jingle* trucks decorated with swirls of red, yellow, and green paint. Silver trinkets dangled across the windows. On the other side of the trucks, heaps of sandbags led up to a massive door that looked as though it belonged to a fort from medieval times. Soldiers carrying guns peered down from a great height. And then came a whirling sound. Yasmine stuck her head out of the car's window and looked up. Helicopters! There were two, she could see their underbellies and guns sticking out each side. They were scary, like giant, killer insects.

"Yasmine, that is the army base, it's called a FOB. It stands for Forward Operation Base. Many soldiers, Canadian and American mostly, from the United Nations, live inside. There is a landing pad for helicopters inside the FOB. But those soldiers . . ." Baba pointed to men wearing helmets, black vests over blue uniforms, their pants tucked into black boots. "They belong to the Afghan National Army, and they work with the UN soldiers. Your grandfather's village is over there." Baba motioned past a row of Afghan vehicles to a walled village across the road and beyond.

The car, and the truck that followed behind carrying their furniture and boxes, nudged through the line of multi-colored trucks and drove into the village. The village was nothing like the villages Yasmine had seen in England. This village was made up of mud houses that had been polished to a smooth yellow shine and winked in the sunlight. All together, the walls, the homes, and the buildings looked as though they had sprung fully formed from the earth.

The two vehicles rumbled down the main street kicking up puffs of dust. People stared. The houses had doors that were made of tin, and many windows were covered with plastic sheets. They passed a man-made stream, its banks covered with grass and leafy trees giving it shade.

"Stop here," said Baba. He got out of the car and walked over to a man tending meat on a grill that lay across a large steel drum. Plastic tables and chairs were on one side of the grill and *toshaks*, on top of old rugs, were on the other side. A grandfather, holding a baby boy with eyelids smudged with black *surma* to ward off flies, sang to the child while tickling him under the chin.

Yasmine pressed her nose against the car window. Across the road a cluster of old men stood in front of a mosque petting their beards and twirling *tasbih* prayer beads.

She could smell bread baking. A line of large flat baskets, filled with milky-white mounds of dough, lay in a row on the ground against a wall. Boys kicked a ball about in the middle of the road.

"What are they doing?" asked Yasmine.

"The boys are playing while they wait their turn. The baker will call out and a boy will take him the dough," said Mother. "Not every family can afford an oven."

Yasmine nodded. She could see the baker squatting beside the hot oven. He was soaked in sweat and there were burn marks on his arms. They looked like chicken bones wrapped in crinkled, brown paper. A boy stood over him holding out a basket. The baker snatched the dough, smacked it flat, sprinkled it with water, then lowered it into the hot oven.

"Is that a school?" Yasmine pointed to a low building beside the mosque.

"It's a *madrassa*, a religious school for boys," said Mother.

"Where is the school for girls?" asked Yasmine.

"Westerners are building a school for boys *and* girls, but it is not ready," she said.

"When will it be ready?"

Mother hesitated. "It may take a long time."

Yasmine said nothing. There was nothing to say.

Baba was still talking to the kebab-seller when a girl plopped a bundle of naan down beside the grill. She looked to be about Yasmine's age. The girl looked towards the car. They stared at each other for just a second. Should she wave? Yasmine was about to lift her hand when the girl turned and ran down the road. She had a limp.

Baba climbed back into the car and gave the driver directions. They didn't have far to go. The house was very near the middle of the village, and the village was small, tiny even. It was only a few moments before the car stopped in front of a great metal door. Baba gave the bell-cord a yank. An old woman with hooded eyes opened the door. She and Baba talked. She nodded then and opened the door wide for Baba to pass into their new home.

Chapter 4

Tamanna

Bazaar-E-Panjwayi, Kandahar Province

Tamanna swept aside the heavy curtain that hung across the doorway separating house from courtyard and looked east to see a weak sun rising.

"*Salaam*, Mor," Tamanna called out to her mother as she slipped her feet into worn sandals.

Mor, hunched in the middle of the courtyard, struck a wooden match and lit the coal fire in the pit under the round *tandoor* oven. A spark landed on her sleeve. It met with one of Mor's mighty smacks.

"Mor?" Tamanna took a step. Her hip suddenly gave way and her foot shot out, knocking her brother's blue, star-tipped sandals to the ground.

"Tamanna!" Mor cried out.

"I am sorry, Mor."

"Tut-tut." Mor's tongue clicked against her teeth. Tamanna took a deep breath and adjusted her *hijab*. She picked up Kabeer's sandals, cleaned them with her sleeve, and placed them back on the step. Kabeer had been missing for five years and, although the sandals fit her perfectly, Tamanna was not allowed to wear them. Kabeer would have big feet by now, but there was no arguing with Mor. The shoes stayed by the door waiting for her brother's return. Was he dead? She and Kabeer were twins, connected forever. Surely she would know when his spirit had left this earth. Would she not have felt it in her bones?

Tamanna hip-hopped around the house, ducked under the clothesline, and crossed the back of the garden. But it wasn't a real garden. Nothing grew there except thistles. Her eyes were fixed on the outhouse straight ahead. She had trained herself not to look in the direction of Uncle Zaman's shed. He was asleep. He was always asleep. There were times when Tamanna thought Uncle never got up and Mor never went to bed. Uncle was ten years older than her mother and, in her opinion, he was mean and as lazy as a slug. Worse, he gambled and smoked *chars*. Maybe he even went to the house where liquor was sold. There were whispers about such a place in the women's bathhouse.

Many months ago, Mor had tried to offer Uncle advice. "What you are doing is against the laws of Islam. You will get hurt," she had said, gently and kindly. Tamanna, holding her breath, had watched it all from the doorway of the house. Uncle Zaman's face had turned as red as a pomegranate. He'd spat on the ground and screamed, "No woman tells me what to do, you *ahmaq*! You woman! I will not be told how to behave in my own house!" But it wasn't his house. It was Mor's house. Then Uncle Zaman shook his fist under Mor's nose. But yelling and shaking a clenched fist did not satisfy him. He slapped Mor and then he punched her, and when Mor crumpled to the ground he kicked her, screaming, "You nothing woman. You have no brain. You must not speak."

"Stop, stop!" Tamanna had run across the courtyard then and pitched herself on top of her mother. Uncle had pulled back his leg and let it fly. When his foot landed on Tamanna's hip, there was a sound, a crack, and searing pain that ricocheted up her body and left her throat scorched.

Three seasons had passed since then, and Tamanna's hip had still not healed properly.

Now Tamanna slammed the outhouse door and bolted it by dropping a length of wood into a slot. The outhouse was just four old pieces of wood surrounding a concrete slab with a hole in the floor. It stank. A new hole needed to be dug, but Uncle would not provide the money, and so they made do.

They could have supported themselves if they had been allowed to keep all that they earned. Mor sold eggs from the chickens Grandfather provided, and she baked naan for Rahim Khan, Mor's cousin the kebab-seller. Tamanna delivered the bread to him twice a day. But almost everything they earned went to Uncle.

Tamanna burst out of the outhouse, poured water out of

a jug and washed her hands. A sound—a sort of groan mixed with a yawn—emanated from Uncle's shed. She tiptoed to the door and peeked inside. She expected to see him sprawled out on his mat, as if tossed there by a large, careless animal. Instead the old wooden door suddenly swung open so wide and so forcefully that it banged against the inside wall. Tamanna reeled backwards.

"What do you want?" Uncle Zaman snarled. He loomed over her like a hawk over prey. He had high, sharp cheekbones and a large, hooked nose. Some might have called him rugged and handsome, but Tamanna thought him menacing and fearsome.

"*Salaam*," Tamanna whispered.

"Go away." He waved his hand at her as if she were a fly. "No, come here."

Go away. Come here. It was always that way with Uncle.

"There is a new customer. He is an important man from Herat. Lots of money. Take him some naan and charge him double," he growled.

Tamanna nodded. A car and a small truck had passed through the village yesterday. There had been a girl inside the car with green eyes, wearing a beautiful gray *hijab*, and the man had spoken to Rahim Khan, the kebab-seller. He'd been dressed in fine, clean clothes. That must have been the man Uncle was talking about.

"He lives in the big house with the blue door. You know it?" he asked.

Tamanna nodded again. No one had lived in that house for years and years. If the man with the fine clothes lived there, then the girl did too. Perhaps she would see her.

"Deliver the bread and do not stop to talk to anyone. I have seen men give you dirty eye. If you get dirty eye again I will make you wear a *burka*. I will not have you spoiled for marriage." He barked out the words while swishing his hands in the air.

"Mor says that I am not to be married for many years. My father said—"

"Your mother is a useless woman. Your father tried to fight the Taliban and look where it got him—in the grave. Dead men do not speak. *I* will say when you get married." He spat out the words.

Tamanna's lower lip trembled, but her hands made small, tight fists. How did he know that her father was dead? There was no proof. She wanted to cry out, to yell, but there was no stopping Uncle.

"Have you any news of your father? Have you received any more of his precious letters?" he jeered.

Tamanna pursed her lips and swallowed hard. A long time ago, travelers passing through the village had brought letters from her father. Mor took her husband's letters to the holy man, the *imam*, to read. The letters were long, many pages, but the *imam* only said, "Your husband sends warm regards and prayers for peace and God's blessings." The *imam* kept the letters. Then, they stopped. They had not received a letter in five years.

Most people would have said that Tamanna was a quiet girl, easily dominated. But they would have been wrong. Anger gave her courage. "My father is a brave man." She looked Uncle square in the face. Uncle raised his hand as if to strike her. Tamanna willed herself not to move. She just waited for the blow. But nothing happened. Uncle laughed and walked past her towards the outhouse.

"*Praise be to Allah*," she whispered as she ran around to the front of the house.

The oven was now bristling hot. Plucking a small mound of dough as white as milk from a basket, Mor pounded it with a closed fist, dipped it into water, then lowered it down into the oven.

"Fetch the wood," said Mor.

Tamanna raced to the far corner of their courtyard, laid down her shawl, a *patoo*, and piled kindling on top. Quickly she tied the corners of the shawl together and heaved the bundle onto her shoulder. Her hip throbbed with pain.

"There, Mor." She dropped the bundle. A small cloud of dust enveloped them both.

"Drink your tea." With a free hand, Mor pointed to a mug and a slab of steaming naan. Tamanna slurped the green tea through her teeth, then pulled back in surprise. Her tea was sprinkled with sugar. Such treats were reserved for Uncle, not for her!

"Mor?" she whispered, but her mother did not turn her attention from the hot *tandoor* oven. Beads of sweat were already forming on Mor's brow. "Uncle says I must take naan to the big house near the mosque," said Tamanna. Mor just nodded.

Tamanna picked up the two steamy bundles of naan that Mor had wrapped in white cotton. With the hot bread clutched tight to her chest, she charged out of the courtyard.

"Be careful! Do not step off the road, there are land mines!"

Tamanna did not look back and so she did not see her mother stroke her *taweez*, the holy charm that hung from a black thread around her neck. Still, she could hear her mother's pleading words following her out through the broken gate and along the rutted path. Soon the path would join a straight road that ran through the village of Bazaar-E-Panjwayi.

"*Salaam.*" Tamanna plopped the naan onto the small plastic table by the stove of the kebab-seller and took a deep breath. The air was ripe with the smell of fried onions, tobacco, and sizzling lamb and goat.

Rahim Khan grunted as he plucked a piece of naan off the pile. He dropped kebabs slathered with onions on top of the flat bread and passed it to a waiting customer. A piece of lamb fell into the coals and crackled. Tamanna's mouth watered. Rahim Khan plucked it out of the coals and handed it to her.

"*Tashakor,*" Tamanna thanked him. Rahim Khan nodded without looking her way.

Tamanna tried not to make eye contact with the customers. It was hard to ignore a bearded old man sitting at one of Rahim Khan's tables, though. He had a face marked with scars, a sharp buzzard nose, and black buzzard eyes.

"*Khoda-hafez.*" She called out her farewell over her shoulder as she dashed off again.

"Watch out!" a woman in a *burka* shouted at her. Tamanna jumped aside as Gul Beebee Akthar, the mother of a martyr, paraded down the road in an old black *burka*. Two more women in *burkas* followed her, calling out, clearing the way.

"*Salaam*," Tamanna said softly.

Tamanna turned into a small passageway between two houses. It was a shortcut across town. The passage bent and curved, and just when she neared the end it came to a dead stop, blocked by rusted farm equipment.

"What are you doing here?"

Tamanna froze.

Noor, fifteen and tall for his age, stood behind her. He riveted his hands to his hips and glared at Tamanna. All the children in the village were afraid of him. He wore a coal-streaked *shalwar kameez* and a beaded cap that covered hair so black it looked blue.

"Where are you going?" he asked.

She didn't answer. It was improper to talk to a boy, and he knew that. Tamanna spun around. Behind her was the old farm equipment and on either side were tall mud walls. There was no way out except straight past Noor. But there would be gossip if someone saw them together in the passage! And then what would Uncle do? Tamanna pulled her *hijab* low over her forehead and came face to face with Noor.

"Do not speak to me ever again," she hissed, then she bolted down the passageway towards the road.

༺࿇༻

The door was big, blue, and made of tin. Tamanna took hold of the bell-cord and gave it a mighty tug. It was many minutes before an old woman, with hooded eyes and a toothless scowl, opened the door. Tamanna had seen her often in the bathhouse. Wordlessly, Tamanna held out the naan.

The woman snatched the bread out of Tamanna's hands. "Come back tomorrow and I will tell you if we want to make an order."

The door was about to close when a girl with bright-green eyes peeked around the wall. "Can you come in and visit?" she asked. It was her, the girl in the car! Visit? Tamanna was astonished. Girls did not visit. Tamanna did not know what to say and so she just stood there, wide-eyed.

"What is your name?" asked the girl.

"Tamanna," she whispered.

"My name is Yasmine."

The old woman slammed the tin door and the girl with the green eyes vanished.

Chapter 5

Warrior Eyes

The next morning Tamanna stood outside the tin door holding a small stack of naan wrapped in cloth. She felt confident. These rich people had to buy bread from someone, and Mor's naan was the best in the village. Tamanna reached up and pulled the bell-cord. Deep breath. She was ready to negotiate a price with the miserable old lady with the hooded eyes.

A man swung open the large door. Tamanna took a step back. The rich man who owned the house stood in front of

37

her. Men or boys almost always answered the door, and she should not have been surprised—it was only that she had been expecting the housekeeper. Tamanna looked down at her feet. She could feel his eyes upon her, but not in a dirty way.

"My wife praises the bread." His voice was nice, not gruff or tinged with anger like Uncle's. The man took the bundle out of Tamanna's arms. She felt her face go hot. She could not speak to a man who was not a relative. How then was she supposed to negotiate a price?

"Would you like to work in my house?" asked the man.

Tamanna stood as still as a stone. It took a moment, maybe two, to understand his meaning. Only Uncle could make such a decision. Still, she nodded without raising her head.

The man left her standing in the road. She heard him talking to someone. A moment later, the old woman who'd opened the door the day before was marching past her, storming down the road, her long skirts flapping around her ankles.

"You may come in and wait," said the man.

Tamanna sat inside the courtyard with her back against the wall. The courtyard was astonishing. There was a tree with a bench under it and beside it a soft *toshak*. There were flowers in earthen jars and herbs growing in a small garden plot. At the end of the courtyard there was a house with a beautiful, multicolored mat in front of the doorway. There was a copper washing pot, a table, a kerosene lamp— Tamanna had never seen such a courtyard. She looked up. A figure loomed over her, blocking the sun.

"You make good bread." Yasmine, the girl with the green

eyes, squatted down beside Tamanna. Both girls were bathed in a soft morning light. Why did this new girl speak so oddly? She spoke all the same words Tamanna did, but they sounded different.

"My mother makes the naan. I just deliver it," Tamanna said.

"I remember your name. It's Tamanna. Do you remember mine?"

"Yasmine," whispered Tamanna. She had been repeating it to herself all night.

"Come and meet my mother." Yasmine pulled Tamanna to her feet. A thin, gold chain sparkled around her neck. Tamanna had not thought it possible for a girl to own such a thing. Yasmine ran across the courtyard and into the house, and Tamanna hurried behind.

The floors in the house were covered with thick rugs. The first room, to welcome guests, held many beautiful pillows. Tiny painted teacups in silver holders sat on a large, circular, brass-topped table. The next room was the family room, with many more pillows, another large, round table, a daybed, and even a foreign-style desk and bookshelves filled with books!

"My father does his work at this desk. One day he will publish a book. That's my room over there!" Yasmine pointed down a tiny hall.

A girl with her own room! Was such a thing possible? There was also a kitchen, an indoor toilet, and a separate room for her parents.

"Come." Yasmine pulled Tamanna's hand. "This is my mother," she said proudly.

A woman with long, black hair streaked with silver, high cheekbones, a mouth curved in a gentle smile, and eyes as bright-green as jade sat up in a wooden bed. She was the most beautiful woman Tamanna had ever seen. She looked like a queen. The queen smiled.

"Welcome, Tamanna. I have tasted your delicious naan. My daughter was waiting for you to come this morning."

Someone had been waiting for her! Tamanna should have been tongue-tied, but instead, the shyness that sometimes threatened to envelope her dissolved like fog in sunlight. "I am happy to be here." There, she'd said it. It might have been the longest sentence she had ever spoken to someone who was not a relative.

They all heard the door to the road open and close.

"The housekeeper is back." Yasmine gabbed Tamanna's hand and both ran through the house and back into the courtyard. The housekeeper came around the privacy wall, a freestanding divider that thwarted prying eyes, and glared at the girls. She was frowning but not because she was angry, that was just how her mouth went. The old woman brushed past them and walked up to Yasmine's father as he sat at his desk. Both girls huddled in the doorway.

"The uncle has no objection to the girl working. She can start with me in the kitchen at sunrise," said the old woman. No one was surprised that Tamanna's uncle had agreed to the conditions. Money was money, after all.

"I have other plans for her," said Yasmine's father. The housekeeper arched her eyebrows, but Baba just kept talking. "She is to be my daughter's companion, at least until the school is opened." Companion? Who had ever heard of such a thing! The woman made a tut-tutting sound.

Yasmine bit her lip. No one had actually asked Tamanna if she wanted to be her friend. But she could tell just by looking at her that they would like each other. Tamanna had a soft, round face. Her eyes were as dark as chocolate, and she was sure that if she smiled it would be a beautiful, wide smile. She turned to Tamanna.

"Would you be my friend?" she asked.

Tamanna nodded. More than anything in this world she wanted to be Yasmine's friend.

Yasmine laughed. "I knew that you would have a beautiful smile."

⟨❊⟩

Next morning, Tamanna woke before the *muezzin* called the faithful to early morning prayers. She collected firewood in the dark, fed the chickens, built the fire under the oven for Mor, and left before the sun peeked over the distant mountains.

The trail from her house to the main road wound through long grass like a kite's tail. The sun-baked ground was hard and her feet fell in and out of ancient donkey tracks. Soon the heat of the day would press down like a flat palm, but for this moment, in the early morning, the weather was glorious. She had never felt so happy.

From then on, every morning Tamanna brought the naan to give Rahim Khan and took a smaller stack of bread to Yasmine's house. Every day the girls drank tea together, ate pomegranates or sweet melons, and bit into Mor's warm naan. They took fruit, tea, and bread into Yasmine's mother's room and listened to stories. Many were from a book, but some were her own stories of places far away, magical places with names like London, Paris, New York, and Montreal. Tamanna repeated everything in her head. When this dream ended and her real life returned, she wanted to relive these moments.

A large *patoo*, a shawl, covered the bed. It was decorated in elaborate and detailed embroidery. It was so beautiful, Tamanna could hardly pull her eyes away. If she could just turn the *patoo* over and see the delicate stitching. Mor said that her stitching was excellent but she had not had the opportunity to work with fine, thin thread.

Yasmine's mother noticed Tamanna's interest and said, "Is it not lovely? It is *cherma dozi,* a traditional form of Afghan needlework."

Tamanna nodded. "I . . ." but she stopped. It would be wrong to tell of her talents.

"Do you know how to embroider?" asked Yasmine's mother.

Tamanna nodded. "But the thread is too expensive and Uncle will not allow it." She felt her face flush red.

"Could you teach me?" Yasmine squealed.

Again, Tamanna nodded.

Later in the day they would study arithmetic under a tree with Yasmine's father. Bent over paper, Yasmine did complicated equations, while Tamanna learned to count by lining up small pebbles in a row. Sometimes they sat under Baba's cozy blanket, the *campal,* and listened to tales of Alexander the Great and Buddhist Afghanistan. But the stories they liked best were of the Silk Road—except it wasn't one road, it was many roads, all filled with adventure.

"And did you know," said Baba one day, "that Genghis Khan, who thundered through Asia in a hail of slings and arrows, gave women equal rights under the law?"

Yasmine always asked Baba lots of questions. Never, not once, had Tamanna managed to ask a question, but then there it was, on the tip of her tongue.

"Did Genghis Khan allow women to work?"

Baba laughed. "A woman could even be a soldier in his army."

Tamanna whispered, "There are woman soldiers in the *kharijis'* army, too. Some walk through the village wearing great equipment and carrying guns."

Baba nodded. "In the West, women may do any job, or join any profession." How could that be? Tamanna wondered. Yasmine's father then went on about the Mongolian warrior who had created the world's biggest empire. There was so much to learn!

And then, each day as the sun began to set, Yasmine's father gave her a few bills, payment for work she had not done. The money was delivered directly to Uncle.

The old housekeeper's mouth curled in disdain. Tamanna grew fearful. If the housekeeper spread gossip, Uncle would not allow her to come back, she was sure of it. As the weeks went on her fear increased. She tried to help with the housework, but Yasmine would not let her. "Leave the vegetables. Mother wants to tell us a story," she'd say, or, "Never mind the laundry, Baba has a map of all of Afghanistan to show us."

The housekeeper went to Mother and complained. "The girl should work. What use is it to educate her?"

Baba overheard, and so did Yasmine and Tamanna. Baba quoted Hajji Zeynalabdin Taghiyev: "An educated woman is an educated mother and, as such, she is able to provide her children with a broad outlook." He spoke gently to the old woman, as if by doing so she would better understand. The housekeeper pursed her lips so tightly they turned white. She had never heard of Hajji Zeynalabdin Taghiyev. Did this man mean to make her feel stupid? Did he think their ways in the village were not good enough for such a learned person as himself?

Tamanna grabbed Yasmine's hand and pulled her into a corner. "Your father must not say such things. There is gossip in the village," she whispered.

"Please, what do they say?" asked Yasmine.

"They say that he is not one of them. That he has been tainted by the outside world."

Yasmine nodded. She remembered the professor who had come to their house after the attack on Mother. It didn't matter that Baba looked like one of them or that he was a *hajji*, they were suspicious of him, as they were of all outsiders.

"What should we do?" Yasmine whispered.

"I do not know." If Yasmine's father let the old woman go, the gossip would only get worse. There didn't seem to be anything that they could do.

One morning, the housekeeper's grandson knocked on the door. He said that his grandmother had taken a pain in her side during the night and died! It was a tragedy. Baba gave the boy paper bills for the old housekeeper's burial. For the moment, anyway, Baba's reputation was safe.

Yasmine's father hired a woman to clean the house after

evening prayers, long after Tamanna had left for the day. Now no knew about their secret lessons, not even Tamanna's mother.

The girls took on a few household jobs, but since they were doing them together it was fun. The hardest job was the laundry. Tamanna filled the copper washing *lagaan* with warm water while Yasmine swished the clothes around, squeezing, swish-swishing, then squeezing again. It was then that Tamanna mustered up her courage to ask, "Why do you speak . . . ?" What was the word she wanted? "You speak Dari but it is different somehow."

Yasmine did not seem to be offended by the nosy question. "My parents spoke Dari to me when I was little but really my first language is English."

Tamanna pulled back so fast it was if she had been hit! "You speak English?"

Yasmine nodded. "And a little French. I wish I had studied more. I thought I had time to learn it. I didn't know that I would be coming here."

Tamanna thought that she sounded sad. "Do you not like it here?" she asked.

Yasmine dried her hands on a piece of cloth. "If I hadn't come here, I would not have met you, so I guess I do like it," she said, smiling.

Tamanna bit her lip. This feeling inside—it was like she was filled with bubbles.

"Why do you speak both Dari and Pashto?" Yasmine asked.

"Everyone in the village speaks Pashto, but my mother is from Parwan Province and there they speak Dari. My uncle does not know how to speak Dari so he cannot understand us when we talk about him." Tamanna laughed.

"What is your uncle like?" asked Yasmine.

Tamanna shook her head. There was nothing to say.

"Would you like to learn English?"

Tamanna nodded, more than nodded. Her head bobbed up and down so fast her headscarf almost came off.

"In the morning you can correct my Dari accent and teach me Pashto, and in the afternoon I will teach you English. I bet that you are the faster learner. You are so smart!" Yasmine laughed.

Tamanna held her breath. Blood rushed to her face. Surely Yasmine did not mean to say such a thing! Embarrassed, Tamanna added, "And will you tell me about England, about how people live?" She would likely never leave this place unless she married a man from the next village, but still, just to hear about the magical world beyond her reach would be enough.

"I will tell you all I remember. I am forgetting things about England, but I haven't forgotten pigs-in-a-blanket!"

Tamanna's mouth dropped open. "You eat pig?" To eat pig was forbidden.

Yasmine laughed. "Mother used to make meat sausages wrapped in pastry, which is like bread, then I'd dip them in ketchup."

"*Ket-up.*" Tamanna tested the word. "Ket-up sounds delicious!" Ketchup was Tamanna's first English word. "Are there buses and rickshaws in England?"

Yasmine told her, "In England, a woman can own and drive her own automobile. And she can wear whatever she wants, no one cares. And young men and women can go out together and even hold hands in the street. I have seen people kiss. And many women live alone in flats." Yasmine giggled.

"Alone? Without family?" Tamanna thumped down in a fog of wonder. Kiss? What was that? Such strange things she was learning!

Twice a week there was a market in the village. Baba always returned with embroidery thread, often silver and gold, but one day he came home with a soccer ball. Even with her bad hip Tamanna could kick the ball through two posts Baba had slammed into the ground. Mother and Baba sat under the tree and cheered every goal.

"Your hip, does it hurt to run?" asked Yasmine as they sank to the ground.

Tamanna shrugged. There was nothing that could be done about it, so why complain?

"You are lucky that you deliver naan," said Yasmine.

Lucky? "I do not understand," said Tamanna.

"In England I walked to school by myself. I was always outside. But here Baba is worried all the time. In Herat, my mother . . ." But her words drifted. They never talked about the attack on Mother. "Never mind. Draw me a map of the village and show me where you live?" Yasmine sat with her knees in the dust and passed Tamanna a pointy stick.

Tamanna scratched a map into the hard ground. "Here is the mosque, and beside it a *madrassa*, and down here is the bathhouse and the public oven, the well, the stream, and my house is here!" It was fun, being the one to teach Yasmine! She stabbed the ground. "Beside my house there are great stalks of wheat and noisy bulbul birds. And there is a burned-out Russian tank right in the middle of the field. It pokes out of the ground like an old tombstone. Kabeer and I used to play on it." She stopped. The image of her brother rose up in her eyes like a flash of light. She closed her eyes tight.

"Tamanna, what's wrong? Who is Kabeer?"

Tamanna shook her head as if the effort would get rid of the memory. "Kabeer is my brother. He is gone now."

"Where did he go?" asked Yasmine, confused.

Tamanna gave her head another shake. There it was again, the picture of her twin brother with a tear-streaked face, arms reaching out for her, pleading, "Mor, Mor, I do not want to go. Tamanna, I do not want to go."

Tamanna squared her shoulders. Again she stabbed the ground with the stick. "A tent school used to be on that spot but it got washed away. The new school will have two rooms, one for boys and one for girls. Each room will have heat! Everyone talks about it."

Yasmine looked down at the scratches in the ground. "Did you go to the tent school?"

Tamanna shook her head. "Uncle would not allow me to go."

It was Yasmine's turn to be surprised. "But you are so smart! Baba and Mother said so. And you can already read and do additions and subtractions. What is wrong?" asked Yasmine.

This time Tamanna let herself hear the compliment. She turned away before Yasmine could see the tears in her eyes.

Mother walked with only one crutch now. Many times Baba had said, "We will go to India or Pakistan and have your leg looked at." Mother brushed him away. "I am healing in my own time, Yasmine is happy, and you are making great progress on your book. Let us enjoy this peace a little while longer." It was true, Baba had filled three large books with his writing. Mother read his work every day, often commenting and sometimes rewriting. Baba said, "Your mother makes me sound smarter than I am."

According to Tamanna, Yasmine no longer had a funny accent and her embroidery had improved, although, truth be told, Yasmine was too impatient to do an excellent job. Tamanna could read, write, multiply, and speak many words in English. And then, everything changed.

"The school building is finished." Tamanna, standing in the courtyard, clutched her side, panting. Yasmine raced across the courtyard and threw her arms around her friend. "Two teachers will arrive tomorrow. And . . ." Tamanna had saved the best for last, "Uncle says that he does not care if I go to school or not, as long as I make my deliveries!"

There was no end to the miracles.

Chapter 6

Education Is Light

The new school was a white building with blue trim. It was beautiful, despite being surrounded by rubble, smashed bricks, bits of wood, shingles, and rocks. Boys gathered on one side of the building, girls on the other. Really, there were hardly any girls, maybe ten or so, but all the boys of the village were there.

Tamanna stood near the building and watched for Yasmine. Uncle had said that he hoped she would enjoy her day at school. She had said thank you, and then her skin had felt prickly. Why was he being nice to her?

Mor had only said, "Wear your *burka*." No, she would not! Anyway, it was not *her* burka, it was *their* burka. They had not the money for two. They'd argued until it was agreed that she would carry it with her.

Praise be to Allah, her life was perfect. Almost perfect. There it was again, that rumble in her stomach. She had felt ill since the day before, and she'd run to the outhouse three times before school. But nothing would be allowed to spoil this day, nothing.

"Tamanna!" She heard her name and turned. Yasmine and her father were walking down the road towards the school. Yasmine raised her hand in a wave, said goodbye to her father, and ran towards her.

"Look!" Tamanna pointed up to a banner above the door of the school. It read, "Education Is Light." The two girls giggled.

The sun was beginning to climb in the sky. Some of the younger children grew tired of waiting and sat in the shade of the building, their backs against the wall. Boys kicked around a ball, while the girls became pensive. Tamanna edged closer to Yasmine. "What if they do not come? What if . . . ?"

"There he is!" Yasmine pointed.

Heads down, eyes up, the girls watched as the teacher strode towards the school. It had to be him. He carried books. What age might he be? Twenty-five? Maybe older. A small beaded skullcap covered his head. He had an elegant nose, large, dark eyes, high cheekbones, and smooth skin—and he wore no beard! He walked with such confidence and assurance that the boys surrounded him like yapping puppies. The girls giggled and covered their faces with the ends of their headscarves.

"*Asalaam alaikum,*" the teacher said to the boys. Then he turned and looked in the direction of the girls. "*Asalaam alaikum,*" he repeated, his hand suspended in the air.

Tamanna and Yasmine stood transfixed, hearts pounding. He was the teacher for the boys, but where was their woman teacher? Tamanna strained to see past him. Nothing. No one.

"You girls," said the teacher. He looked at them! He spoke to them! "Your teacher is delayed."

The heads of the girls slumped. Tamanna swallowed hard. Delayed? Was she coming at all? Some girls turned and started for home.

"No, no, today we will all be together. Come," said the teacher.

Boys and girls together? The girls whispered to one another. Was it allowed? Would they get into trouble?

"Girls will sit at the back," said the teacher.

"Yasmine, perhaps we should go home," Tamanna whispered.

"It will be all right. In England, boys and girls always sit together!" Yasmine grinned and tugged at Tamanna's hand. She was outside, she was with other girls, she could not go home, not yet.

The boys barged into the school first. The smaller boys crumpled like balls of paper onto the rugs at the very front of the room while the bigger boys took the seats behind. Immediately they pounded the desks that were attached to the chairs. Girls were expected to behave well, but could and would do what they liked. Noor took the best seat. That was expected, too.

"*Alaikum asalaam*," mumbled the girls as they passed the teacher's desk and made their way to the back of the class. Some stopped in the doorway and peered around, frightened and unsure. Eventually they all took a place on the tall benches that ran the length of the room. Tamanna's legs dangled beneath her. It was hard to sit so far off the ground, and harder still to keep from slumping forward.

Large, long windows were at their backs and in front the teacher stood beside a black chalkboard. He said, "*As salaam wa alaikum*. My name is Nasir Akhtar, but you will call me *Moalim sahib* or Teacher." Tamanna reached out and squeezed Yasmine's hand. Teacher wrote words on the blackboard:

May God protect us.
May God bring us peace.
May God give us strength to continue our education.

He thumped the blackboard and said, "Repeat these words."

Tamanna and Yasmine exchanged looks, then stared down at their toes. Should they admit that they could read? No one spoke. Teacher pointed to each sentence then reread the words out loud.

"Yasmine?" Tamanna put her hand to her ear then motioned with her head. Yasmine nodded. She heard it too. Vehicles, trucks maybe, outside the school.

Suddenly they all heard it. Girls snuggled closer; little sisters reached for their big sisters; even the boys looked alarmed. There were loud footsteps outside of the classroom. The door burst open. It happened so suddenly that no one had time to react. There, on the threshold, stood a grinning *khariji* lady, two *khariji* soldiers, and two Afghan National Army soldiers dressed in blue. Yasmine was comfortable around foreigners, but the rest of the students were used to seeing *kharijis* in the distance, not like this, not close up.

Teacher motioned to the *kharijis*. "Come, come," he said with his hands. "In the name of Allah, most beneficent and most merciful, I welcome you to Afghanistan." Tamanna and Yasmine exchanged looks. He was speaking in English!

The ANA soldiers left the classroom to stand guard outside. The others came in carrying cardboard boxes. A small, worried-looking Afghan man followed. "*Salaam*," said the adults, one to the other. The *khariji* woman wore a head-scarf covered in yellow flowers. Her skin was brown from the sun and her gray eyes were sparkly, despite being almost buried in a nest of wrinkles, and like most *kharijis* she had teeth that were very white and very straight. Hardly any adults Tamanna knew smiled. Hardly any adults she knew had all their teeth!

"This is our 'terp,'" said the *khariji* woman while nodding towards the Afghan man. The interpreter gave a little bow. He looked embarrassed and befuddled, and his eyes kept darting towards the back window.

The *khariji* woman took out a small knife and *zip, zip,* slit the boxes open and lifted out wondrous gifts: pencils, small pink rubber erasers, rulers, little cases with zippered tops, bound paper, and cloth bags, for every student in the room. The boys leaped up, reached into the boxes, and grabbed what they could.

"Boys, boys!" Teacher clapped his hands. Only when the really tall soldier removed his helmet and stepped forward, brow furrowed, did the boys sit back in their seats. It was hard not to stare at the soldier. His hair was orange and his eyebrows were bushy.

"My name is Dan, or you can call me Danny." The soldier punched himself in the chest. The boys laughed and the girls covered their mouths with the fringes of their headscarves and giggled.

The foreign lady spoke, and the translator translated. "This school was built by a group of women in the West who care about the children of Afghanistan," she said. She talked, too, about the UN forces and how they wanted to keep the people of Afghanistan safe. The girls sat and listened respectfully, although the meaning of the lady's words was lost on them. The boys mostly punched each other. And then, with a clap of her hands, the foreign lady was finished. The interpreter clasped and unclasped his hands. All the adults looked nervous now.

"*Khoda-hafez*," said Teacher to the lady and the soldiers. He put his hands together and bowed. The *khariji* woman and the interpreter also bowed and repeated, "*Khoda-hafez.*" Dan-Danny waved and bellowed, "See ya later, alligator," then turned back at the doorway and said, "In a while, crocodile!" When he winked, his giant eyebrows came down over his eyes like a curtain.

"What did he say?" Tamanna whispered to Yasmine. Her English lessons had not extended to foreign animals.

"He says that we are alligators and he is a crocodile." Yasmine laughed while Tamanna sat back, eyes wide. *Alligators in Afghanistan? Crocodiles, too?* "Do not feel bad," said Yasmine. "Perhaps he is American or Canadian, I cannot tell. They come from North America and do not speak the same English as the British. Some people say that they don't speak English at all."

Suddenly they were alone with Teacher, and in that moment even the boys behaved. Standing in front of the long, magnificent blackboard, he said, "Today is a special day. The government of Afghanistan has a difficult curriculum planned, but today I want to ask you, what is it that you want to learn?"

The boys' hands shot up in the air. "English," shouted two boys at once. The girls nodded their heads vigorously.

Teacher looked to the back of the room, at the girls. "I would like to hear what you girls would like to learn."

"Girls cannot learn. They should all be sent home. They should not be in the room with boys," yelled Noor from the top of the class.

Before Teacher could respond, Yasmine stood and said, "We want to learn about our country." Tamanna's jaw dropped. Her friend was fearless.

"Our history is noble, often heroic, and violent, too," said Teacher. "Many outsiders—the Macedonians, Sassanians, Arabs, Mongols, Greeks, Tartars, the British, and the Russians —have tried to conquer us, and now our government has invited the United Nations into this country to free us from the domination of the Taliban. But listen carefully." Teacher wagged his finger. "We have been occupied but never conquered. To know about history is to know that dark times pass and after the dark there is light. You must remember that always."

This time when Tamanna looked around the room she saw more than a flash of anger in Noor's eyes, she saw something else. Disdain? Hatred? It was a funny look.

Noor bounced up. "We must study *halal*," he said, his chest puffed out and his hands on his hips.

"Yes, we may talk about the Muslim code of behavior," said Teacher.

"Infidels are unbelievers," said Noor. "The *kharijis* eat pork—that is forbidden, *haraam*. They let their women walk naked. They drink alcohol, and they will molest women if they have the chance." He took a breath. "'Persecution is worse than slaughter,' that is what we are taught. It is better to die fighting the invaders than to live with them on our land."

Yasmine watched Teacher's face grow dark. "To whom are you referring? The *kharijis* are here to fight the Taliban, they are guests invited by the government. They have built this school and given us books." He cleared his throat and turned to the class. "Today, we will start with arithmetic." His hand flew across the blackboard as he wrote simple questions. Noor sat down, his body hitting the wooden seat with a purposeful thud.

The morning passed. Heat filled the room. A few of the smaller boys sitting cross-legged at the front fell asleep, their heads lolling forward or dropping sideways on the shoulder of a friend.

Finally, Teacher picked up a large school bell and shook it. The older boys raced out of the room while the younger ones, startled out of their naps, screwed their fists into balls and rubbed their sleepy eyes. One by one they leaped up and ran out of the room. Respectfully, the girls began filing past Teacher's desk.

Tamanna stopped.

"What is it?" asked Yasmine.

Tamanna shook her head and listened more intently. There was a sound—a distant whining, menacing hum. It grew louder. Now all the girls left in the room stopped to listen. It wasn't the sound of big UN tanks. This sound was more like a vibration than a rumble. Tamanna was the first to recognize it.

"Yasmine!" cried Tamanna, pointing. All the girls turned and ran to the back windows.

Three black Toyotas materialized out of gusts of billowing sand.

Taliban.

Every girl froze. Not a breath escaped their lips, not a muscle twitched.

"*Burkas!*" someone yelled. Yards of indigo-blue and saffron-red cloth spilled out of bags. Up went the cloth then down again as bodies burrowed inside.

Teacher hollered above the din, "Stay together. Be calm." It was no use.

"Tamanna, I do not have a *burka*." Yasmine's green eyes were huge in a face as pale as ice.

Gunshots pierced the air. There were footsteps in the hall. The Taliban had entered the school.

"Everyone out!" the Taliban shouted. More gunfire.

"Run, Yasmine!" Tamanna cried.

Yasmine jumped up onto the windowsill. Poised like a cat, her head swiveled back and forth. She jumped and dropped over the side, out of sight.

"*Allah, protect my friend,*" Tamanna whispered.

"Out! Out!" More yelling and more gunfire.

The padded headpiece of her *burka* clamped down onto Tamanna's head like a lid on a pot. Almost instantly she lost her bearings. Their faces hidden and their eyes covered by a grille, the girls stumbled around with outstretched arms.

"Stay together, stay close!" cried Teacher. There was panic in his voice.

Tamanna took a few steps and fell. She gathered up the cloth in her hands and tried again. Directly in front of her a girl wore white sandals. Tamanna tried to focus on the girl's feet and follow her out of the room. The girl slipped. As she flailed about, hands outstretched, Tamanna heard the *clink-clink* of bracelets. She knew the laws of the Taliban, every girl did. The Taliban would beat a woman, sometimes to death, for making any sound. In one fluid movement Tamanna reached over, pulled off the two bangles, and yanked the girl to her feet.

Finally all the girls stumbled out of the school building and stood quivering on the rocky ground. Tamanna raised her head and with one hand pulled the grille of the burka tight against her face. With the grille pressed against her eyes she could see a little better, but the cloth covering her mouth and nose made it hard to pull in a deep breath.

Under a searing white-yellow sun, the girls shook as if freezing from the cold. More Taliban scrambled out of the cars. In menacing poses, with guns propped on hips and thin whips called *duras* coiled in their hands, they stood in a semicircle around the students. Black *surma* was smeared around blank eyes, making them look as savage as attack dogs. Shaggy beards meandered across their chests and limp tails of black turbans were draped over their shoulders. All carried big guns, and most wore braces of bullets around their necks and across their chests. The Russian Kalashnikov rifles were large and fierce-looking. Some cradled them in their arms, while others waved the guns over their heads like flags. How many Taliban were there? It was hard to count, maybe fifteen, maybe fewer.

Tamanna wanted to look over her shoulder but was afraid to move. Where were the *khariji* soldiers? But if the soldiers returned there would be shooting, children would die, and likely the villagers would blame the deaths on the *kharijis*. It had happened before.

A few of the Taliban stormed into the school while the rest stood on guard, their guns pointed at the students. One Talib sauntered over to a group of young boys and began talking. He gave his gun to a boy who looked to be eight or nine years old. Fear instantly turned to joy as the boy's grin spread from ear to ear.

"Up." The Talib lifted the muzzle of the gun until it pointed towards the sky. The boy pulled the trigger. The *rat-a-tat* startled the girls and made all the boys laugh and clap. "Me next!" "No, *me* next!" With hands waving in the air, they leaped and jumped, while the Talib grinned and patted the boys on the back. The Talib spoke to each boy. Tamanna could hear bits of conversation. He asked, "Which girl in your village behaves in an un-Islamic way? Who does not pray five times a day?"

One Talib leaned against the car, rested his gun on his knee, and opened his little box of *naswar*. Slowly he picked out a pinch of chewing tobacco, chopped it in his hand with the lid of the box, then tossed it into his mouth as though it were a handful of nuts.

A young Talib carrying a smaller rifle paced up and down directly in front of Tamanna. He seemed anxious, troubled even. She caught a glimpse of him, his nose, his forehead, his eyes. There was something familiar about him. The boy stopped and stood in front of her. Eyes down, she could see his shabby sandals, his dirty, broken toenails, his hardened, scabbed feet. And something else, his feet were lined with brown marks, as if they had been burned.

"Has your family no pride or honor?" the boy screamed. Was he talking to her? What was he yelling about? Tamanna shuddered, her stomach . . . she was going to embarrass herself. His voice waned. Wait, he was yelling at the girl in the white sandals. Why?

"To wear white on your feet is to break our law. White is a holy color, the color of peace. You may not walk on it."

As he spoke he lifted his gun and put his finger on the trigger. The girl shook so hard that the hem of her *burka* bounced on and off the ground. Tiny, muted sounds could be heard through the grille of her *burka*. She kicked off her sandals.

A commotion—thuds, bangs, and yells—came from inside the school. A body came hurtling out the door, a jumble of flailing arms and legs. Teacher crashed to the ground. He lay there twitching and sputtering. The gunfire stopped. The laughing boys quieted. And then, the crunch of rocks underfoot as an old Talib stepped out of his car and walked towards Teacher. Stillness prickled the back of the neck as the air emptied of sound. No birds, no wind, no hum or echo—nothing, just the hammering of hearts in ears.

The old Talib spat a dark, green lump of chewing tobacco on the ground, then gazed around with the eyes of a snake lying on a hot rock. His face was covered with raised, dark scars. Spittle collected in the corners of his mouth, and his sneer revealed black, rotting teeth.

"Look up! You students, you girls, watch what happens to a man who breaks our law." He spoke in a high-pitched, nasal voice that sounded almost—silly. He leaned down over Teacher, grabbed a fistful of his black hair, and yelled in his ear, "Girls and boys that are not related must not be in the same room. Girls must not be educated. You think you can teach girls to be immodest? You want girls to forget Islam? You want them to go to Hell? What do you teach? You teach them to talk to *shaitan*, to the Devil. You are worthless. Allah and the Prophet, peace be upon Him, will punish you." The old man drew a pistol from his belt and pointed it at Teacher's head. Teacher lay motionless on the ground. Was he dead already?

Tamanna's head drooped. The young Talib who had threatened the girl in white sandals jammed the muzzle of his gun under her chin, forcing her head up. Through the netting she looked directly into his eyes. It was surprising how clearly she could see through the grille when a person was really close.

"Look up. Do you not hear? Are you deaf? You do as you are told, you stupid, nothing girl," snarled the young Talib. There was yelling from behind. The young Talib looked past her, over her shoulder.

"We caught her escaping." A scuffling sound in the sand, and a girl was shoved, face first, onto the ground next to the motionless Teacher. Yasmine. A young, grinning Talib rolled her over with his foot. Yasmine, her face exposed, looked up into the sun.

Tamanna took quick breaths. *No, no, no. Yasmine, I am here. I love you. You are the sister of my heart.* Screams were trapped in her throat.

"See this girl?" The old man poked Yasmine with his foot. "She has dishonored Islam, and for that she will die." More bullets pierced the sky. The boys from the village were cheering too.

Tamanna closed her eyes and murmured, "*In the Name of God, the Most Gracious, the Most Merciful. All Praise is due to God alone, the Sustainer of all the worlds, the Most Merciful, the Most Compassionate, Master of Judgment Day . . .*"

The young Talib soldier yanked Yasmine to her feet. She turned, and for a moment her beautiful green eyes locked on the grille of Tamanna's *burka*.

"*See me, see me,*" whispered Tamanna. "*I am here.*"

Yasmine did not cry. Her face was a mask! *She is not afraid,* thought Tamanna. *Look, she is not afraid!*

"What is her punishment?" the old man yelled.

"Death," the Talib shouted. The young Talib who had stood in front of Tamanna picked up his gun and aimed it at Yasmine. As he did so, Yasmine turned her head. Her gold necklace shone in the sun. Eyes wide with delight, the Talib reached down to rip it off her neck. The clasp held fast.

"No," whispered Tamanna. Like a bullet through glass, she shrieked, "ENOUGH! Don't hurt her!" The strain of her cry seared her throat. Tamanna lunged towards the boy with the gun. The Talib pivoted and turned the gun on her.

Tamanna's hand went down under her *burka* and with one swift movement she flipped it up to reveal her face.

"Kabeer," she said. "It is me, Tamanna, your sister!"

There was silence. The girls within hearing seemed to pull in their breath; the others just looked on, quivering with fear. The Talib peered into Tamanna's face. They were twins, their features identical—round, black eyes, high cheekbones, full lips. Shocked, he stood still for a moment. Then he turned and walked over to the old Talib. Kabeer spoke, but she could not hear his words. The old Talib came towards her. Tamanna covered her face. She could not stop herself from rocking back and forth. She thought she might faint.

"This is your sister?" The old Talib pointed to Tamanna but spoke to Kabeer.

"Yes," was all he said.

"And this one." He pointed to Yasmine, who lay on the ground. "Is she your sister also?"

"No," said Kabeer.

"Then we will make an example of her. We will show everyone that educating girls is against the law of the Taliban."

Prayers ran through Tamanna's head. She looked to the ground and could not see the old Talib's expression but she felt movement. Her head reared back and she looked up in time to see the old Talib raise his gun and point it at Yasmine's head. He fired. Tamanna squeezed her eyes shut, clenched her fists, her nails biting into her palms. *No, no, no.* And then she heard laughter, long peals of foul laughter that spilled out of mouths and into the air. She opened her eyes. The bullet had gone into the sand inches from Yasmine's head.

The old Talib stood close to Tamanna. "Your brother wants me to spare your life. I will do it for him. You tell everyone how your friend and your teacher were spared on this day. Your brother is good. All Taliban are good. You tell people that."

❁

"Mor!" Tamanna ran into the courtyard of her mother's house and looked around. "MOR!" She drew back the rug that covered the doorway and peered into the dim.

"Daughter, I am here," said Mor.

It took a moment for Tamanna's eyes to adjust to the light that filtered in through a small window. Her mother sat slumped on a pillow. The Qur'an, encased in soft cloth, sat on a raised pillow in front of her.

Tamanna stumbled towards her mother. "I must tell you—"

Mor held up a flat palm. "I have something to say also."

"No, listen. At the school . . . Kabeer . . . he is alive. Mor, he is alive! He is with the Taliban." Tamanna lowered her voice and whispered directly in her mother's ear, "Kabeer is alive."

Mor's eyes widened with shock. "Kabeer?" she whispered. Her eyebrows arched, she took in a sharp breath, and then she rocked back and forth, back and forth.

"Praise be to Allah, it is what we dreamed of," said Tamanna as she picked up her mother's hand and rubbed it against her own cheek. "What is it, Mor? Why are you not happy? What is wrong?"

A sorrowful sound came out of Mor's mouth. Mor put her head in her hands. "Your grandfather insists that your uncle's gambling debts be paid."

Tamanna sat back on her heels. She was confused. What had this to do with Kabeer?

"Must we sell the house?" Tamanna, fearful, eyes wide, pulled away from her mother.

"No. It's not the house that your grandfather wants sold." Mor, suddenly still, stopped and looked up at Tamanna with dead eyes.

"No!" Tamanna moaned. "No, no!" She stood and backed towards the door, her face contorted in shock.

"Allah has made women to suffer," said Mor. Silently she stroked the *taweez* that hung around her neck. "I want you to remember that had your father lived he would have found a good husband for you. Remember, your father loved you. He was a good man. There are many good men in our country."

Tamanna dropped to her knees and grew quiet. So this was why Uncle had been so pleasant about letting her go to school—he knew it would not last. She did not ask Mor about her would-be husband. Likely Mor knew nothing.

"When?" asked Tamanna in a low, flat voice.

"Before the new moon—an unlucky time to marry. *Muharram* is a month of mourning."

Ten days, thought Tamanna.

Chapter 7

Yellow Walls, Dusty Birds

Yasmine could hear the comforting, warbling prayer of the *Allahu Akbar, Allahu Akbar* echoing from a speaker on the top of a minaret. She lifted her head to look through her small bedroom window and crimped her eyes against the morning sun. How did one mark time when one was asleep? Turning her head slowly, she saw a haggard old man with red-rimmed eyes sitting on a stool.

"Baba?"

"Praise be to Allah, you have returned to us, Daughter."
Baba's voice was filled with anguish and relief.

In the shadows she saw her mother, who sat among
pillows that bolstered her on either side. "Mother?"

The woman lurched towards her daughter and, with
all her strength, gathered her in her arms.

"How long?" It was hard for Yasmine to form words.
Her tongue felt thick and the words seemed to scratch her
throat.

"You have been in Allah's hands for two days, Daughter."
Mother pulled away and sank back into the pillows. "We
were wrong, Yasmine. Wrong to bring you here. Your father
and I have agreed. We will leave this place, this country. He
is making plans. As soon as you are better, we will leave."

Yasmine looked past her mother to Tamanna, who stood
in the doorway. Reluctantly, she closed her eyes again.

⟨⋇⟩

Another day passed, then two. Every day Tamanna had helped
her get out of bed, dressed her, and coaxed her forward.

Today she would do it all on her own. Tentatively, gin-
gerly, Yasmine stood and slowly, silently shuffled across the
room. She walked through the house, occasionally reaching
for the back of a chair or the wall. Finally, Yasmine stood
looking out into the courtyard.

The yellow walls that surrounded the house glimmered
in the pale dawn light. Dusty birds twittered in the tree, and
Baba, always up before dawn to say his prayers, sat on a
bench surrounded by three thick notebooks. Beside him on

the ground was the *toshak* that the girls used to sit on to listen to his readings and lessons.

Yasmine let go of the doorframe and stood unsteadily.

Tamanna, in a heartbeat, was at her side. "What are you doing out of bed? Come, before your father sees you." She wrapped her arm around Yasmine's waist and led her back to her pillow. "Lie down. I will get you some tea."

Tamanna disappeared from view as Yasmine closed her eyes and felt the memories wash over her. She remembered lying on the stones in front of the school. She could see Tamanna hovering above her. She looked as though she was praying.

Tamanna, I see you. I see you. Why are you praying?

"Here, sip." Tamanna reappeared holding an earthen mug of sweetened green tea. Tamanna supported Yasmine's back while lifting the cup to her lips. "Your poor neck. Does it hurt?" she asked.

Yasmine touched her neck and felt the rough, raised skin that circled it.

"My brother did that to you. He yanked at your necklace but it did not break. I am sorry." Ashamed, Tamanna bit down on her lip. But he had been a good boy once, a kind brother. Somewhere inside him, that boy must still exist.

"It is not your fault, and anyway, it does not feel bad." In truth, while badly bruised, she did not feel terrible, although there was a ringing in her right ear that refused to go away.

"What happened to Teacher?" Yasmine asked.

"He is alive. The foreign soldiers came back. Someone must have called on a cell phone. They heard the sounds of the tanks and got back into their cars."

"I remember you carrying me. You saved me," said Yasmine simply.

"No, it was not me. It was Kabeer, my brother, who saved you. He went to the Taliban leader and made him stop hurting you."

No, it was you, thought Yasmine, but she said nothing. It was not often that Yasmine heard such pride in Tamanna's voice. "Has your brother returned to your house?"

Tamanna shook her head. "Perhaps he cannot forgive me," she said, her voice soft and low.

Surprised, Yasmine asked, "But what is there to forgive?"

Tamanna just shook her head. "Rest now. I must bring tea to your mother."

Yasmine lay back on her pillow and thought of Tamanna and her brother Kabeer. Something gnawed at the corners of her memory. Something was not right. She closed her eyes and slept.

(⋙⋘)

Another day passed. Yasmine, stronger and steadier on her feet, stood in the doorway looking out at the courtyard. Father was writing in his notebook, while Tamanna pulled laundry out of the copper *lagaan* and did her best to wring it dry. With squared shoulders, Yasmine crossed towards her.

"Yasmine!" Tamanna looked up from the laundry.

"Shush." Yasmine put a finger to her lips and pointed to her father. "Let me help," she said softly. She pulled back her sleeves and reached into the brown water.

Tamanna saw the purple bruises etched in pale yellow.

"No. Look how hurt you are." She surprised herself. It wasn't like her to be so bossy. Her tan face went pink with embarrassment.

"But I am much better, and besides, you do not look well either." Yasmine peered at her friend. Tamanna's cheeks had thinned and her eyes looked hollow. "Why have you lost weight?"

Baba, suddenly aware of his daughter's presence, put down his notebook and rushed over. "Yasmine, my dear, you must not do any work."

"Baba, look." She pointed to a mound of laundry. "This is too much for Tamanna, and I am feeling fine."

"*I* will help Tamanna," said Baba as he reached for the laundry.

Tamanna could not contain her amazement. A man help with the laundry? It would be more likely that a goat would make a bargain with a butcher!

Yasmine looked nervously towards the open gate. The door and a freestanding wall prevented prying eyes from getting a clear view of the courtyard, but still, she knew that if the men of the village saw Father helping with the laundry they would call him a fool, or worse. Yasmine and Tamanna had not talked about the gossip around the village since the housekeeper's death, but both girls knew it had not gone away.

"If you leave the laundry alone, I promise I will sit with Mother," Yasmine said firmly.

Baba made a pained, funny face but nodded, kissed Yasmine on the forehead, and picked up a book by the poet Rumi.

"Go, be with your mother," Tamanna agreed. "She is not well."

"Is it her leg?"

Tamanna shook her head. "No, it is something else. Her skin is not a good color and she has not slept well since you were attacked. Go."

"I will if you eat something." Yasmine pointed to a bowl of fruit.

"Yes, go." Tamanna nodded.

Head high, shoulders back, and standing as straight as she could, Yasmine walked into the house.

Mother lay on a bed, her body so long and thin under the quilt that it hardly looked as if there was a person there at all.

"Mother, are you awake?" whispered Yasmine.

"I am, my daughter. Do you feel better?" Mother struggled to sit up.

"Lie still. I am much better. But now it is you who are sick. Are you warm enough?" Yasmine covered Mother with her favorite embroidered *patoo* and sat on a three-legged stool beside her cot. Tamanna was right. Even Mother's eyes had a yellow tinge about them.

"Here, Mother, sip." Yasmine held a cup of water to her mother's lips then dabbed her mouth with a cool, soft cloth. "Does that feel better?" Mother nodded and Yasmine slipped a cassette into the tape deck. "Would you like to listen to music?" This time Mother smiled and nodded.

An Afghan woman sang a song of longing for death. She asked that she die and become the water in a stream, the wind over the desert, the grass of the plains. Yasmine closed her eyes and let the words float around her.

"Yasmine, are you still here?" whispered Mother.

"Yes, Mother. I was just daydreaming." Yasmine picked up a damp cloth and used it to cool her mother's cheeks. Mother took Yasmine's hand. "Yasmine, remember that there is kindness in the world, freedom to follow your heart." Spikes of pain broke Mother's voice. Yasmine had a better understanding of pain now. But while she was getting better, it was clear that Mother was getting worse.

Asleep, Mother's face was a mask of calm. Yasmine took a deep breath and put her head in her hands. How had it come to this? Mother, an educated woman who had attended Le Sorbonne in Paris and Radcliffe College in America and spoke of dogs in buns, of girlfriends named Linda and Melissa, of popcorn and movies. Where was the medical help that she needed now? If they had stayed in Oxford, surely she would have been better by now, back on her feet.

The tape came to an end. Except for her mother's soft breathing, the room was silent.

༼༈༽

"She is sleeping, Baba." Yasmine walked out into the courtyard and gazed around in amazement. A long line of laundry, scrubbed and wrung, hung on the line. She looked over to Tamanna, who made a half-hearted attempt to hide a smile. "Oh, Baba," Yasmine sighed. He had helped with the laundry after all.

She put her hand affectionately on her father's shoulder. "Baba, what is wrong with Mother? It's more than her leg."

Baba nodded. "She would not leave your bedside, and the effort and the worry has been hard on her health. Visit with your friend, my daughter. I will sit with your mother. Even asleep your mother is good company to me."

Respectful as always, the girls fell silent until Yasmine's father had collected his precious notebooks and disappeared into the house. Yasmine looked over at Tamanna as she collected the soap. It was very rude to make comments about another's body but Yasmine couldn't help herself.

"Tell me, why you are so thin? It seems that while I slept both my mother and my best friend have become ill." Yasmine reached for her friend's hand.

Tamanna looked away. *Best friend.* She took a breath and shook her head. It was too embarrassing to discuss.

"Please, Tamanna. You are getting smaller and smaller." There was a time when Tamanna had been the bigger and stronger of the two.

"Food does not want to stay in me. It leaves as quickly as I eat it." She was ashamed.

"Then you must go to one of the clinics the *khariji* doctors set up. They have medicine," said Yasmine.

Again Tamanna shook her head. "The *khariji* doctors do not charge for their diagnosis but medicine must be paid for, and Uncle will not pay."

"But Father will. You know that to be true! Both he and Mother love you like a daughter. And the *kharijis* charge very little for their medicine." Yasmine gripped Tamanna's hand even more tightly.

"No, you must not tell your father. It is too . . . humiliating. He has done too much for me as it is. Promise me, Yasmine, that you will not ask him for anything more. Besides, it is too late." Tamanna stopped, dithered, and then blurted out, "I will be married soon."

The news hung as heavy in the air as wet laundry on the line.

"Married? Married? When?" The words slipped through Yasmine's clenched teeth.

"In two days. I wanted to tell you before but you were so ill and then I thought that if I told you our last days would be sad. Uncle says that the sooner I am married, the less chance there is of me being spoiled. The first day of school . . . Noor . . . I was seen running away from him. They say that I was not spoiled because there was not enough time, but next time . . ." She stopped talking. Tamanna did not add that the price her future husband agreed to give her family would pay off Uncle's debts. "The *Nekahnama* certificate has been drawn up. Nothing can be done."

"Do you know who will be your . . . ?" Yasmine could not bear to say the word *husband*.

Tamanna shook her head. "It is good that you are leaving, Yasmine. You belong in the big world, not here. This was a gift, this time together. But now it has come to a close, and every day I thank Allah for bringing you here. It's like a window opened, but now it is closing, and everything has returned to its rightful place."

Chapter 8

Tears

"A car will come from Kandahar City. We will leave in a few days."

"Kandahar? Not Herat?" asked Yasmine. She had assumed that they would return to the city where Baba worked.

"No, my dear. We will fly from Kandahar to Dhabi and then on to London."

Home. England. Yasmine sat very still. This was what she wanted, and yet Oxford didn't seem like home anymore. Would any place feel like home now?

Baba and Yasmine sat under the tree in the courtyard and looked up, past the wall that surrounded their yard, to the distant mountain. Even in the dying light it was possible to see the deep paths the *khariji* soldiers had carved into the mountainside. Toy-like tanks rested on strategic high points. Their long barrels pointed down into the village. The *kharijis'* FOB was like a world within a world.

"Mother is so ill. Can she travel?" Yasmine asked.

"I have talked with the soldiers about your mother. I told the medic that she has a high temperature and her skin has a yellowish look. But the medic said it is not their policy to treat people who are ill." Baba shook his head.

"What does he mean, not their policy?" Yasmine leaned in towards her father. "The medic is a doctor, isn't he? How can it not be his policy to treat sick people?"

"The medic was a woman and is neither a doctor nor a nurse, as I understand it, but someone specially trained in field medicine."

Yasmine nodded. It was easy to forget that only a few yards away, in the big FOB, there was equality between men and women. "But that does not explain this *policy*," Yasmine persisted.

"It means that there are limitations to what they will do for civilians like us. Their commitment is to care for anyone who has been hurt by the war." Baba spoke like a very tired man. "However, perhaps it is because I speak English, or perhaps the medic was just being kind—she said that if I can bring your mother to the fort tomorrow she will be examined."

To Yasmine, Baba was a handsome man, tall and strong, but for the first time since the attack on Mother in Herat, Yasmine saw defeat in her father's eyes.

"Baba?" Yasmine reached for her father's hand. "If a civilian was being forced to do something she didn't want to do, something that might be against the law in other countries, would the *kharijis* help? Would they help a girl who is being told she has to marry someone she doesn't even know?"

"No, Daughter. They cannot help Tamanna." He let out a deep sigh. "They are invited guests of the government and must not interfere with local customs."

Tomorrow was Tamanna's wedding day. It seemed that nothing would stop the day from coming. "Will we go to the FOB tomorrow?" she asked.

"Your mother and I will go. I have arranged for a cart to come before dawn. You will stay here."

"But—"

"No, Daughter, I do not want you to be seen going into the FOB. There is no reason for you to come. Your mother and I will leave at first light and come home to a good meal that you will prepare for us." Baba tapped her hand. His voice was kind, as always. Even so, she knew better than to argue. Besides, no daughter would contradict her father.

The evening light had turned the air pink, the earth gold, the sky cobalt blue, and the distant mountains a ruby red. Night descended like a velvet cloth, and soon they would be sitting in the dark.

"Baba, we are almost out of kerosene." A small red jug sat beside their generator.

"We can do without lighting the lantern tonight," said Baba. They sat in silence as millions upon millions of stars lit up the night sky. "I have seen the lights of New York and London, but behold the magnificence of nature," said Baba.

"Ours is a country of pebbles and rocks, and yet the stars shine down from the heavens like stones polished to a glittering shine."

Yasmine tried not to giggle. Sometimes she thought Baba should be a poet . . . sometimes not!

"There is Little Bear . . . and Great Bear." She knew all the constellations. Soon Sirius, the brightest of all stars, would shine in the south.

"Shall I tell you the story of Ulugh Beg?" asked Baba.

"Baba, you have told me the story so often I could tell it to you, word for word."

"Take my *campal*." Baba wrapped the blanket around her. "And I will sit and listen to my knowledgeable daughter."

"Prince Ulugh Beg, the fifteenth century's greatest astronomer, built an observatory and catalogued thousands of stars. He founded a school for boys and girls and inscribed the words of the Prophet Muhammad—*The seeking of knowledge is incumbent upon all Muslim men and Muslim women*—on the wall." Yasmine looked up to the starry sky and smiled. "Peace be upon Him."

"And what happened to this brilliant man?" asked Baba.

"He was assassinated by extremists on October 27, 1449." And as Yasmine looked up to the starry night she had a thought. "Baba, do you wish that we had not come here?"

"I wish with all my heart that you were in school. I love my country, Daughter, but here we have been robbed of our most precious gifts: thought and imagination. Only in an atmosphere of peace and security can artists, poets, and writers flourish. Without our artists and storytellers, we have no history, and without history our future is unmoored—we drift. It is art, never war, that carries culture forward."

(~❈~)

The wail of the *Allahu Akbar, Allahu Akbar* woke Yasmine the next morning. In that moment between sleep and waking, unconsciousness and consciousness, she knew something was wrong.

Pop, pop, pop. Gunfire!

"Mother?" she called out. "Baba?" Yasmine leaped up and ran through the house in seconds. Empty. "Baba!?" Had they left already to go to see the medic at the FOB?

There were cries and shouts from outside their compound. Yasmine grabbed her *hijab*, flung open the door, slipped her feet into sandals, and ran across the courtyard and out onto the road.

Noor was standing in front of her house. "Your parents have been shot," he told her.

There was no time to scream, no time to cry out, no time to think. She raced down the road, Noor's words ringing in her ears: "Your father was seen going into the fort. He talks the *kharijis'* language. He is a spy. Your parents will be dead by the time the soldiers come with their army ambulance."

Gulping air, Yasmine kept going. *Your parents will be dead.* That meant that they were not dead yet. *Not dead. Not dead. Not dead.* Her feet hit the ground with such force that swirls of sand rose up behind her.

Yasmine did not have to go far before she saw a puddle of saffron material and a body beside it, splayed as if tossed from an airplane. Nearby was an upside-down cart, its wheels spinning in the air. The driver and donkey were nowhere to be seen. Mother's old *burka*, the one the driver had made Baba buy so very long ago, was blood-soaked. Baba, too, was lying in a pool of blood. Children hovered. Yasmine threw herself onto the ground and touched her father's hand while whispering into her mother's ear, "Mother, Mother."

"Yasmine? Daughter?" The words gurgled up Mother's throat. "Run, hide!" Mother lifted a heavy hand and pushed her daughter away.

"No, no!" Yasmine buried her face in her mother's *burka*. And then a sound, a groan, from her father.

"Baba!" Yasmine crawled over to her father. "Baba, do not leave me here."

A truck pulled up, and soldiers jumped down and took charge. "Secure the area. Move! Get these kids back." The commanding voice belonged to a woman soldier.

Yasmine scrambled up and melted into the crowd of children, who had left their chores, their baskets of dough, and their games to gather and watch. More soldiers leaped out of their vehicles, formed a circle around her parents, dropped down onto one knee and pointed their guns out towards the village and surrounding hills.

"Stand back." The command was in English but all the children seemed to understand.

Two medics jumped out of the truck. "Let me through." A small woman with yellow hair poking out under her helmet and a red cross sewn on her sleeve went directly to Mother. She dropped to her knees and split open a bag filled with medical supplies. Yasmine watched as the woman pulled the *burka* off Mother's face. She took out a flashlight and peered into Mother's eyes. "Jaundice," she hollered to the male medic, who was treating Baba. Time was both still and fleeting in the same moment. The truck with lights, bundles of supplies, and all manner of things dangling off it had its back door hanging open. Inside were beds.

"The female has lost a lot of blood," shouted the yellow-haired woman.

Yasmine edged as close as she could to the medic looking after Baba and peered over his shoulder. She felt hot air on the back of her neck. She turned. Noor was close behind her.

The woman medic glanced over at Baba. "I know that guy. He came into the FOB yesterday. He speaks perfect English. Educated, big time. He said that his wife had a broken leg and back problems, an old injury. He was going to bring her into the FOB today. This must be her. Get me a neck and leg brace. Private, get over here and help me."

A soldier pulled a stretcher out of the truck.

"How's he doing?" The woman tending Mother looked over to the medic caring for Baba.

"A couple of hits to the shoulder, one to the chest. His left arm is a pizza. He took a few to the thigh, too." Then the medic pushed a needle into Baba's good arm. "He's ready for transport," he shouted. Another soldier, young and pink-faced, picked up one end of the stretcher.

Yasmine's heart hammered in her chest and ears. Her teeth began to chatter.

"Okay, the braces are secure. Where's the terp? Tell him to find out who these people are and if they have any family.

Ask the kids. That girl there looks scared to death. She must know something." The female medic was pointing directly at Yasmine.

Yasmine recognized the interpreter—it was the one who had come to the school.

"You, who are these people?" He stared at Yasmine and spoke Dari. His eyes blinked and his head twitched. He was nervous.

The children around her answered for her. "Daughter! Daughter! She is the daughter of spies!" The words seemed to ignite the children as they all leaped and howled with laughter.

"Yasmine?" Tamanna was running down the road towards her. She was out of breath. "I was delivering the naan. I heard the men talking. I came as fast as I could."

Yasmine opened her mouth to speak, but no words came out.

In that moment, the interpreter called out and motioned to her to step towards him. "Are these your parents?"

Yasmine nodded. He turned and yelled words that she did not understand.

A female soldier rushed towards her. "*Asalaam alaikum.*" The soldier's accent was funny.

"*Alaikum asalaam,*" Yasmine replied.

The soldier said to the interpreter, "Tell her that I am just going to touch her, gently. Tell her that I won't hurt her." Still smiling at Yasmine, the female soldier bent down and touched her with fluttering fingers. "It's okay, sweetie," she said softly, as though she was afraid Yasmine might fly away. "Clean," she yelled.

Yasmine looked back at Tamanna. Clean? What did that mean? What was happening?

"Get in." The female soldier motioned towards the armored ambulance. Both parents lay on cots inside the truck. Yasmine leaped in. Mother was on one side, Baba on the other.

"Tell her to get to the back and sit. There's not much room," hollered the nurse. She did not need the interpreter. Yasmine understood, but everyone was too busy to notice. Children, soldiers, even the interpreter—everyone was shouting as soldiers scrambled into trucks and tanks. The door on the ambulance slammed shut, and for a moment everything went black. There were no windows.

In that last second Yasmine cried, "Tamanna!" But Tamanna was gone.

A light came on inside the ambulance. Yasmine crouched down and watched as two medics—one hovering over Baba, the other over Mother—went to work.

Chapter 9

Wedding Day

Black spots remained on the road where the blood of Yasmine's parents had seeped into the ground. Excitement over, the children scattered.

Tamanna stood still and watched as the dust from the truck's wheels wafted back to the ground. Was this it? These people, who had come into her life and changed her forever, were gone. She had not even said thank you or goodbye. Tears pooled in Tamanna's eyes. Suddenly, abruptly, she was alone. She wanted to crumple into a ball and cry. *Yasmine, don't forget me.* She whispered the words in her heart. This strange gift of friendship, of learning, of feeling treasured was over, and she had to accept it. She turned and looked directly into Noor's face.

"They will die, you know," he sneered. "Yasmine's parents—dead. Allah wills it. They are traitors, just like your friend. You must stay away from her or you will get hurt too." His words burned like kerosene poured on an open wound.

Tamanna picked up the edge of her scarf, covered her face, and sobbed, "Noor means *light*. What light do you cast? What good do you do?" She spun on her heels and ran all the way home.

Breathless, Tamanna leaned against the inside wall of her own courtyard, closed her eyes, and waited for her heart to stop pounding. There, tethered to a rope, in the middle of the yard, was an old, angry billy goat. The goat pawed the dry ground and bleated. Tamanna, suddenly tired, walked up to the goat and patted its head. Did it know that it would soon be kebabs for the wedding feast? "Poor goat." She ran her fingers through its knotted hair.

A wedding usually cost much money and lasted for many days. Uncle was insisting that there be a feast—at least he was willing to pay for that, and many people in the village had been invited. But she would have no pieces of furniture, cloth, or jewelry to take with her to the marriage.

Her wedding should have been the most important event in her life, but to Tamanna it did not *feel* like her wedding day. Perhaps if she had done the things that most brides do to prepare . . . but her hands and feet were not painted with henna, and no one had yet troubled to help her remove the hair from her body. Except for the hair on her head, eye-lashes, and eyebrows, a bride was to go to her new husband hairless. But what did it matter what she looked like? Her husband would not think her pretty. A truly beautiful Afghan woman was tall, with almond-shaped eyes, a small mouth, pale, delicate skin, and a round tummy. Tamanna looked down. Yasmine was right. She was very thin, and the sickness left her tired, too. She'd thought she was getting better but really, she was getting worse. The only way she could control her trips to the outhouse was to not eat at all. She had eaten nothing for two days.

Tamanna gazed around the courtyard. In the evening, as the sun set on this day, she would receive the blessings of the *mullah*, sign the *Nekahnama*, the marriage certificate, and she and her husband would exchange thin gold bands. "*Mobarak*," everyone would congratulate the couple. They would clap. She would be a married woman. She imagined it all. Men would hug one another out in the courtyard right where she was standing now. The women would hug one another in the house. Mor's precious glass bowl filled with sugar-dusted almonds would be passed around. Along with the goat kebabs there would be saffron rice, and rice with raisins and nuts, spinach, *manto* filled with meat, and eggplant with yogurt sauce.

Tamanna felt that funny rumbling in her stomach again. How could she make it stop?

"Tamanna, come and eat," Mor called from inside the house.

"In a minute, Mor." Tamanna ran past Uncle's shack and into the outhouse. She burned with equal parts of pain and shame. Her legs quivered and her heart thumped hard in her chest. She felt weak, cold, and sweaty, all at the same time. What would happen when her husband found out that she could not control her bowels? Would he beat her?

"Are you still ill, my daughter?" asked Mor.

Tamanna, head down and dragging tired feet, walked back around the house and sank down onto an old *toshak*. She put her head on her mother's shoulder. "I will be fine," she whispered. Tamanna picked up a tiny potato and began to peel it. Only then did she notice her mother's shoulders heaving up and down. "Mor, are you crying?"

Mor's voice drifted as her hands peeled vegetables. "I have lost my son to the Taliban and now I have lost my daughter, too . . ."

"Mor, you have lost me to a husband. What other life is there for me? Aren't all girls told from birth that they must marry? Think of Kabeer. Did we not think him gone from this earth? And how could he truly be a Talib if he saved Yasmine and Teacher?"

"My sweet little boy." Mor nodded.

"Mor, what will become of you?" Lines creased her mother's forehead, and she was so thin that the bones of her wrists looked like knots of rope under a thin blanket. But Mor was old, almost twenty-nine.

"I will go to your grandfather's house. I will be taken care of."

"Will I ever see you again?" Tamanna leaned over and wiped the tears from her mother's face with the end of her *hijab*.

"It is in the hands of the Prophet, peace be upon Him.

Take the naan to Rahim Khan. He will be waiting." Mor nodded towards the stack of bread. "Be quick. Your uncle must not see you on the street. He is—"

"Smoking *chars*." Uncle had been celebrating his freedom from debt by smoking opium. And they both knew, without going to the well or bathhouse to hear the gossip, that he was drinking and gambling, too.

"Go, go. Go before he returns." Mor swished her hands in the air, shooing her away like a fly.

Tamanna kissed her mother's cheek, stood, then turned back and fell on her knees. "Mor Mora, grand Mora, Mora, Mora, grand Mora."

They were the wrong words to say. Mor put her face in her hands and cried.

"Don't cry, Mor. I did not mean to make you cry," Tamanna whispered.

Chapter 10

Forward Operation Base: Masum Ghar

Inside the ambulance the two medics talked to each other and into their headsets while bending over Mother and Baba. They did not pay any attention to Yasmine. Had they forgotten that she was even there? She listened carefully. As long as they didn't use too much slang their words were easy to understand. Baba and Mother needed blood, she understood that. They had to be cross-matched, stat. What was "stat"? Both Mother and Baba had needles in their arms attached to tubes that led to bags of clear fluid. The bags swung from the ceiling of the vehicle.

The armored ambulance stopped several times, but finally the back door dropped open. "Whatta ya got?" Yasmine couldn't quite see the soldier who was speaking, but his voice was familiar.

"Two locals," said one medic as both jumped out of the ambulance. "The male took three bullets, female took two. Female has an old leg injury. She needs to be immobilized before transport. I think she's septic, too, and seriously vitamin D deprived. The male might lose an arm, but the bullets missed major organs. Girl, about fourteen or fifteen years old, not involved in the hit. We're assuming that she's their daughter but the terp hasn't interrogated her." As they talked they slid the stretchers out of the ambulance and, in a heartbeat, her parents disappeared behind the swinging doors of a small building.

"Has she been checked?"

"Clean. Where's the terp?" The female soldier, talking and walking, barged back out of the building.

"Terps are busy with a local down at the front gate. They're sending up an ANA who speaks Dari and a little English."

The female soldier peered into the ambulance. Yasmine sat crouched between a metal tank and a stack of medical kits. "Come on out, honey, it's okay. Come on." She motioned with her hand. Standing behind her was a tall soldier, gun slung over his shoulder, helmet pushed back revealing a clump of red hair. He was the soldier who had come to her school and talked about alligators and crocodiles.

Hunched over, with her head down, Yasmine scrambled out of the ambulance. *"Asalaam alaikum,"* she whispered, but more to her feet than to the soldiers in front of her. She looked over the soldier's shoulder. Where were her parents?

"Hey, I know her. She was at that school, the one that got attacked. Hi there, Princess, remember me? My name is Dan or Danny—you choose."

Yasmine drew the ends of her *hijab* over her mouth and nose, looked up, then down. His eyes were so blue they looked liked water. He was grinning.

"She doesn't understand. Stop scaring her," snapped the female soldier.

"I am not scaring her. I'm great with girls. Look here." Dan-Danny fumbled for something in his pocket just as an Afghan soldier came up from behind the *khariji* soldier.

"Daraysh. Stop. Identify yourself. You will be shot by the *kharijis* if you misbehave," barked the soldier in Dari. He was dressed in blue, wore a heavy black vest, and carried a gun. Yasmine shrank backwards.

"Hey, what are you saying to her? She's just a kid." The female soldier, clearly annoyed, gave Yasmine a pained smile full of sympathy and concern.

Grateful, Yasmine looked up into the eyes of the woman soldier. They were light brown with streaks of green. She was young, very tall, and had soft yellow hair tied back in a round bun. She wore the spotty camouflage clothes soldiers wore to blend into their surroundings, big boots, and a gun was strapped against her leg.

"I'll take charge of her," she said.

The Afghan soldier shrugged before walking away, but

the female soldier said nothing. Yasmine was surprised. Did she not know that a shrug was a sign of disrespect?

"My name is Brenda. BRENDA." The female soldier tapped her chest. "The doctor and medics are with your parents. You sit." The medic was talking with her hands. She handed Yasmine an orange and a bottle of ice-cold water.

"My name is Yasmine," Yasmine whispered.

Brenda stopped and peered down at Yasmine. "Did you hear that? She speaks English!"

Dan-Danny, still searching his pockets, looked up. "No way. Maybe she knows a few words. I took French for ten years and all I can say is, '_Je n'suis pas parley Français._' Hey, I found it." Dan-Danny held up a photo. "Sister—Haley—she's fourteen." He held up a picture of a smiling girl standing in snow, wearing a big coat, scarf, and funny wool hat.

"I am also fourteen," said Yasmine.

"She can speak English, all right," announced Brenda.

"Holy . . ." Suddenly there was nothing to say. Both Brenda and Dan-Danny were looking at her as if they had just discovered a kitten who could bark.

"Please, could I see my parents?"

"Come on, I'll take you."

Brenda led the way into a wooden building. The air was cool. Yasmine had forgotten about air conditioning. Everything was modern, clean, spotless. There were four beds, two on each side. Blinking machines were pushed next to the beds. Equipment hung from the ceiling. This wasn't exactly like the hospital she'd been to once in England, but it was certainly nothing like the one in Herat that stank of unwashed bodies and cigarettes.

"This is the trauma room. It's where we bring wounded people for initial assessment, to see how hurt they are. Your parents are in the next room, through those doors. That's the ICU, Intensive Care Unit. Come." Brenda pushed the door.

No, no, no. Yasmine covered her mouth. Her parents lay in high beds, eyes closed, their faces pale as the white sheets that covered them. Baba's face was almost hidden by a mask, a tube ran under Mother's nose, and there were machines flashing and beeping beside both of them.

"It only looks bad. See? The mask is giving your father oxygen. That is your father, isn't it?" asked Brenda.

Yasmine nodded. She couldn't open her mouth for fear of what might come tumbling out.

"Mother?" Yasmine took hold of her mother's hand. It felt bony and crumpled, like paper. Worse, the metal band around her head made it look as if she was being tortured! And she was tied to the bed. Why? Did they think her mother might run away?

"Your mother is not in any pain. We have secured her head, back, and legs so she can't move. Now, listen to me." The medic spoke softly into Yasmine's ear. "Most people die from an assault like this because of loss of blood. It was dumb luck that we were out on patrol in the area. Your father took shrapnel to the leg and arm. But here's the thing, he has a bullet lodged in his lung. We have given him a very strong sedative. He is in a very deep sleep. We have just given your mother a mild sedative, but in a few minutes we will give her a very strong one so that she sleeps through the flight. There are surgeons at KAF. They will operate on your parents. They are very good, the best in the world."

"What's KAF?" Yasmine felt faint.

"Kandahar Airfield, it's near Kandahar City. By road it would take about three, four hours but we're transporting your parents by helicopter. It will take only twenty, thirty minutes. It's where all the United Nations Forces are— Canadians, Dutch, French, British, Australians, Americans, Romanians, everyone. Come, sit with me and I'll tell you all about the operations. Drink some water." Brenda opened a tiny fridge, pulled out a bottle of water, and twisted off the cap.

They were going to take her parents away. What would happen to her? Did the soldiers understand that a girl her age could not be left alone without family? As Yasmine forced water down her throat a young soldier poked his head around the corner.

"Lieutenant, two more cases of the Kandahar-crappies just reported. What should I do with them?"

"Great, that makes five. That's all we need, an epidemic ripping through the camp. I'll be right there." Brenda turned back to Yasmine. "Honey, I have to handle this. Talk to your mother. Stand on this stool so that she can see you without turning her head. She is not to move. I'll be back in a few minutes, okay?"

Yasmine nodded. She tiptoed over to her mother's bed.

"Mother, Mother."

Mother's eyelashes fluttered. "Your father! Where is your father?" She struggled to lift her head up and pushed against the restraints that tied her to the bed.

"Hush, hush, he is sleeping. Please, do not move!" Yasmine cried.

She sank back into the pillow as Yasmine buried her head in Mother's blanket. She must not cry in this place, and she must not be selfish. What would happen to her after they took Mother and Baba away did not matter.

Mother coughed. There was a glass with a straw poking out of it on the little table beside her bed. Yasmine held the straw close to her mother's lips. "Here, Mother, sip." Mother swallowed, then lifted a heavy hand and pushed it away. Tears streamed down her face to settle in her hair and pillow. "Mother, Mother, please, please don't cry." Yasmine stroked her mother's cheek.

"Yasmine, I am sorry. We are so sorry." Mother was sputtering. "Yasmine, you are the *noor* of your father's heart. If only more Afghani men loved their daughters like your father does you, perhaps our country would not be in such peril." Mother took a deep breath and closed her eyes.

"Mother, Mother . . ." Yasmine laid her head on the pillow.

Behind her a door opened and closed, bringing with it a stream of hot air. Brenda came in and sat down on a bench.

"Yasmine, come sit beside me," she said.

Yasmine kissed her mother's cheek, dried her tears with the fringe of her scarf, and sat, hands folded, ankles crossed, on a bench at the foot of her mother's bed.

"Eat this." Brenda handed Yasmine a peeled banana. "So tell me, why do you speak English with a British accent?"

"I don't understand." Yasmine choked down a bite then put the banana aside. She kept her eyes on her parents, afraid to look away in case they vanished forever.

"Your accent, you speak like someone from England. Did you have a British teacher?"

Yasmine nodded. "I had lots of British teachers when I went to school in England. My father was a teacher, a professor. And my mother was a lawyer who studied in the United States." Yasmine sat up a little taller. Allah forgive her, she was guilty of pride.

"But you and your parents are Afghans, correct?" asked Brenda.

Yasmine nodded.

Brenda let out a big sigh as she slumped back. "And I guess they came back here to help their country, and brought you with them."

Yasmine watched her parents for some movement; even a flicker of an eyelash would have made her feel better. *Mother, Baba, don't leave me. Don't go. I do not know what will happen to me*, she thought.

Brenda looked Yasmine in the eyes and said, "This is important, Yasmine, really, really important. Is there a special place in your home where your father keeps important papers? A box perhaps, or maybe a big envelope or file?"

"Please, I do not care about papers. I care about my parents, my father—"

The door banged open and a soldier filled the doorway. "Incoming. One down. Shrapnel to the abdomen. ETA six minutes."

Brenda leaped up. "Mike, call Dan and tell him to take Yasmine here back down to the gate. The civilians are ready for transport. There are five bottles of ciprofloxacin on the shelf. If any more cases of the Kandahar-crappies report in, have them fill out the form and give each one a five-day dose. Tell Dan to take a few bottles down to the gate.

Michelle says that a couple of ANA soldiers have come down with it too."

As Brenda talked she strapped on a holster, checked a small gun, and donned a heavy-looking vest and helmet. She spun on the heels of her big boots and spoke quickly to Yasmine.

"Dan will take you down to the front gate. There's a female soldier there named Michelle. I'll call her on my cell. Is there anyone living in your house? Are you safe there?" Brenda spoke quickly, eyes wide. There was no time to hesitate.

Yasmine nodded. "I am safe in my home."

"Good. I want you to go and find all the documents you can. Bring back anything that looks official, and look for passports. Tell Michelle that you are to be let out of the FOB and back in. Do not stand outside the gate." As she spoke, she replenished a medical kit and bolted for the door.

Yasmine stood in the middle of the room. What now?

"Hey there, Princess, your chauffeur is at your service." Dan-Danny laughed. It was a big laugh, like the rest of him. Mike was on his heels. "What gives? Isn't Princess here flying out to KAF with her parents?" Dan-Danny's eyebrows came together to create two deep ridges between his eyes. Yasmine watched. Baba's forehead looked the same when he was worried.

"Can't take locals in military transport unless they've been wounded. Her parents are scheduled to be vacced out in an hour, but this place is going to be hopping any minute. Another IED just called in. That makes two," said Mike as he opened Mother's chart.

Dan-Danny's face, which had been pale to begin with and dotted with freckles, went white. "Okay, Princess, let's hit the road." He hoisted his gun onto his shoulder.

So, she would be left behind—her skin grew clammy and her heart began to race. But she must not think of herself. Her parents would be helped. That's what was important.

She took a deep breath. "Please, I must say goodbye to my father, even if he is asleep." Yasmine ran over to her father's bed. She kissed him on one cheek, then the other once, twice, ten times, then whispered, "*Allah, You make night pass into day and You make day pass into night, and You bring forth the living from the dead . . . Allah, give sustenance to us.*"

"Best to get out of here before this place heats up." Dan-Danny swung open the door.

"Hey, Dan, take a few bottles of Kandahar candies down to the front gate." Mike shoved a handful of pill bottles into a cloth bag. "I swear half the camp will be in the can before nightfall. One pop a day for five days. Not five pills in one day!"

"Yeah, got it." Dan grabbed the bag.

Yasmine followed Dan-Danny outside. They trailed up a stony path and then stopped at the top of the hill where a jeep was waiting. In one easy swoop he bounced up in the air and almost magically landed behind the steering wheel. Yasmine hesitated, then did her best to climb in gracefully. And then, over the hill, she saw an amazing sight. All she could do was stare.

Three mountains surrounded a space that housed dozens and dozens of fearsome tanks all lined up in front of massive concrete walls. There were hundreds of tents and long tin buildings, and as many more vehicles and tall cranes. Ten, twenty villages could have fit into that space. Flags flew over buildings. She recognized the American flag and the Canadian flag—they were also on the sleeves of the soldiers that patrolled the village. Everywhere she looked, soldiers, men and women, walked around with big guns hanging off their shoulders. The *kharijis* had brought their world to Afghanistan. How could the Taliban, how could anything or anyone, stand up to such might?

"Pretty amazing, huh?" said Dan-Danny. "You drove right through it in the ambulance. Now, hang on as we blast off to all of your favorite destinations!"

As Dan-Danny put his foot to the floor, the jeep took off. Yasmine grabbed the overhead bar. The wind snapped her head back and took her breath away. They plunged down the hill and bounced along the flat middle ground, passing the long line of ferocious-looking vehicles with long guns. Dan-Danny moved a stick beside his leg. The jeep growled like a dog then made a great leap forward and raced back up a small hill. It lurched and pitched, and just as it felt as if it might actually leave the ground, it came to a sudden stop in a cloud of dust at the top. They perched there, peering down like birds onto the little encampment at the front gate.

Yasmine adjusted her headscarf, then pulled the ends across her face. Down below, a female soldier was arguing with a local man.

"Do you know him?" Dan-Danny asked.

Yasmine shook her head. A girl might not recognize her own neighbor if he was a male, but he might recognize her even though she was seldom outside the walls of her house. It was funny that the *kharijis* had been in the country for such a long time and yet seemed to know so little about their customs. What else did they not know?

The female soldier's voice rose up like smoke. "I repeat, we cannot interfere in local politics or your culture. We are not an occupying army. We have been *invited* here by your government. We cannot provide shelter for your nephew. That would be kidnapping. Children who come to our door must be returned to their parents. It's the rules."

The man flapped his hands in the air. "Why are you in my country? All you do is make more war. When we ask for help you have your *rules*." He turned his back on the female soldier and stomped back towards the gate. Two ANA soldiers tried to keep up with him.

Dan took giant strides down the hill, and Yasmine did her best to keep up. "Looks like you're making friends with the locals. Catch." Dan-Danny tossed the cloth bag down to Michelle.

"Yeah, I'm a hit. He thinks his nephew is in danger of being recruited by the Taliban and he wants us to give him a job inside the FOB. Every boy is in danger. We're not babysitters. What's this?" Michelle held up the bag.

"Kandahar candies for the ANA. It looks like we're all going to come down with the Kandahar-crappies before too long. Directions are on the container."

Michelle looked over at Yasmine and smiled. "Hi there, Yasmine. Brenda told me about you." Michelle was heavy-set, with wide hazel eyes and a huge smile. "You speak English, right?"

Yasmine nodded.

"I'm not sure what's going on here. Brenda was in a hurry. I do know that you are to go to your house, collect whatever it is Brenda asked for, and come straight back. Straight back!" Michelle spoke gently but firmly. Yasmine nodded again. "And you are going to have to hurry. I mean run, really run. I'll be waiting for you here. Take this. I bet you haven't eaten a thing today." Michelle shoved a chocolate bar into her hands.

Chocolate—it had been so long! "Thank you. Please, the soldiers that are coming into the hospital were hurt by IEDs. What is an IED?"

"An improvised explosive device."

"A land mine?" said Yasmine.

"Yep, but bigger."

"I am sorry that the soldiers got hurt," said Yasmine.

"Oh honey, it's not your fault. Now go," said Michelle. Yasmine ran for the gate.

Chapter 11

Goodbye, Tamanna

Yasmine held the ends of her scarf over her face and crossed the road, skulking between the *jingle* trucks, rickshaws, cars, and *millie* buses. It would not do to be seen. Everyone seemed to think that her parents were spies. What would they do if they saw her going back to her house? She ran towards the middle of the village, ducked behind a wall, and watched as Rahim Khan, the kebab-seller, turned his meat. There was one slice of naan left on the small table beside the grill. Today was Tamanna's wedding day, but no

103

matter, she would still be told to deliver the naan, Yasmine was sure of it . . . almost sure. *Please Tamanna, come, come*, she begged silently. How long should she wait?

Minutes passed, and more minutes. It was no use. And then there she was! Tamanna, her eyes fixed on the ground, came down the road and placed the bread on the table.

"Tamanna," Yasmine called out in the loudest whisper she dared.

Tamanna spun on her heels and saw Yasmine's head bob up briefly from behind the wall. Casually, eyes glued to the ground, she walked over to Yasmine's hiding spot then ducked down beside her.

"I thought you were gone!" Tamanna said, taking her friend's hands with delight.

"Have you been crying?" asked Yasmine. Tamanna's eyes were as red as saffron.

Tamanna shook her head. To admit to such a thing, even to a friend, was too humiliating. "Your parents . . . are they . . . ?" Tamanna could hardly form the question.

"They are alive. The *kharijis* will put them in a helicopter and take them to Kandahar. I have something for you." Yasmine handed Tamanna the chocolate bar that was now soft in its package. "But I cannot stay. I just wanted to see you, to tell you that they are all right. I have to go to my house, then return to the FOB with papers."

"I will go to the house with you." Tamanna reached for Yasmine's hand.

"But your wedding?" said Yasmine.

"I do not get married for hours." Never mind that Mor needed her to help, or that Uncle would be angry that she was away so long. He would not beat her on the day of her wedding. Her future husband might object to having her damaged.

Hugging walls, their eyes averted, they made their way through the village to the door of the courtyard. Quickly, Yasmine twisted the knob, the bolt slipped, and they ducked inside.

"What are we looking for?" asked Tamanna.

"I'm not sure, but there is a box under Mother's bed." Yasmine ran into Mother's room and reached under the bed. Carefully, she pulled out a large metal box. It was heavy, too heavy to lift, so they slid it across the floor. "It's locked." Yasmine sat back on the floor.

"Where would your father hide a key?"

"His desk?" Yasmine ran to the desk and began opening the drawers. Nothing. In England she'd once seen a detective show where a key was taped under a desk. She crawled under and looked up. Nothing. And then a thought. Baba's favorite poet was Rumi. He was seldom without a copy of the poems. Yasmine pulled a book off the shelf, held it by its spine, and shook the pages. Still nothing.

"What about Rabi'a Balkhi?" suggested Tamanna. Baba had read her poems to both girls many times.

Yasmine searched the shelves. "Here." She pulled it out of its leather case and gave it a shake. Still nothing.

"Could you carry the big box back to the fort?" Tamanna asked.

Yasmine shook her head. It was too heavy for one person, and if Tamanna helped, she would certainly be accused of helping spies.

"Wait." Tamanna held up the book of Rumi's poems. "There is a pocket in the back. The key!" She held it up triumphantly.

"You are so smart!" Yasmine laughed, while Tamanna blushed.

Yasmine turned the key in the lock and lifted the lid of the box. What she found were colorful rolls of paper as thick as a clenched fist. "Look! These are British pounds, these are American dollars . . . but I don't recognize the rest."

"What are these?" Tamanna pulled out three little books. Two were the same color but the third was a dark red.

"Passports! I need those. But look at this." She held up a scroll of paper. It had a great gold seal on the bottom. There were others, too, some small with strange lettering. One had a red seal. "Some of these used to be on the walls of our home in England."

Tamanna leaped up and grabbed a cloth bag. "Go, take them back to the fort and do not return." The sudden movement made her double over in pain.

"Is it any better, the illness?" Even now Yasmine did not want to use the embarrassing word *diarrhea*.

"It does not matter. Go." Tamanna pushed the cloth bag into Yasmine's hands. "Hurry, before everyone knows that you are here."

In that instant, both girls understood that they would never see each other again.

"Take this. Baba and Mother would want it so." Yasmine peeled American paper bills from the roll of money.

Tamanna waved her away. "It is no good to me."

"But you could buy medicine." Yasmine tried to force the bills into Tamanna's hands.

"It will only be found . . . or worse, I will be accused of theft." Tamanna looked at the ground. The pain of losing her friend was worse than feeling Uncle's foot as it broke her hip, worse than seeing her mother cry, worse than thinking that soon she would be married to an old man.

"Then you will take this. It will be your dowry." Yasmine tried to undo the gold chain from her neck, the one Baba had given her when she was ten years old.

"No, it will only be stolen from me by the other . . ." She stopped. She could not bear to say *other wives*. All she did was shake her head. Yasmine must not know about the life that was in store for her, it would not be fair.

"Then what *can* I do?" Yasmine asked.

"You can go, now." Tamanna gathered up the papers and shoved them into the bag. "Your father's notebooks!" she cried. Tamanna ran to his desk. There were three of them, and together they weighed as much as a good-sized bag of apples. Tamanna put them in the cloth bag and looped its shoulder strap over Yasmine's neck.

"I will be sure to tell Baba that it was you who remembered the notebooks." Yasmine kissed her friend's cheeks one, two, ten times. The kisses tasted salty.

"Tell your parents that I thank them, that in my heart they are my parents, too. I will love them forever." Tamanna stood tall and strong.

It was Yasmine who began to cry.

∽⁂∾

The ANA soldier curled his lip as he swung open the huge gate. Yasmine wasn't afraid, not this time. She turned to the sound of rocks crunching under boots. Michelle swung her arm over Yasmine's shoulder.

"Yasmine, your parents have been evacuated. We don't have enough staff to take care of them and our soldiers, and your father is going to need immediate surgery."

"To KAF?" The words stuck in her throat.

Michelle nodded. "They are being flown to Kandahar Airfield. They should be arriving any minute."

Yasmine's legs felt rubbery. The sun, the heat, running, no food—everything conspired to make her feel confused and dizzy.

"Come, sit." Michelle guided Yasmine to a chair and kneeled in front of her. "Brenda told me everything. Is this it?"

Yasmine handed Michelle the bag.

"Hey, there. The Princess is back!" Dan-Danny slung his gun over his shoulder and grinned. "Anyone call for a car?"

"Yeah, me. We're sending Yasmine to KAF. Fill that old daypack by the fridge with power bars and water bottles, will you? She can take them with her. And there are some oranges there, too. Just fill the bag."

"Please, I am going to KAF?" Eyes wide, Yasmine couldn't believe what she was hearing. She was going to KAF after all?

"Yes, of course. Did you think we'd leave you on your own?" Michelle sounded equally surprised.

Yasmine's heart began to pound. "But the man who asked that his son be taken in . . . you said that you cannot interfere with local customs. You are not . . ." What was the word Michelle had used? "Childminders." Yasmine's voice trailed away. She took a deep breath to ward off tears. She would not be alone.

"Childminders? You mean babysitters?" She smiled. "Honey, your circumstances are totally different—"

"Excuse me." An ANA soldier came up from behind. "My soldiers need the medicine for the diarrhea," he said, looking directly at Brenda and ignoring Yasmine entirely.

Yasmine spun around. Diarrhea?

"Medicine, three." He held up three fingers.

Brenda nodded and handed him three little bottles of pills, the same bottles that Dan-Danny had brought from the hospital. But Dan-Danny had called them *candy*.

"One bottle per person, one pill a day in the morning with food. ONE!" Brenda held up a finger. "After five days the men must go see the medics."

The ANA soldier nodded, took the pills, and left.

"Is that not candy?" asked Yasmine.

"Candy? Oh, I get it. They call the pills Kandahar candy because we eat them like candy. It's really medicine." Michelle was shifting through the papers.

"What is the medicine for?" asked Yasmine.

Brenda was not listening. She pulled out the parchment. "Jeeze. Dan, look."

Dan leaned over Michelle's shoulder and whistled. "Your father has a Ph.D. from Oxford! I can't even afford the shoes."

"Excuse me," whispered Yasmine. "The medicine—what is it for?"

"That's not all, look at this." Michelle held up another paper. "Radcliffe. Her mother went to Radcliffe! So how in . . . Look, Brenda was right." Michelle waved the three passports. "Outstanding!" Dan cheered. "Dan, have the driver bring the car right into the FOB so that no one can see her get in."

Grinning, Dan spun around. "Yes, ma'am." He headed off at a steady clip in the direction of the front gate.

Yasmine turned back and this time spoke a little louder. "Pardon, but what does it mean, Kandahar-crappies?"

Brenda held the telephone receiver with one hand while she riffled through Mother's and Baba's papers. "Get me the Brits . . . Anyone will do . . . Yeah, well I have one of their citizens . . . No, not a soldier, a girl, a girl with a British passport . . . Yep, I'll hold." Michelle turned back to Yasmine and held up one of the passports. "Do you have any family living in Britain?"

Yasmine nodded. "Grandfather."

"You are getting out of here, sweetheart . . . Yes, I'm still here. I am holding her passport . . . Yeah, it's current . . . Hold on a sec." Michelle covered the phone. "You are fourteen, right?"

Yasmine nodded. "But about the *crappies* and the *candies* . . . ?"

"Yep, she's fourteen. Wait . . ." Michelle put down the phone and sifted through the papers before finding a small one with tiny writing on it. "I have her birth certificate. Born in Brighton, that's by the sea in England, and you are going to love this part, she speaks English with a British accent. Her parents are at KAF in the hospital . . . Yes, yes. We will send her by car . . . Right. Who will meet her? . . . Lieutenant Trish Stenson, got it." Michelle hung up the phone, looked over at Yasmine, and grinned.

"Please, what are the pills for?"

"We call it *the runs* or diarrhea. I think you Brits call it *the trots*—it makes you want to run to the toilet often." Michelle pointed to a cluster of tall, blue, tin boxes that looked like upright coffins. "Wait, you're not sick, are you?"

Yasmine shook her head. "Do those cure the sickness?" She pointed to the pill bottles.

"It depends on what caused the illness in the first place. People have to be tested to find the cause." Michelle smiled. "Honey, you are not responsible for the soldiers. Now, let's get moving. The drive to KAF is three to four hours, but with these roads it can take longer." Michelle pointed to Baba's notebooks. "What are those?"

"They belong to my father."

"Hang on, I'll find you a knapsack . . . or should I say *haversack*? That's what you Brits call it, what?" Michelle laughed as she disappeared through a door and returned holding an army backpack in desert camouflage. "It's all I have that will hold the books besides a dozen Hello Kitty bags, but they're too small. They were a donation." Michelle stacked the notebooks and papers then slipped everything into the backpack. "No matter what, do not lose this bag. Put it over your shoulder or strap it on your back. It's even waterproof. When you get to KAF give it to Lieutenant Stenson. We will pay for the car."

"I can pay." Yasmine reached into a pocket and pulled out the roll of money.

"Mother of . . ." Michelle stopped in her tracks. "Child, you are no end of surprises."

Yasmine handed her the roll.

"There must be a couple of thousand U.S. dollars here, British pounds, these blue banknotes are Afghanis, and I think these are Pakistani bills. See these?" Michelle held up two green American bills with the number fifty on the corner. "These could feed an Afghan family in a city like Kabul for six months. Give me a minute," said Michelle as she again disappeared through the door.

Now was her chance. Never in her life had Yasmine stolen anything. Perhaps if she just asked, Michelle would give her the pills. But what if she said no? What if she said that it was against *policy* to give pills to a local person? There was no time to reason it out. Yasmine grabbed a bottle of pills and jammed it deep into a pocket. A long time ago thieves had their right hands cut off. As far as she knew that was something that had happened many centuries ago, and in Taliban times too, but it didn't happen anymore. Still, Baba would have said that stealing was shameful and would weigh heavily on one's conscience.

Michelle reemerged holding what looked like a long, skinny piece of cloth. "This is a moneybelt my grandma gave me. Apparently she thought I might get mugged in Afghanistan. I think it's made of kryptonite. It goes around your waist. See?" Michelle held it against her own waist. "No one will know that you are wearing it. I'll put the money inside. It has a little zipper. There! Now, lift your shirt."

Tentatively, Yasmine stepped in close and let Michelle clip the belt around her middle and tuck it under the waistband of her skirt. Michelle was right. It could not be seen.

"The limo has arrived." Dan-Danny ambled towards them.

"Is the car inside the FOB?" she asked.

"Yep. Except it's not a car, it's one of those rickshaw things with one front wheel, room for the driver in the front seat and two skinny people in the back. Kinda looks like a garbage can on wheels. Frankly, I wouldn't ship a goat in it," replied Dan-Danny.

"As long as it gets her there in one piece," muttered Michelle as she gathered up Yasmine's two bags. "Come on, then, Yasmine. Freedom is just a few hours away."

As Yasmine fingered the bottle of pills in her pocket, Michelle kissed her on the top of her head. "Be safe," she whispered.

The rickshaw was very old, likely brought to Afghanistan from Pakistan. Like all the other cars, *jingle* trucks, *millie* buses, and rickshaws, it was decorated with toys and bright fabric and painted with brilliant colors—lime, scarlet, gold, sky blue—all mixed in swirls, curls, and rainbows. A small, bearded man wearing traditional clothes, chewing on a stick, stood beside the car. His beard hung down over a gleaming white *shalwar*.

"Don't be a stranger now, Princess. We expect to hear how this story ends." Dan-Danny strolled up to the rickshaw. There were no doors, just material as thick as a rug hanging across the space where a door might have been.

Yasmine felt blood rush to her face. "Mr. Dan-Danny, I am not a member of the royal family."

"You are to me, Princess."

The driver raised an eyebrow. *He now knows that I speak English*, thought Yasmine. *He will think I am a spy, or worse, that I am tainted by the outside world.*

Michelle came up from behind. "We will get a call from KAF when you arrive. Here are your two bags. There are lots of treats and some extra water bottles in here, but remember, hang on to this one. It's heavy." Michelle rattled the bigger haversack holding the passport, papers, and Baba's notebooks.

Yasmine looked at Michelle and Dan-Danny. "Thank you. And please, tell Brenda thank you." Yasmine thought of Tamanna. How many times had Tamanna said that she had no way to repay Yasmine's family for their kindness? Yasmine had simply laughed. Now she understood. These people, these foreigners, had saved her parents, and now they were saving her. *Thank you* did not seem like enough.

"You can thank us by having a great life, sweetheart. Now go." Michelle smiled.

"Get in," the driver snarled.

"Whoa, Nelly. Excuse me, you speak English, there, pal?" Dan-Danny walked up to the driver and peered down at him from his great height. All the men in the foreign army loomed large over the men of Afghanistan.

The driver nodded. "A little bit."

"What's your name?" Dan-Danny slung his gun over his shoulder and put his hands on his hips.

"Mahmood," said the driver, with a note of defiance in his voice.

"Here's the thing, Mahmood. This girl is a friend of ours.

You might say she's like my little sister." Dan-Danny bent down until he was nose to nose with the driver. "And I'm thinking that you might want to change that there tone of yours, or maybe we can find another driver."

"Take it easy, Private." Michelle's voice was low—not angry, but almost.

"Yes, ma'am, I'll do just that in just a sec. I just want to come to an understanding with my new pal Mahmood. I think he needs to *comprendo* that the Princess here is his boss for the ride to Kandahar Airfield. You do understand that, right, Mahmood?" This time Dan-Danny was almost growling.

Yasmine looked from Dan-Danny to Michelle and back to Dan-Danny. What was he doing? The driver was losing face. *Please, Dan-Danny,* she thought, *an Afghan man who loses face can become very angry.*

"Okay, *sahib,* sir," said the driver. His mouth smiled but his eyes did not. "I take very good care of the girl. I deliver her to Kandahar Airfield."

"And you will do what she says," said Dan-Danny.

"Yes, yes, *sahib.*" The driver bobbed his head several times, turned, and fanned himself with his hands. He was performing a *du'a,* a prayer for a safe journey.

"Private, get over here," said Michelle. Now she sounded annoyed. "Don't make it any worse for her. These guys can be dangerous," she muttered under her breath.

Yasmine climbed into the rickshaw and looked back through a plastic window. Dan-Danny was waving, his arm as big as a broom sweeping the sky.

Chapter 12

To Drown in Fire

Except for a few stray dogs, too tired or too hot to bark, and a group of young children playing in the dust, the streets were empty. Yasmine took a deep breath. It was now or never.

"Stop here." Yasmine spoke in Dari as loudly as she could. Over and over she repeated to herself, *I am a British girl. I am a British girl. British girls speak up for themselves. British girls are not afraid.* But the truth was, she didn't *feel* brave anymore. She didn't feel British, either, or like an Afghan. She didn't feel like anything.

The driver ignored her.

"Stop!" she cried. The driver hit the brakes. She jolted forward. "I must go to my house . . . I must . . ." What should she say? "I will not be long." Yasmine jumped out of the rickshaw. She left the bags on the seat. To carry them with her would have attracted attention.

Yasmine dug her hand deep into her pocket and held the pill bottle tight. She would go to Tamanna's house, pretend to be a wedding guest, and slip into the room with the other women. The pills would be Tamanna's wedding present. She looked up at the sun. Tamanna would be getting married any minute. Perhaps she would be in time to hold Tamanna's hand as she agreed to become a wife. Wife? It was still hard for her to believe.

Yasmine stood at the crossroad and tried to visualize the sand map Tamanna had scratched in the dirt many months before. She took a breath, skirted the center of the village, left the road, and followed the twisty trail through long, wavy grass. Tamanna had once said that she and her brother used to play on a burned-out Russian tank. She saw the wheat fields . . . and there! Pointing upward was the rusted muzzle of an old tank. Yasmine stopped outside a walled compound. Was this Tamanna's house? The walls were uncared for and the gate to the courtyard hung on its hinges. Fear prickled the back of her neck. Why were there no sounds coming from the house? Where was the wedding?

Slowly, tentatively, Yasmine pushed the broken gate open and stood outside the privacy wall. "*Asalaam alaikum,*" she called out, and listened for a response. Nothing. Where were the wedding guests? The *mullah*? She called out again. Still nothing. Perhaps this was not the house after all. She looked around—the wheat fields, the tank, and there were no other houses nearby. This *had* to be it. She stepped around the wall, even knowing that to enter a home without an invitation was a terrible thing to do. "*Asalaam alaikum.*"

Yasmine stopped. Rounds of naan had been ground into the dust. Shards of glass were strewn among spoiled fruits, peeled vegetables, and candy. Worse, the *tandoor* oven was smashed and lay in pieces. It was as if an angry animal had been let loose in the courtyard. And then . . . and then! Yasmine clapped a hand over her mouth and muffled a scream. "Tamanna?"

Slumped in the doorway across the courtyard was the figure of a female. Her head lolled back and forth on her shoulders. A *hijab*, pulled down, hid her face.

"TAMANNA!"

The figure looked up—bloodied lips, bloated face, one eye swollen shut, dried blood rimming her nose. Yasmine took a breath then ran towards her and fell to her knees. Bending down, Yasmine cupped Tamanna's chin in her hand and gently lifted her face towards the sun.

Startled, Yasmine reared back. It wasn't Tamanna. It was Tamanna's mother. "What has happened?" Yasmine, catching her breath, touched the woman's battered hands. It was the woman's turn to react. She drew in a breath and raised her arm across her face as if to stave off a blow. "Do not be afraid. It is Yasmine, your daughter's friend. Who did this to you?"

The woman sank back against the door frame. She mumbled something, but her words were garbled.

"I do not understand. Say it again," whispered Yasmine. She took a shallow breath and spat. A bloody tooth landed on the ground. "Zaman . . . huban broter . . . wedting . . ." The effort exhausted her and again the woman slumped forward.

"Zaman, Tamanna's uncle? Where is she? Where is Tamanna!" Yasmine leaped to her feet. "Tamanna! Where are you?" She barged into the little house, ran across the stone floor, and yanked back the curtain that separated the sleeping areas. "TAMANNA!" Yasmine's heart pounded in her chest. The house was empty.

Breathless, Yasmine returned to the little, broken woman. "Where is she?"

"Zaman—left. Tamanna—gone. I told—run—hide—do not return." Yasmine's eyes darted around the yard, half expecting the uncle to come roaring across the courtyard.

"I will get you water." Yasmine filled an earthen mug with water from the cistern and returned, too, with a small, damp rag. "Why did this happen?" Water spilled over the lip of the cup, and Yasmine willed her hands to stop shaking. She held up the mug and Tamanna's mother grasped it and pulled it towards herself, wincing as she sipped. She took a breath and spoke slowly, carefully forming each word.

"Man to be Tamanna's husband—watched her as she delivered naan to Rahim, the kebab-seller. He saw her limp . . . thinks it is a birth defect . . . she will bear defective children. He says he was lied to. He will not sign . . . the marriage certificate."

"So, Tamanna will not get married. Her uncle will just have to accept it. Things will be as they were." As Yasmine spoke she dabbed the dampened cloth on the woman's face, gently cleaning as much of the dried blood as she could.

"No. Zaman's debt will not be paid. He blames my daughter. Says she is worthless—will never get a husband—she shames our family. He says that no man will want her. If he finds her, he will murder her—call it an honor killing. What honor is there in . . . killing a girl? A perfect girl . . . who he himself maimed? If she limps, it is his fault!" Struggling, her hands inching up the door frame, the woman stood. "He is taking strong drugs. He is in a rage."

A hope, a thought, brewed in Yasmine. "Please, please, I'm leaving for Kandahar City, right now. Let her come with me," she begged.

The woman looked up at Yasmine as if she were a spirit. She sputtered and wobbled on her feet. "No," she wailed. Her head shook.

"Dear Aunt, I beg you. A driver in a rickshaw will take us there."

"No, no, no." Tears ran from the woman's eyes. She reeled back, stumbled, and fell. "Allah, have mercy on me," she cried.

"I beg you. Dear Aunt, please, please. You know there is no life for her here. My parents love her as I do. She will be my sister. She will be cared for, go to school. Please. You said yourself that her uncle will kill her." Yasmine, still on her knees, clutched at the woman's skirt.

"No, you have to understand . . . it's too late. Tamanna has gone to her brother, in the mountains. See, she took . . . his shoes." The woman pointed with a quivering hand towards a vacant spot by the door.

What shoes? What was the woman talking about? The world seemed to shift around Yasmine. Tamanna gone to the mountains? A Talib . . . help a *girl*? It was more likely that the Taliban would give aid to an American! And no girl would last long in the desert alone. Danger was everywhere. Travelers attacked unaccompanied girls. It was assumed that any girl walking without a man was unpure and deserved to be raped. Near breathless, Yasmine bent forward, holding her stomach as if punched. Words rattled around in her head: *Find her, find her.*

"My daughter is the love of my life . . . the *noor* of my heart. But I was afraid to tell her . . . afraid . . . my heart would break, afraid my love . . . would make her weak. I loved her too much. I tempted fate. She is doomed." The woman crumpled into a ball, cupped her hands around her wounded head, and sobbed.

"It is not your fault, none of this is your fault. Tamanna knows that you love her." Gently, Yasmine ran her hand over the woman's bony back. She was skeletal, starving. "What will happen to you?" she whispered.

"I am to go to my father-in-law's house today, like this . . . ugly . . . damaged. They are poor. They will call me a parasite."

Yasmine reached into her money pouch and drew out a fistful of the green American bills. "Perhaps if you give this to your father-in-law he will better protect you, at least for a little while." Yasmine tucked the money into the woman's clenched fist. Opening her hand the woman stared down at the paper money. She did not know what it was. "Hide it. Others may try and steal it from you. Give it only to your father-in-law."

Yasmine left the woman as she found her. There was no consoling her. She stepped out onto the road and began to retrace her steps. The rickshaw driver would be getting impatient, but he would not leave, he wanted the money. She stopped and thought. How could it be that Tamanna had gone into the mountains to find her brother? It didn't make sense. Tamanna would not have left the village in daylight, she would have hidden until the stars came out. And standing on the road, in full view of the village, Yasmine suddenly knew exactly where Tamanna would hide.

༼ར᠍ᠯ༽

Yasmine stood outside her own house and rattled the door. The gate was bolted from the inside. "Tamanna," she called through the slats of the corrugated tin. Nothing, not a sound, not a peep came from the other side of the wall. Even now she could feel the eyes of the neighbors upon her.

Pushing her face up against the gate she called out again, and again. There was a funny smell. What was it? Her skin grew cold. It was the smell of kerosene.

"Tamanna? Tamanna, what are you doing?" Yasmine cried out. She pulled the bell-cord again and again and again. The neighbors would hear but it no longer mattered what anyone thought. Nothing mattered.

"Tamanna!" Still no response. Yasmine hammered the gate with a closed fist. Sharp ridges of tin cut into her hands and made them bleed. She gulped air, stepped back, and looked at the wall that surrounded the courtyard. It was smooth and at least six feet tall, but unlike many walls that surrounded homes, Baba had refused to imbed glass shards in the top or surround the house with barbed wire to ward off thieves. If she could find a way to scale the wall she could jump down to the other side. All she needed was something to climb up on.

"You don't belong here. Your father is a spy. He deserves to die." Noor stood in the middle of the road. He jutted out his chin and yelled, "Why do you care about her?"

Yasmine stopped. Why was he just standing there? He must have known that Tamanna was inside. She glared at him. "Why do you hate us? What are we to you?" There was no time to wait for an answer. She spotted a broken barrel lying on its side across the road. Noor just stood and watched as Yasmine dragged it across the road, turned it over, and pushed it up against the wall. But as she jumped up, her foot went through the top splitting the barrel into pieces. Gasping, Yasmine sprawled flat-out on the ground. When she looked up, Noor was there.

"Come." Noor stood above her. He motioned with his hand.

Yasmine's eyes narrowed as Noor walked around the side of the house out of view of the road and the neighbors. She did not trust him, and yet she scrambled to her feet and followed. Then he did something startling. He knelt down on all fours and sidled up against the back wall of her house. Yasmine stopped, unsure of what to do. Was it a trick?

"Hurry," he hissed. He wanted her to stand on his back! She looked at him hard and had a funny thought. Was it possible that he cared about Tamanna? That he *liked* her? Boys and girls were not allowed to *like* each other. Besides, he might never marry any girl until he himself was in his middle years and made money. He was poor, too poor to afford a bride-price.

"You care for her!" Yasmine blurted out the words before her thought was fully realized.

Noor's face darkened. He shifted back and forth like a goat in a pen. There was no time to talk, let alone think. Yasmine climbed on his back and reached up. She stretched. The top of the wall was still out of reach. Noor grunted. He started to stand, and as he did Yasmine rose higher and higher.

"Climb up," he huffed.

Yasmine hoisted herself up until her elbows were on the top of the wall. She could see Tamanna standing in the middle of the courtyard, the red plastic jug of kerosene dangling from her hand. Kerosene! In her other hand—matches. Tamanna meant to douse herself with the flammable liquid. She meant to set herself on fire!

"TAMANNA!"

Slowly, Tamanna raised her head. Her eyes were blank. Yasmine swung one leg up and over, then the second leg, until she sat on the wall. She looked back at Noor. There was a strange, pleading look in his eyes.

"She is alive," Yasmine called out over her shoulder.

Noor nodded, turned, and ran.

Yasmine leaped down from the wall and stumbled towards her friend with outstretched arms.

"Yasmine?" Tamanna spoke as if in a trance. "There was not . . . not enough kerosene," she stammered. Sitting in swirls of dust, the girls held on to each other as if drowning.

"Tell me, what has happened?" Yasmine asked while holding her tight.

"A boy came to our home and told Mor that the man who was to be my husband fought with Uncle in the place where they sell liquor. I will not be married now." Tamanna spoke in gasps. "Mor told me to run away. She is afraid that my uncle will kill me because he will not get the bride-price money and because he will say that I have brought shame to my family." She was confused, each word sliding into the next.

"I went to your house," whispered Yasmine.

"Is Mor all right? He will return in a rage!" Tamanna bolted upright.

Yasmine dithered, but just for a second. If Tamanna went back to her house she might meet her uncle. And then what?

"Your mother is well."

"Did Uncle return? Did he harm her?"

"No. She is well."

Chapter 13

Two *Burkas*

"*Burkas!*" Yasmine ran into her house.

Tamanna followed. "What is happening? I do not understand."

"It's best if no one sees you leave. Hurry." Yasmine opened a trunk and pulled out two silk, indigo-blue *burkas*, each with a crown made of silver thread—the same ones Baba bought when they'd left Herat. Yasmine flung a *burka* at Tamanna and grabbed the second one for herself.

"Leave?" Confused and wide-eyed, Tamanna watched

126

as her friend kicked off her sandals and slipped on a pair of her mother's shoes. They were foreign-made, of thick and heavy leather, and by the looks of them they had never been worn.

"We are going to a place the *kharijis* call KAF near Kandahar City. Hurry," said Yasmine. She looked down at the star-tipped sandals on Tamanna's feet but said nothing.

Kandahar! Never in her dreams had Tamanna thought that she would see a city. "How would we travel to such a place?" she asked.

"The *kharijis* in the FOB, the fort, arranged for a rickshaw. It is waiting just outside the village." Yasmine spoke in snatches of breath as she grabbed her father's blanket. She turned and ran towards the door.

"I d-do not understand," Tamanna stuttered.

"I will explain later. Wait." Yasmine bolted back into the house. "Put this under your *burka*." She stripped Mother's bed and handed Tamanna the beautiful embroidered *patoo*.

Tamanna did not know what to do, so she did as Yasmine had asked. Both girls adjusted their *burkas* before stepping out onto the road. Yasmine turned back and pulled hard at the door and listened for the *thunk* of the bolt slipping into place. But really, what did it matter if the house was locked or not? Allah willing, they would never return. "Hurry," she hissed as she took the lead.

Heads down, *burkas* billowing out behind, they walked as quickly as possible without tripping or drawing attention. Neither was used to wearing the *burka*. The thin, silver thread around the headpiece clamped down on their heads and glistened in the sun. Hearing was difficult, seeing was almost impossible, and the air underneath the *burka* was stale, making it hard to breathe.

Tamanna's star-tipped sandals had hardly been worn by her brother and the leather was stiff. Yasmine's toes in her mother's shoes chafed. Worse, the shoes were heavy and made it hard to run. Hopping on one foot and then the other, barely slowing down, Yasmine yanked the shoes off her feet and, along with Baba's blanket, clutched them to her chest under her *burka*. Never mind that the ground was littered with old plastic buckets, garbage, broken glass, and that she might cut her feet, she needed to run.

As the heat of the day ebbed, men, boys, and small children emerged from their houses. Both girls could feel eyes upon them. The men hissed and pointed. Who were these women? *Burkas* were expensive things, and new *burkas*, without rips and tears, were a rare sight in the village.

They came to a clearing. To the left was the school building, or where the school was supposed to be. Had they torn it down completely? Men stood around the damaged building with their hands on their hips, *tsk-tsk*-ing. Yasmine and Tamanna slowed down.

Someone shouted, "Run!" Yasmine turned back. Who had said that? Noor? Yes, it was him. With Tamanna close behind, Yasmine made a dash for the rickshaw.

The driver took a long drag off a hand-rolled cigarette, narrowed his eyes, and watched as the girls darted towards him. Yasmine reached out, batted the thick curtain aside, and lunged for the backseat. Thank goodness, the haversack and bag remained untouched on the back seat.

"Get in." Yasmine pushed the bags onto the floor.

Tamanna tumbled in, with Yasmine behind her. "Drive," she pleaded.

The driver paused. His thoughts were plain. He would not get paid unless he delivered the girl to KAF, to Kandahar Airfield, but now there were two girls, not one.

"Drive!" This time Yasmine shouted. The sound of her own voice shocked her. The driver tossed away his cigarette and climbed into the driver's seat. "Get down." Yasmine pushed Tamanna to the floor.

Only when they had left the village, when they were sure no one could see, did Yasmine and Tamanna unfurl themselves from the floor. Both girls flung back the *burkas*, exposing flushed, red faces. Clutching the straps that hung beside the curtains, they slid and bounced around the seat as the rickshaw jolted down the road. With her free hand, Yasmine reached deep into her pocket and pulled out the small pill bottle.

"It is medicine from the *kharijis*. This pill will stop you from running to the outhouse. One pill a day for five days." Yasmine shook a long, white pill out of the bottle and held it out in an open palm. "In five days you will be cured."

Tamanna peered at the pill. "I do not understand." What was she to do with it?

"Put it at the back of your throat, then drink." Yasmine reached into the bag and pulled out a bottle of water. The top cracked as she twisted off the cap. "Drink," repeated Yasmine.

Tentatively, Tamanna placed the pill on her tongue, gulped water, and tried to swallow. She coughed. The pill came up, or rather did not go down.

"Try again," said Yasmine.

On the second try the pill slid down Tamanna's throat. Only then did Yasmine take a deep breath, lean back in the seat, and think, *What have we done?*

The rickshaw picked up speed. Brightly painted *jingle* trucks, with their bells and toys dangling across the windshield, lined the shoulder of the road. Raggedy, stick-wielding boys maneuvered long-eared goats around the vehicles. Occasionally *millie* buses packed with travelers passed by, coughing black clouds. The buses had religious sayings written on the sides, although few people could read.

Women in indigo and saffron *burkas* walked along the road gripping the hands of small children while balancing bundles of firewood on their heads. Everything whizzed by so quickly that it was difficult to focus on objects outside the car. "It's as if we can fly," whispered Tamanna. Yasmine caught the eye of the driver in his rear-view mirror. He was staring back at them with unmistakable contempt. Dirty hands gripped the wheel as he pressed his foot down on the pedal.

"I do not understand, why have the *kharijis* provided this transportation?" Tamanna tried to be heard above the motor's high-pitched whine. She was almost shouting.

Yasmine leaned to one side and whispered into Tamanna's ear, "My parents are there. You will be safe with them. You will be their daughter, too."

Tamanna pulled back. "Their daughter? But such a thing is not allowed under our law!"

Yasmine put one finger to her lips and motioned towards the driver.

Tamanna sat back, confused. Moments ago, she'd had

no future. Moments ago, she had made her peace with this life. She had decided to die. She had not thought of Heaven or Hell, of right or wrong. She had said a prayer, asked for protection for her mother, then reached for the red jug of kerosene that Yasmine's father used to fill the lamp. When she'd tipped it and found it was empty, she knew that Allah had willed that today was not her day to die.

They passed through villages. One or two of the walled compounds would look inhabited, then the next two would be empty, the next occupied, the next empty, and so it went—like missing teeth in a mouth. Occasionally they passed fields of flags and cement tombstones marking the deaths of martyrs. *Burkas* weaved among the flags.

Twice the car slowed to a crawl only to zigzag between small herds of one-humped camels. Yasmine sat back, and for the first time since she had stood beside Michelle at the fort, she allowed herself to think of the future. Mother and Baba would get well and they would all go back to England. Tamanna would come too. Grandfather would be there. Her memory of him was growing vague—a tall man who lifted her high in the air and laughed. He was like Baba, kind and smart. She looked out at the stony land that seemed to pass by at the speed of light. She would leave this country, possibly forever. Why did she feel sad?

The car suddenly stopped. Both girls bolted forward, slamming into the back of the driver's seat. Tamanna cried out as a tooth cut into her lip. Yasmine looked out to barren, rocky land. What was wrong? She looked ahead to see what might be blocking the road. Nothing. She looked behind. Nothing. The road was empty.

The driver leaped out of the car and hissed, "I will not be given orders by girls, you daughters of devils. Get out. You have polluted my rickshaw with your filth."

Even before his last words were uttered Yasmine had grabbed the two bags, the blanket, Tamanna's hand, and scrambled out of the car. The heavy haversack unbalanced her. She slipped on the gravel and crashed down on her already skinned knees. She felt she should say something to the driver, remind him that he would not get paid, that he would not work for the *kharijis* ever again, but the driver's contempt had turned into rage, and rage could kill.

"Daughters of dogs," he screamed, then spat at their feet. He turned and spotted the foreign, leather shoes on the floor of the back seat. In a hail of more foul words he reached into the cab and hurled both shoes at the girls, hitting Yasmine in the forehead and Tamanna in the chest. Then without looking back he climbed into his rickshaw, spun it in a circle, and, in a plume of orange dust, headed back towards the village.

For a moment they just stood still. Slowly Yasmine turned and looked west. KAF was at least two hours by car in one direction, and nightfall was two hours in either direction. Two girls alone on a road in the desert at night would not last long.

"Uncle will come after me," whispered Tamanna.

Yasmine nodded. The driver would tell everyone in the village that he had not taken the girls to Kandahar City, that he had left them stranded on the side of the road, that he would not take orders from daughters of dogs. He would brag. The men would cheer him.

"Uncle does many drugs. Perhaps he will think that bandits will kill us instead."

Yasmine nodded. There were scorpions in the desert, sandstorms, thirst and hunger. There were many ways to die in the desert.

"Yasmine, what do we do?" Tamanna's voice wobbled and caught.

Yasmine forced air into her lungs. "We walk."

"To Kandahar City?" Astonished, Tamanna turned towards her friend. Yasmine's profile was perfect, like a queen's. Her green eyes stood out like emeralds in the sand. They were warrior eyes, fierce and determined.

"No, that is what would be expected. We will do the unexpected," said Yasmine with pretend confidence.

Startled, Tamanna pulled back. "Where will we go?"

"We will go up into the mountains." Yasmine looked across the flat desert and beyond to the darkening mountains of Pakistan.

Tamanna was astounded. This was madness! But Yasmine continued. "We must go back, pass the village, pass the FOB, go up into the mountains and cross over into Pakistan," she said. "We cannot use the roads. We must take goat paths and old caravan trails."

"But Yasmine, it will take days, maybe weeks to reach the border on foot, and everywhere there are land mines, and the Taliban live in the mountains," said Tamanna.

"We have no choice," said Yasmine.

It was Tamanna's turn to look out into the pale desert, as raw and smooth as a lion's pelt, and to the fierce gray mountains beyond. In that moment she understood that when there are no reasonable choices, one must make an unreasonable decision.

"They will not come after us in the mountains. They will think we are afraid."

"Are we afraid?" whispered Tamanna.

"Yes."

Chapter 14

Shadow of the Sky

White-hot terror pinioned them in place. Neither drew a breath. And then Yasmine said, "We cannot wear these *burkas*. They attract attention. They are too new, too beautiful." She spoke quickly and with authority.

"I know what to do. Look." Tamanna pointed to a large family group led by an old man clutching a hooked staff. They were walking, one after another, across the flat, desert plain, pushing a herd of bony goats ahead. The goats fanned out in different directions. She also knew what they were

135

hoping—that a goat, rather than a man or a valuable donkey, would trigger a land mine. The old man and young children followed the goats, and behind him came a line of women carrying babies and leading burdened donkeys.

"Give me your *burka*, hurry." Tamanna pulled her *burka* up over her head, balled it under her arm, and knotted her headscarf under her chin.

"Why?" Yasmine took off her *burka* and handed it to Tamanna. She, too, covered her hair with the scarf that lay around her neck.

"I'll explain later." Tamanna kicked off her shoes, pivoted on bare feet, and ran towards the family. Yasmine watched as Tamanna moved across the sand with unexpected grace. She was amazed. Tamanna, so shy, seemed to have transformed right in front of her!

"*Asalaam alaikum*," she called out to the women.

A girl carrying a baby at the end of the column turned back and stared at Tamanna. She called out to the other women in the group. Then all the women stopped and turned. One, two, five, then six women gathered around Tamanna. Even the children nudged into the circle to listen. Unaware, the goats and the old man trudged on. Yasmine, sitting on her haunches, almost laughed out loud at the thought of the old man and his goats walking alone, forever, until they fell off the face of the earth.

The women and girls passed the blue *burkas* around, fingering the material. Yasmine watched from a distance as heads bobbed like pecking birds and hands flew up in the air, a sign that the bargaining had begun. Twice Tamanna turned as if to walk away. Twice the woman pulled her back into the negotiating circle. Even the children and animals seemed to be in on the discussion. And then the circle broke up and Tamanna came running across the sand towards Yasmine.

"I wanted to make an exchange—beautiful *burkas* for old, dirty ones—but there was mistrust." She was holding her side and puffing. "So, I demanded . . . money . . . too." Tamanna opened a clenched fist to reveal the paper money. Under her arm were two filthy, torn *burkas*. They were both the color of mud, full of holes, and frayed at the hem.

Tamanna peered into the distance. It looked as though a small sandstorm was rolling along the road towards them. "Quickly, put it on." Tamanna tossed Yasmine the nicer of the two *burkas*, put the food bag over her shoulder, threw the other *burka* overtop, and clutched the embroidered *patoo* to her chest. "Put your shoes in the bag. They will be recognized as foreign-made." Tamanna was now in full command.

The cloud of dust kicked up by a bus was getting closer. Yasmine slipped the black shoes into the bag filled with her parents' papers, draped it over her neck and shoulder, and pulled the *burka* overtop.

"Dirty your hands," whispered Tamanna as she dropped to her knees. Both dragged their nails across the ground and rubbed their feet with sand.

A lone flatbed truck charged towards them. Tamanna lifted her dusty hand and waved. She had never been in a truck but she had seen them stop at the village many times. The truck wobbled from side to side, then lurched back and forward before coming to a grinding stop. In the back of the truck men and boys sat on benches on one side, women and girls on the other. The middle was filled with goats, chickens in cages, and multicolored bundles. Two large dogs with clipped ears and leather straps binding their muzzles pushed their noses through wooden slats and growled. They were valuable dogs, fighting dogs.

Tamanna divided the paper money between her two hands and approached the driver.

"Where is your *maharam*, the man to accompany you? You cannot travel alone." He was like the dogs, snarly. Tamanna opened a fist revealing paper bills. "Get in." The driver snatched the money out of her hand and yelled over his shoulder to the other passengers, "These are my sisters."

The travelers did not believe him, but the lie was proper and expected and nothing more was said. The girls climbed into the back. The truck reared back, coughed, and leaped forward.

An hour had passed, maybe more, when Yasmine gripped Tamanna's hand and pointed. "Tamanna, look!" They were approaching their village. Yasmine tucked the haversack between her feet and under her *burka*. Coming towards them on the other side of the road was a *millie* bus.

Tamanna closed her eyes, but Yasmine peered intently through the grille of her *burka*. Neither took a breath. Tamanna's eyes flew open and in that second she spotted Uncle Zaman. Perhaps Uncle had bribed the driver, because the *millie* bus slowed. If the driver of the bus flagged the truck, both vehicles would stop. The bus came to a crawl, as did the truck. Even at a distance Tamanna could see Uncle's eyes flick up and down, searching, searching. Likely the driver of the rickshaw would have told him to look for blue *burkas.* Had they not exchanged their new blue *burkas* for old ones . . . Had they walked towards Kandahar City instead of doubling back . . . Had they not flagged down the truck . . . Had the driver not taken the bribe . . .

The bus passed the truck. Yasmine collapsed against the rail behind her back. Tamanna sat as still as stone.

As the sun turned the desert sands to ruby-red they passed the FOB to one side and the village to the other. Brenda, Michelle, and Dan-Danny would be inside the FOB. What would happen if they just climbed off the truck, pounded on the great door, and asked for help? She knew the answer. They would help her but not Tamanna. To take a girl away from her home, help her run away—that was kidnapping, against *the policy*. But passing the FOB was harder than Yasmine had expected.

Tamanna was not looking at the FOB, she was staring intently towards the village. "Mor," she whispered.

Yasmine squeezed her friend's hand. If she told Tamanna the truth, that her mother had been beaten by her uncle, she was sure Tamanna would leap out of the truck and run home. But what good would that do? Was she right or wrong to keep the truth from Tamanna? Yasmine closed her eyes and said a prayer. When she opened them, she looked ahead to pale-gray mountains that stretched across the horizon. The border crossing was in the hills. There was no turning back.

The truck stopped at different villages. People got off and more passengers got on. There were no greetings or farewells. Stars came out. Finally, the truck stopped near a village and the children, people, goats, dogs, chickens, bundles tumbled to the ground. Women and children set up camp while the men smoked hand-rolled cigarettes. Exhausted, many of the smaller children simply curled into balls on the ground and fell asleep. Everyone was careful not to point the soles of their feet towards Mecca.

The driver glared at Tamanna. "Yasmine, we must go," she whispered. The girls lumbered off into the dark desert, Yasmine weighed down by the haversack, Tamanna hampered by her bad hip and the bag with the food. One clutched the *campal*, the other the embroidered *patoo*. Yasmine glanced back at Tamanna, and for the briefest of moments she laughed. "Look, we are two little hunchbacks trudging across the desert." It was agreed that walking during the night was safer. They carried on.

Once away from prying eyes they pushed back the hoods of their *burkas* and felt the cool night air on their faces.

"See, that is the Big Dipper, and that is the North Star. We have to keep the North Star on our left." Yasmine pointed to the brightest star in the sky. The moon was late rising, but when it did come out and the stars dimmed, they could see the shapes and shades of the desert all around them. The desert rolled and meandered, the shadows of the dunes disguising its dips and crevices.

Once in a while they heard whistles—eerie echoes that pierced the night air. It was like birdsong, in a way beautiful. "Goat or sheep herders," said Yasmine, although she sounded neither convinced nor convincing. It was the howls of dogs running in packs that frightened them most.

Yasmine's shoes were of no use. Sand collected in them, weighing her down. She walked barefoot. Many times

Yasmine looked back at her friend. If Tamanna's hip was bothering her, she did not let on.

"It is almost dawn," said Yasmine. Tamanna nodded. A buttery sun, masked by floating dust particles, was rising in the east. The mountains were still a day's walk away but rocks that looked rooted deep in the earth were starting to emerge from the sand.

"Look." Tamanna pointed to three large boulders. "If we string your father's *campal* across the top and hold it in place with stones, we can hide underneath." The blanket was red-gold, the color of the desert. Even from a distance they would not be spotted. Exhausted but determined, the girls worked quickly, and in no time they were scrambling under their makeshift tarp to sit on the *burkas*. Mother's embroidered *patoo* went across their shoulders. Like all Afghan girls, they had learned how to blend in, to hide.

"Your lip is still big from where you hit the back of the seat in the car," said Yasmine.

"And you have a big bump on your head from where the driver hit you with a shoe. We are like soldiers after a battle," said Tamanna. For a moment they laughed, or at least they made the sounds of laughter.

"How are you feeling?" asked Yasmine. She opened a bottle of water and passed it to Tamanna.

"The medicine is working." Tamanna gulped and paused as she searched for words. "I think that you risked your life to bring me this medicine. The driver would have taken you to Kandahar City if I had not been with you."

"Risk? At the school, when the Taliban wanted to kill me, you stood up for me. How could I do any less for you? I am your sister. I love you." Yasmine touched Tamanna's hand. Tamanna hung her head. To be told that she was loved left her breathless with wonder. "The driver would have left me anyway, and if he had, I would now be alone." Despite exhaustion, Yasmine spoke in a matter-of-fact voice.

"And I would be dead, or dying," whispered Tamanna.

Joints ached, heads thumped, and legs, unused to such exercise, quivered. They were too tired even to eat. Both fell into a long and uncomfortable sleep.

Sometime later Yasmine woke with a startled cry. Jolted awake, Tamanna reached for her. "What is it?"

Yasmine, more asleep than awake, sputtered, "I dreamed of fish, their bodies shimmering in water under a brilliant full moon."

For the first time in a very long time Tamanna really laughed. "If you dream of a fish and the moon then you will be a king."

"A girl can never be king. Besides, I have told the dream out loud. It will never come true now," said Yasmine, searching for the water bottle.

"Then you will not be a prince but a beautiful princess instead, like Scheherazade," said Tamanna as she pulled back the blanket and looked at the sunset. Everything was confused. It was almost night again. They had slept the whole day through.

"Scheherazade told stories to keep herself alive. She had to be smart and brave," said Yasmine.

"Like us," said Tamanna, although there was no conviction in her voice.

"Do you remember the red-faced soldier with hair like a copper pot who came to our school? He said his name was

Dan-but-you-can call-me-Danny. Do you remember?" asked Yasmine. Tamanna nodded. "At the fort he kept calling me 'Princess.' He showed me a picture of his sister."

"Maybe in the West all brothers call their sisters 'Princess,'" said Tamanna as she flipped back the edge of the blanket.

This time Yasmine laughed for real. "That is not how I remember brothers and sisters together."

The setting sun threw a thin stream of light onto the ground, turning the brown sky to gray.

"YASMINE!" Tamanna screamed as she gave Yasmine a mighty shove. Yasmine fell back into the sand, taking the blanket with her. A scorpion, its shell translucent and its tail curled into an arc, passed Yasmine's foot by a few inches. Yasmine and Tamanna just sat for a moment. The only sounds were their sharp intakes of breath. Yasmine looked into her friend's eyes. They were getting used to keeping each other safe. It was what friends and sisters did.

"Come, we will perform *wudu*." Yasmine picked up a bottle of water, intending to pour out the tiniest bit of liquid into the palm of her hand.

"No, save the water," said Tamanna. And so in the desert the two girls performed the morning ritual by pretending to sprinkle water over their heads and wash themselves.

"*Bismillah al-Rahman al-Raheem, In the Name of God, the Most Gracious, the Most Merciful. All Praise is due to God alone, the Sustainer of all the worlds, the Most Merciful, the Most Compassionate, Master of Judgment Day,*" they repeated.

"We have food." Yasmine dumped out the bag Dan-Danny had filled. She laid all that they had in a row. "This is called a *power bar*. I don't know what magical power it's supposed to have, but in England, I ate them all the time." She laid out four bars, three bottles of water, including the one that had been opened, a bag of nuts, an apple, an orange, and some candies wrapped in gold foil.

"It is a feast," said Tamanna.

"Now I will tell you everything. I will start with Noor. I think he is not the person we thought him to be. I think perhaps, in his heart, he is good. Eat!" Yasmine snapped the power bar in half. "Let us see if we become powerful."

⟨⟩

They reached the foothills of the mountain range that separated Afghanistan from Pakistan on the second night. Walking through a grove of cypress trees, they came to a mountain path, likely carved out by sheep or goats but hammered down by the feet of shepherds who had climbed this way for thousands of years. The mountains were riddled with such paths and passages, tunnels and rock bridges in streams below and rope bridges up on top.

It was spring, the new month of *Safar*. Mist enveloped the girls, leaving a shine on their *burkas* that starlight turned into sparkles. Thistles scratched their legs until thin streams of blood dribbled down into their shoes. As they climbed, the air grew colder. Toes turned into frozen nubs that rubbed and burned, and fingers grew so stiff they turned into claws.

The second night of steady climbing plunged them both into a sleep so thick and deep no fear could penetrate it. Twice they awoke, but only briefly, to the clank of bells as donkey caravans passed nearby.

Groggy and bleary-eyed, they slept the days away. On the third night they dragged themselves up and followed the stars. Rutty roads, hairpin turns, and stony paths that led nowhere constantly took them in the wrong direction. Thankfully, the donkey droppings they passed told them when they were headed the right way. It had become harder and harder to talk and climb at the same time, and as the air thinned, their heads began to ache.

"Listen." Yasmine, in the lead, stopped. "Mountain music!" she said as they listened to the muted braying of long-necked, soft-eared karakul sheep. The sheep, bedded down for the night, were no threat, but a barking dog might alert a young shepherd, who might run to his father or brothers and tell them about two unaccompanied girls walking in the mountains. While all tribes had a code to provide asylum to strangers, runaway girls would not be given such consideration. Yasmine motioned with her head as the two gave the small herd a wide berth.

The cliffs in the moonlight were sharp-edged, the rock the color of the corrugated metal used for roofs of mud homes in the village. Boulders threatened to roll down from above and crush them. Their hands were raw from gripping rocks, their ankles swollen, and their toes stubbed numb. The discomfort Tamanna had felt in her stomach was replaced with a grinding pain in her hip. Using a thick branch as a walking stick, she carried on, uncomplaining. Whenever the path allowed, without speaking, Yasmine draped Tamanna's arm over her shoulder and the two struggled on side by side. They had refilled the plastic water bottles from glacial streams dozens of times. They were beginning to feel the sting of hunger. Once a day they ate from the bag of food. At the foothills of the mountains they found berries, but it was early in the season and they were small and tough.

They were taking a short midnight break. They would not rest for long; the longer they sat, the harder it was to get up again. Yasmine pointed up to the dark hills illuminated in the moonlight. "See? The mountains look like elephants. In England, Mother read me a story about Babar."

"Your father once spoke of Barbur, the founder of the Mogul dynasty," said Tamanna, her voice edged with exhaustion.

"No, Babar the Elephant," said Yasmine as she pulled Tamanna up onto her feet and took her arm, placing it over her shoulder.

"Do you mean Emperor Babur, the first emperor of India? He loved Kabul and grew tulips." Tamanna, stumbling, was confused.

"Babar the Elephant. He wore a green suit!" Yasmine grabbed tree roots and branches to pull herself along.

"What is *suit*?" With her free hand, Tamanna rammed her stick into the dirt and pulled herself forward

"It is what Western men wear."

"Emperor Babur had an elephant, but I do not think it was made to wear Western clothes," said Tamanna.

"No! Babar was not a real elephant, silly. He was a drawing. He was made up." They had to stop for a moment and catch their breath.

"I do not understand. Did Barbur or Babur have a pretend elephant that was made to wear Western *suits*?" Tamanna did not find the idea of dressing animals totally unreasonable. Elephants in Pakistan and India were often decorated in strange ways.

Yasmine took a deep breath. "In Europe there are books just for children. A writer makes a story and an artist matches the story with drawings. Babar is French," said Yasmine.

"But you met him in England?"

"I did not meet him. I told you, he is made up."

"Is he British or French?"

"He comes from Africa."

"An elephant wears a suit, comes from Africa, but lives in England and France. Yasmine, I do not understand."

Yasmine took another breath. Explaining seemed hopeless, but she would give it one more try! "Babar's mother was killed by hunters in Africa so he ran away to Paris, France. He met an old lady in Paris who took care of him, bought him clothes, and even sent him to school."

"This elephant reads!"

Yasmine thought for a minute and then said, "Yes. Now, while Babar was in Paris eating bonbons, his father, who was the King of the Elephant realm, ate poisonous mushrooms and died." Yasmine walked a little faster. Tamanna did not seem as tired as before.

"What is a bonbon?"

"A candy." A memory flashed through her mind. She was in her bedroom, in their flat: a yellow quilt, toys on the floor. She was just four or five years old. "Just one quick story. Baba and I are having dinner with the Chancellor," said Mother. She wore a pretty dress, high heels, and her hair was long and flipped over her shoulders. Baba came to the door. He told Mother that she was beautiful. Mother laughed.

"He became an orphan?" asked Tamanna.

"Who?" Yasmine was still in the shadowy world of a child's memory. She swallowed hard.

"Babar. You said his father ate bad mushrooms," said Tamanna as she let go of Yasmine and began to walk on her own.

"His cousins Celeste and Arthur came from the Elephant realm and found him in Paris. They asked him to return home and become the new king since he was now educated. Soon everyone in the Elephant realm dressed like the French." The path was steep. They climbed hand over hand.

"How do the French dress?" huffed Tamanna as she yanked her walking stick out of a tangle of thorns. She knew a little bit about France. Yasmine's father had taught them geography. France was part of Europe and across the water from the little island of England, which was ruled by a queen, except that there was no king so really she was the king. France was a beautiful country that produced an alcohol called wine, which was illegal in Afghanistan. Afghanistan produced opium, which was a drug and illegal in France.

"Mother says that French women are the best-dressed people in the world," puffed Yasmine. Without asking, Yasmine took Tamanna's walking stick and put it on her back, wedging it under the haversack. The stick was useless, even a hindrance, when climbing up steep embankments, but they dared not throw it away. Trees were getting scarce and it was harder and harder to replace the walking stick.

Once in a while Yasmine could see Tamanna's movements in the moonlight. They were stilted and pained. But not once had she complained.

"What happened to the old lady, the one who took Babar in and cared for him?" asked Tamanna.

"She came with Babar to the Elephant realm."

"Are there any more Babar stories?" asked Tamanna.

"Of course."

And so a gray elephant in a green suit accompanied the girls as they climbed.

Chapter 15

Blameless Stars

As another dawn broke they stood on a hilltop. Above, the soaring mountains, streaked in ruby, yellow, and muted silver, looked cold and foreboding. Below, poplar trees flashed silver and green leaves. Small white almond flowers blanketed the hills. But down deep, in the gullies and crevices, were graveyards of trucks, tanks, donkey bones, and maybe human bones, too.

A twig snapped. Yasmine grabbed Tamanna's arm and pulled her down behind a rock. "There!" She pointed. Above, standing on a rock face, a boy waved to them.

150

"What should we do?" Tamanna whispered.

Yasmine shook her head. They could not have outrun him even if they had wanted to. He was young, maybe eight or nine years old. Carrying a shepherd's crook, he leaped from rock to rock, skipping with the grace of a mountain goat. He came closer, then stopped in front of them and grinned. He looked to be made of dirt and dust, but he was beautiful all the same, red-cheeked and clear-skinned, wearing an old, dirty, western-style snow jacket with a zipper and hood.

Waving his crook like a flag, he whirled it over his head and pointed to a crevice in the rocks. "Follow." He spoke Pashto. Tamanna understood perfectly, but Yasmine struggled with the language. Still, she had learned much from Tamanna over the past months.

Yasmine pulled back. "Tamanna, he could be the child of a Talib or the son of a warlord. He could be anyone."

Tamanna did not respond. Yasmine looked closely at her friend. Her face was gray, her eyes half closed and dull. Worse, she was sweating. *She has a fever*, thought Yasmine. It was a snap decision. She looked back at the boy, who continued to motion to them, then reached over and pulled Tamanna to her feet. "Lean on me." They followed the boy.

A stone hut stood in the middle of what had once been a compound. Dilapidated beyond use, the outside wall at the very front was a pile of stones jumbled together with handmade bricks. Soaring rocks protected it on three sides. Inside the courtyard, bleached bones—they looked as though they might have been the hip bones of horses—were piled against the hut to be used as spades and shovels. Scrawny chickens ran in and out of a small twig pen. A fat cat, more black than white, sat on bricks warmed by the sun. A half-dug garden of newly planted herbs and vegetables lay beside the wall.

The boy plunged ahead of them, grinning, shouting, and leaping. As the wooden door was flung open each girl pulled her *burka* down over her face and peered through the grille. A tiny old woman, so bent she looked as though she might topple forward, clung to the door frame and gazed up at them through eyes nearly buried in wrinkles. Soft white hair fell out of her headscarf.

"Grandmother, visitors!" yelled the boy in Pashto, laughing.

A cackle erupted out of the old woman's mouth. Both girls recoiled from the sound as she raised her hand in greeting. Just like the boy, she motioned to them to come closer. Another rasping noise arose from her throat. The boy, still bouncing and laughing, bolted ahead of them.

Yasmine entered the hut first, Tamanna followed. It was a very poor home but as tidy as the wind-swept, mountainous land around them allowed. A worn rug covered the floor and a large *toshak*, also old but clean, was pushed against the wall. Yasmine and Tamanna removed their shoes.

Sit, sit, said the old woman with her hands. The boy had already put a pot on a small wood stove that sat in the corner. It was a surprise to see such an expensive stove in a poor house. A small kerosene heater was tucked away in a corner, another surprise. A plastic jug lay on its side near the heater.

The woman cackled. The boy nodded. He could decipher the noises coming from the old woman, but to Yasmine's and Tamanna's ears the sounds were indecipherable.

"My grandmother wants to welcome you." The boy's grin never left his face, and he had blank, dreamy eyes. Tamanna realized it first. He was *bool*—sweet, gentle, but not intelligent. Tamanna looked at him with kindness. Such a child might be treated with indulgence by his family, but in the villages or in the city he would be an object of disdain.

He darted out of the house, returning with the cat in his arms. "Beelow," he yelled. Tamanna and Yasmine nodded, yes, yes, the cat's name was Beelow. Each took a turn petting it. The old woman tapped her grandson's arm, nodded her head vigorously, and made another screeching noise.

"Grandma says, '*Chai, chai!*'" The boy dropped the cat and danced in circles. Tamanna and Yasmine sat on the pillow as the boy passed them each an earthen mug filled with green tea. "My name Zmarak. Means lion cub. Father, Zmaray, lion!" The boy thumped his chest.

"Is your father here?" Yasmine asked, tentatively.

"He is martyr," said the boy, loudly and proudly.

Both girls exhaled and relaxed a little. Even the pain in Tamanna's hip seemed to dull, though she was still sweating. They sipped their tea as the fire under the stove warmed them. It was hard to keep their eyes open.

✦

"Speak, before I shoot!"

Yasmine instantly awoke to the sound of a bullet as it was released into a firing chamber of a gun. The cocked rifle rested against Tamanna's temple. Tamanna, too, awoke with a jolt. Both looked down the barrel of an old-fashioned gun, the kind Yasmine had seen in old western movies she and Baba used to watch on the television in England. Instinctively they covered their faces, Tamanna with her hands, Yasmine with the end of her headscarf.

"Tell me who you are and what you want."

Then, from the other side of the room, the grandmother's long, guttural whine filled the air. The man with the gun understood the woman's squawking and pulled back. The old woman, sounding like a crow, cried out again and again. She was pleading with him, her hands folded over her chest. The man stared first at Yasmine and then at Tamanna with eyes lined with black *surma*. He wore a dirt-brown *shalwar kameez*, leather boots under baggy pants, and a turban, its trailing ends wrapped around his nose and mouth.

"Why do you walk through the mountains alone? Where is your man?" He seemed to be asking the old woman and the girls at the same time. Zmarak, the boy, sat in the corner petting the cat.

"Please, we are travelers. This woman and boy gave us refuge. We will leave now," Tamanna answered in Pashto. In that moment she caught a glimpse of the early-morning sun through a paneless window. How long had they slept? Tamanna struggled to stand but her hip gave out and she tumbled back to the ground with a muffled thump. A woolly sheepskin and the *toshak* padded her fall.

Yasmine, trying to keep her face covered with one hand, reached out to help Tamanna with the other. She was about to speak when the gunman turned the gun on her. The old woman's screeching had turned into a long, slow moan, the gunman paced back and forth, but the boy only smiled as he murmured into the cat's ear. For a few moments there was silence. Tamanna's eyes darted around the room. She spied the place where the boy and old woman must have slept. The ground was as hard as iron and covered only by a thin sheepskin. The gunman stood between them and the door. There was no escape.

"Who are they?" the gunman asked the grandmother.

The old woman turned away. The cat screeched and jumped out of Zmarak's arms. The boy leaped up and threw his arms around the gunman's legs. Tamanna took a breath, expecting the man to beat the boy. But instead of shoving Zmarak into the dirt floor, he reached down and patted the boy's head. The gunman's hands were small and dirty, the nails bitten, and to Tamanna's ears, his voice seemed strange.

"We mean you no harm. We are trying to reach the border," said Tamanna. Perhaps it was the fever that made her brave, perhaps her judgment was impaired, but she spoke out, unafraid of the consequences. She revealed her face and looked the gunman in the eye.

There was a pause, no one spoke. The gun was lowered, and the wrapping around the gunman's face was pulled away. The man was a woman.

"Welcome," she said.

Zmarak clapped his hands and reeled with laughter as the old woman sighed and pulled herself up to stoke the fire.

"My name is Ariana. This is my mother, and you have met my son, Zmarak," she said.

Tamanna was about to say something but instead she sniffed. They all did. Chicken!

Ariana's gun stood propped up by the door. They sat around a long cloth, the family's *dastarkhoan*, having feasted on chicken stuffed with grain and nuts. There was fried eggplant and yogurt dip and many rounds of naan. It was overwhelming.

Tamanna, too sick to eat more than a few mouthfuls, paused and thought of the wedding feast Mor had planned. *Mor, Mor . . . be well, be well. May Allah protect you.* The tears that crawled up her throat were sudden and unexpected. She swallowed. Mor would tell her to watch for signs of good luck and bad. *Good follows good, bad follows bad.* Tamanna looked at the bowl now emptied of food, then around at the company. This was a welcoming home. They were warm, full, and, for the moment, safe. Surely this was a good sign.

"It is a miracle that you have got this far on your own. It is strange . . ." Ariana's voice trailed off.

"You have been kind. We thank you," said Tamanna. The old woman beamed.

"You have made my son and mother happy. You can thank us better with a story." Ariana smiled.

"I am not good at speaking, but perhaps I can try and tell you the story of an elephant who wears a suit," said Tamanna, mustering all her energy. Neither knew this word *suit*, but Zmarak and his grandmother laughed anyway. Even the cat seemed to be listening. Tamanna was unused to being the center of attention and certainly, in her whole life, she had never told a story. Sitting around a dying fire, she told the young lion cub and his grandmother the story of Babar.

Ariana stood, took her gun, and went outside. Her back against the wall of the house, she looked up at the stars.

"My Pashto is not as good as my friend's, but may I speak?" asked Yasmine, standing in the doorway.

Ariana nodded. "Sit."

Yasmine crouched beside her. "Thank you. Without your help . . . I am not sure how much farther we could have gone."

"Your friend is sick. My mother will take care of her," said Ariana.

"Why do you dress like a man?" It took Yasmine courage to ask such a personal question.

"Because there is no man in this house, so I am the man," she said simply.

"To dress like a man is against the rules of the Taliban. The hills are filled with Taliban, and warlords, too. Why do they let you live as you do?" asked Yasmine.

"What? Do you think the Taliban follow their own rules? Their laws are to control others, not themselves! They do what is convenient. It is not convenient for them to kill me. They have uses for a woman beyond marriage." Ariana turned and faced Yasmine.

In the dim of the hut Yasmine had not looked at the woman closely. Now, under starlight bright enough to read by, Yasmine saw a face so sharp and lean it might have been chiseled in stone. Ariana was beautiful. In the British world that she had once lived in, Ariana would have graced the covers of magazines. People with cameras would have followed her. Then Yasmine looked more closely. Mother and daughter had similar features. That old woman had once been beautiful too.

"Why do the Taliban let you travel as you do?" Ariana asked.

Yasmine reared back in shock. "I do not understand."

"You have walked into a nest of hornets. I want to understand why you have not been stung," said Ariana.

"We have traveled only at night. They do not know we are here," said Yasmine.

"When a sheep dies in these mountains, they know. Do not underestimate the Taliban. Tell me, do you hear whistles in the night?"

Yasmine nodded and instantly realized what a fool she had been. Of course, the whistles were Taliban signaling to each other.

"If they let you travel these mountains it is because they do not care or have more important plans," said Ariana.

Yasmine rested her chin on her knees. She had to believe that they had not been spotted. "How is it that your mother cannot speak?"

Ariana shrugged. "I was a child when the Russians invaded my country. They attacked the *mujahideen*, our courageous defenders, on a mountain pass. There was a battle. My father was tending to our flock of sheep. He was not a soldier but he loved this country, and so when he was given a gun—an old gun that did not work—he went with the *mujahideen* to fight the Russian invaders. When he did not return, my mother went up the mountain in search of him. The last words she spoke were, 'I will find your father and bring him home.'

"It has been said that instead of finding my father she found a dying Russian soldier. He cried out to her and she gave him a sip of water. She was a young, compassionate mother, and he was a young soldier. He died as she held the cup to his lips. A *mujahideen* spied her giving comfort to the enemy. They could not stone her because my father was a martyr, so they took pity on her and only cut out her tongue." Ariana looked up at the stars. "My mother cannot read or write. We can only guess if this story is true. But what is true is that my mother has no tongue."

For a long time they sat. "What of your husband?" asked Yasmine.

"He was from the city of Herat. I was tending the sheep and he was walking towards Pakistan. Herat is a city of poets. Do you know this city?"

Yasmine nodded.

"My mother offered him shelter for the night and he never left." She paused as if waiting for a reaction. "Does that shock you?"

"You are very beautiful. I am not shocked."

Ariana let out a small laugh. "An explosion killed all of his family, and so he was free to take a wife of his own choosing, and he chose me." Ariana paused as if trying to reason the miracle of it. "He and I were the same in many ways. In a country where women are expected to have many children, we were both without siblings. Like him, I had lost my father and my three brothers had died as infants. My mother did not demand a bride-price, she asked only that we stay together.

"For a short while we were happy, and then the Taliban came for him one night. I was hiding, but they knew I was there with my mother and our newborn baby. They said that he could join them or watch them murder me and our son.

He went with them and was killed by the Americans. The Taliban pay the family of those who have been martyred. When the foreign soldiers kill our men, do they offer such compensation? Tell me, who is more just?"

They could hear laughter from inside the house. The words *Paris*, *France*, and *Babar* rang out.

"But if it is as you say, and the Taliban know everything, why do they let you live as you do?" asked Yasmine. There was something not right about Ariana's story, but Yasmine had never lied or known liars and so it was hard for her to judge.

"The wars have taken my father, maimed my mother, and martyred my husband. That is why the Taliban leave me alone, at least for now," added Ariana.

The two sat under the stars for a long while. "And your son, Zmarak?" Yasmine asked.

"He was born as you see him—happy with the world and his circumstances. Do we all not wish such a life?" replied Ariana with a shrug.

Yasmine reached into the moneybelt that circled her waist and held out many thousand Afghani banknotes.

Ariana lurched back. "How dare you offer money in exchange for hospitality freely given?" She was tall and strong, but in that moment so was Yasmine.

"I offer this not as an exchange for hospitality but as a gift independent of hospitality. You have a stove. The kerosene jug lies on its side. It is empty. This is for kerosene to keep your son and mother warm during the winter. That is all." Yasmine placed the money on the ground in front of Ariana.

A moment passed. Ariana sat back on her haunches. "That will pay for much more than kerosene," she said, but gently. She picked up the money and tucked it into a deep pocket. "Rest for a few days. My mother will care for your friend and make her well. It is her nature."

Yasmine was about to give thanks but, as usual, Ariana ignored her and kept talking.

"Beyond that mountain range there is a large, open pasture. In five days many tribes will come together for a game of *buzkashi*. Thousands will gather. *Buzkashi* is more than a game, it's a way of life. The Taliban might not care about two girls and a boy walking through the mountains. In six days, Zmarak will take you along the high paths and through a village. Do not stop. Zmarak must not go too far. He is always in danger of being kidnapped by the Taliban."

"Surely Zmarak would not make a good soldier."

Ariana sniffed. "A suicide bomber does not have to be smart, only tortured into submission. They would make a simple boy into a bomber and tell him that when his body blows up into a million pieces he will smell sweet almonds and go to Allah's warm embrace."

"But how would he know how to do such a thing? He is not . . ." Yasmine did not want to use the word.

"You think he is not capable? Young suicide bombers are often wired so that they can be detonated from afar. Even dead, their bodies can kill. The Taliban operate by fear, not loyalty. You think that only girls are under attack but boys, too, must hide, not only from the Taliban but from the warlords. Warlords put bells around the ankles of young boys, dress them like women, and make them into *bacha bazi*, dancing boys. They are used like women. It is an old, filthy tradition that must die." Ariana stood and dusted herself off. "When you leave here you must move quickly. Besides the Taliban and wandering bandits, there are many foreign soldiers in the area. And if foreign soldiers are near, so are land mines and suicide bombers."

Yasmine nodded.

"You must change your *burkas*. Come."

Yasmine followed Ariana back into the house. The boy and his grandmother were already asleep and curled up under the sheepskin. Tamanna lay on the pillow, awake but sleepy.

Ariana opened a wooden trunk, took out two old *burkas*, and gave them a shake. "My husband brought these from a bazaar just after we were married, one for me and the other for my mother. They are old and worn now." Ariana held up a tattered green *burka* and fingered the material. "Do you know the history of this thing?"

Again, Yasmine looked at the woman with surprise. She shook her head.

Ariana stared hard at Yasmine. "The *burka* has been around for centuries, but hardly anyone would wear it in the past. Have you heard of Habibullah?" There was pride in her voice.

"He ruled only a hundred or so years ago," said Yasmine. For the first time in her life, she was embarrassed to have answered correctly. She did not want to appear to be a know-it-all in Ariana's company.

"Yes, and he had a harem of two hundred women. The princesses were clothed in silk *burkas* stitched with gold thread. The *burka* was only for the upper class. And do you know that it was the Christians, not the Muslims, who first hid their women? Even now many women believe that wearing the *burka* is an honor. They feel naked without it." Suddenly Ariana scoffed and threw the *burkas* at Yasmine. "They are walking prisons, shrouds for the living dead. Take them and leave the ones you are wearing."

"How do you know such things?" Yasmine asked quietly.

"What do you mean?" Ariana stood tall.

"How do you know about Habibullah?" The question was no sooner out of Yasmine's mouth than she regretted having asked it.

"My husband was a teacher and I a good student. You think that I am ignorant because I live in the mountains. I am strong. All the women of Afghanistan are strong. We will endure." Ariana looked away, but it was too late. Yasmine could see tears in her eyes.

⚜

When they awoke the next day Ariana was gone. Where had she gone? Ariana's mother could tell them nothing, and the boy would not have understood the questions.

Five days passed. Ariana was right, the old woman took great care of Tamanna. She served Tamanna cold food for her fever—goat yogurt, eggs, chicken, walnuts, and spring fruit. Hot food—beef, ginger, spice—was for colds. Soup was the exception. Chicken and coriander soup cured everything. Tamanna ate all that she was given. With the old woman's care, Tamanna grew strong.

On their last morning, while Tamanna slept, Yasmine closed her eyes and silently made *du'a*.

Insh'Allah, I am doing the right thing.
Insh'Allah, my friend will stay well.
Insh'Allah, my parents are safe.
Insh'Allah, good things will come to these kind people.

She stood, stretched, and sniffed. She could smell soup brewing in the pot. "*Salaam*," Yasmine said to the old woman, then she skipped out to the courtyard. Streaks of light in the eastern sky promised a fine day.

"Good work!" Yasmine called out. Zmarak, holding a crumbly yellow brick, turned and beamed a boy-smile. Over the past five days, and under the watchful eyes of Beelow the cat, Yasmine and Zmarak had rebuilt the wall in the front of the house and even remade the chicken coop to keep the chickens out of the fledgling herb-and-vegetable patch. Yasmine picked up a stone and slammed it into the pile.

"*Salaam*." Tamanna stood at the doorway holding a mug of soup. "You are a good worker," she called out to Yasmine. To see Yasmine do such work made Tamanna laugh.

Yasmine looked back at Tamanna and then up at the surrounding mountains. She took a deep breath of clean mountain air. *Imagine always living in peace, imagine always feeling at peace.* She wiped her forehead and said, "We must get ready to leave." Tamanna nodded. Yasmine caught a look, something in Tamanna's eyes. Fear? No, not fear. Was it regret?

Zmarak gave Tamanna a present, a newly carved walking

stick. He had shaped the bottom into a point so that it might easily drive into the ground. The old woman packed provisions for their travels, dried goat and naan. Yasmine shook out their food bag. All that was left were some of the candies wrapped in gold foil and the near-flattened water bottles. She gave all but two candies to Zmarak and his grandmother. They kissed. They cried. The old woman bellowed, but now they were used to her sounds and sometimes could understand her meaning. She thumped her chest, clasped her hands, fingers to fingers, palm to palm, and cried out to Allah. Tears fell down her face, running in and out of wrinkles until they pooled on her cheeks. She was haggard and spent, but Tamanna, especially, saw only beauty.

Zmarak was about to translate when Tamanna said, "She says that she will carry our memory in her heart and remember the joy we brought to this house."

The boy's laughter was a familiar sound now, too.

"May Allah bless you," Tamanna whispered as she held the woman in her arms.

Yasmine handed Tamanna her mother's embroidered *patoo* and nodded. Tamanna understood. She tossed the *patoo* over the woman's head and shoulders. The old woman picked up the fringe and covered her nose and mouth. Her eyes, as black as pebbles under water, glistened.

With Only the Sky to Hold

Zmarak took the lead while Yasmine and Tamanna followed behind. As long as a male was in their company they
could walk freely during the day, but that did not mean they
were any less cautious. Yasmine's eyes were never still. But if
it was as Ariana had said, that the Taliban knew everything,
why did they not attack?

Walking during the day gave them a new perspective.
With full bellies and uncovered faces they could occasionally
stop and admire the soaring mountains, plummeting gorges,

and protected valleys that harbored delicate white and yellow flowers. A crisp wind blew off the snow-capped mountains. "Our land is beautiful," said Yasmine. She was beginning to feel something for this country. What had Mother called it? *A call back to the land.*

The path underfoot disappeared and reappeared, but Zmarak plunged on, undaunted. He was quick, sometimes too quick, leaping from rock to path, then back to rock. He stopped often to let Yasmine and Tamanna catch up.

The girls turned a corner, their hands grasping at scrub, their feet feeling their way along a narrow track. And he was gone.

"Where is he?" There was panic in Tamanna's voice.

"There!" Yasmine pointed. They could see the top of Zmarak's skullcap disappearing around a small hill.

"Zmarak!" Tamanna called out. He turned, waved, and bounded down another path towards home.

"He has gone as far as he's allowed," said Yasmine.

"Zmarak, may Allah protect you and your family!" Tamanna's words were carried off by the wind. In this short time, Tamanna had come to care for him as she would a brother.

They carried on down the path, both deep in thought. Suddenly Yasmine stopped, and Tamanna banged right into her. "Down," Tamanna muttered. They crouched behind a boulder, then peeked around it. In front of them they could see a dozen or so huts made of branches, mud, and bits of tin, clinging precariously to the mountainside. A child wearing a necklace of yellow glass played in front of a dilapidated shed. There were no other signs of life.

"Where is everyone? Where are the dogs?" Yasmine whispered. It was usually the barking dogs, clucking chickens, and sometimes braying donkeys that told them a village was near. Yasmine shook her head, then pointed to an overhanging rocky ledge. They would make the climb and avoid the village.

"What are you doing?" It was a man's voice, deep and raspy. He had approached silently from behind. Startled, both girls pulled their *burkas* over their faces and looked through the grilles into the dull, vacant eyes of a grandfather. His cheeks were shrunken, his nose hooked, his face gaunt and skeletal, and his clothes were so filthy that they looked to be made of mud rather than cloth. Strands of hair falling from his gray turban were matted into his straggly beard, and white spittle collected in the corners of his mouth.

Yasmine was about to speak when he abruptly turned and stumbled down the path. They watched as he stopped in front of a hut and kicked aside a torn rug that hung over the opening. A puff of smoke drifted out as he entered and the rug fell back into place.

Tamanna sniffed. She recognized the sweet smell that went up the nose and stayed there. It had often come from Uncle's hut behind her house. "We must get away," she hissed.

At that moment, the child with the necklace reappeared. Startled, Yasmine turned and looked down into huge, liquid eyes. The child smiled, slipped her small fingers into Yasmine's hand, and pulled her forward.

"Yasmine, no!" Tamanna grabbed Yasmine's skirt.

"It's all right. She's just a child," said Yasmine as her feet inched forward. The child led Yasmine towards the rotting, wooden steps of the hut.

Tamanna, right behind her, held her breath. "Yasmine, do not go in," she whispered.

"It does not look dangerous," she whispered back.

"*Asalaam alaikum*," Yasmine spoke as she stepped closer to the doorway. "*Asalaam alaikum*," she said again.

"Yasmine, no."

Yasmine pulled back the rug that covered the door. It took a moment for her eyes to adjust to the dim light, and then a small cry bubbled up her throat. Three children—one a baby and two others who looked to be no more than four or five—lay nearly naked on the floor beside their sleeping mother. Despite twitching limbs, they all looked more dead than alive. The tip of a pipe dangled from the mother's lips. Smoke curled up from the bowl of the water-pipe.

Tamanna tugged at Yasmine's sleeve. "They are opium addicts. We must not stay here."

Shaken, Yasmine looked towards the other mud huts in the tiny village. "Is everyone here addicted?"

Tamanna nodded. "There is no medicine so they use opium for pain. The mother blows smoke into the child's mouth. Soon everyone, even little children, becomes addicted."

"How do you know such things?" Yasmine looked at her friend with both shock and amazement.

"In the bathhouse, women talk. And I know the smell, my uncle . . ." Tamanna said nothing more. There was nothing more to say.

Yasmine looked at the little girl, then gazed up at the surrounding mountains. Suddenly, almost inexplicably, rage filled her body. If one was good, worked hard, and trusted in Allah, life would unfold as it should. That was what she had been taught. That was her belief. But at every turn there was only misery and pain. Her body grew cold, so very cold, as she covered her face with her hands. The cries came from deep within. They seemed to grow until she was enveloped with grief. She leaned down, dropped the heavy haversack, and collapsed on the ground. All of it—the hunger, the fear, the senseless violence—felt as though it were piled on top of her, as though she might collapse under its weight.

When Yasmine looked up at last, her eyes burning, she saw Tamanna and the child sitting silently nearby. "I'm sorry," Yasmine said. She wiped she face with a flat palm.

Tamanna extended her hand and they walked away. The child with the necklace toddled behind, oblivious to her surroundings or destiny.

Yasmine turned back and stared at the child. "What can we do for her?"

"Wait, we can give her something." Tamanna took out the last two candies wrapped in gold foil and handed them to the child. The girl plunked down in a puff of sand and grinned.

There was nothing to fear, and so the girls walked past the tumbledown huts, picked their way through strewn garbage and rubble that littered the ground, and kept going until they came to where the rutted road turned back into a path.

This time, neither looked back.

Chapter 17

Taliban

Once again, they walked by the light of the stars. The paths were steep and slick with frost. The moon was full as they crossed a rope bridge cobbled together with wooden slats, most rotten and some missing. They couldn't see the river rushing beneath them but they could hear it.

Down in the gullies, where only the thinnest moonbeams reached, they hopped across rock bridges. White water ran so fast around the boulders that a wrong step would have carried them away. The soles of Yasmine's shoes were flat and on the wet rocks they became slippery. Bare feet were best. Her toes soon went numb in the icy water. More frightening was the thought of breaking an ankle or leg. What then— to die slowly of the cold and hunger? No, it was better to drown quickly.

The haversack holding Baba's notebooks weighed Yasmine down and occasionally slipped to one side, throwing her off balance. Tamanna repeatedly offered to carry it. Yasmine shook her head vehemently. The added weight would only increase the pressure on Tamanna's hip. As it was, she was limping badly again.

"Tamanna!" Yasmine cried as she stumbled. The haversack shifted. Tamanna, in the lead, turned back and grabbed it. Yasmine let out a muted sob as it was lifted off her back. The straps had cut deep welts into her shoulders.

"Sit," said Tamanna.

Yasmine shook her head. "We should keep going. Listen." Both cocked their ears to a familiar sound. They could hear the beating of helicopter propellers. The border could not be far.

"Just rest for a few minutes," said Tamanna.

Yasmine sank to the ground. For a moment they sat there in silence. Tamanna took a sip of water and passed the bottle to Yasmine. Up until then the idea that they might actually succeed had been unimaginable. And in truth, Tamanna felt that she was not walking *to* anything, she was walking *away* from something. But now, with the border so near, the possibility of a future was creeping into her thoughts.

"Once, you said that many women in the West live

without family. Is that true? Are they all very lonely?" asked Tamanna.

"If they live alone, it is their choice. I remember a friend of my parents, a doctor, who lived alone. I remember her as being happy," said Yasmine. "Come, if we stay any longer we will not get up at all." Yasmine stood and eased the haversack back across her shoulder, pursing her lips tight to swallow the sting.

A day and night had passed since they had said goodbye to Zmarak.

The sun was rising. There were roads nearby but, without a male to accompany them, Yasmine and Tamanna kept to the deserted paths. The routes criss-crossed, backtracked, some simply petered out, while others fanned out so broadly that the trail became a road large enough to accommodate tanks and trucks. It was easy to tell that the Russians had once used these routes. Rusted, broken Russian equipment was scattered about like weeds.

They climbed up a hill. Again, the road to the border was in sight. Even at this early hour they could see a string of colorful *burkas*, horses decorated with bells and blankets, *jingle* trucks, caravans of fat donkeys trailing bony goats and dusty children, and businessmen carrying large cases of mysterious goods, clogging the road. Once again they plunged into a valley.

"Look." Yasmine stopped short and pointed to an ugly black lump on the ground. "What is it?"

"*Naswar*," whispered Tamanna. A great plug of chewing tobacco lay like a donkey turd in the middle of the path. Tamanna stared down at it. It was of high quality. Uncle chewed such tobacco, spitting it out in the corners of the house and courtyard. In these parts, only the Taliban would have been able to afford such expensive tobacco.

"It could be from someone driving a caravan," said Yasmine. They had seen many caravans. Most were carrying ragtag refugees, though once they had seen what might have been a foreign medical caravan—it was hard to tell from a distance.

Tamanna said nothing. They plodded on. Not even Babar stories would help them now.

Exhausted, they looked for shelter to wait out the daylight hours. Yasmine motioned towards an abandoned hut, its tin roof almost flattened and the mud walls around it partially caved in. *Come, come,* Yasmine signaled with her hand. Talk was too exhausting, and besides, they were on the cusp of a great ravine and sound carried.

Yasmine stepped towards the entrance of the hut and stopped. There was something underfoot. She froze. "Stop!" she cried.

Tamanna halted mere feet away from where Yasmine stood, still as a statue, her eyes wide with terror. The Russians, Americans, and even Afghans themselves had buried millions of land mines. They were all over the place. Some had even been made to look like toys.

"Get away," Yasmine muttered. "Get back."

"Stay still," Tamanna whispered, approaching her on tiptoe.

"No, get away. Get away!" Yasmine brushed Tamanna's shoulder with her hands.

"Hush." Tamanna knelt down and, with her fingertips, lightly swept the ground. Some of the mines were triggered by a reverse pressure. One could step down on a mine and nothing would happen, but once the pressure was removed the land mine would be set off. Others were connected to a can of petrol or stick of dynamite.

Tamanna picked up a twig and began to dig a little trough around Yasmine's foot. There were dozens of shell casings scattered around but no wires that led to a buried fuel source. Nor could she see a plank of wood that might be pressing on a detonator.

"No mine," she said with a shudder.

Yasmine crumpled onto her knees and took in long breaths.

"Come," said Tamanna gently.

The ground around the hut had been beaten down. Strewn about were more shell casings, a broken wind-up radio, empty water bottles, plugs of chewed tobacco, and dead batteries. A broad-leafed tree had draped itself over the hut, looking both protective and ominous at the same time.

Yasmine pushed open a wooden door and peered into a filthy, garbage-strewn room. Light filtered in through a small window beside a stack of thin mattresses, but still it was hard to see anything. Another tattered rug, almost more holes than cloth, covered the hard dirt between the door and the mattresses. Drawing a deep breath, Tamanna stumbled in behind.

"Tamanna, look!" Yasmine picked up a crumpled newspaper and held it up to the light streaming in through the window. On one side there was a story written in Pashto about infidels and beside it pictures of American soldiers. They looked huge in their military uniforms. On the flip side of the paper, an Indian woman wearing a glittering pink sari held up a bottled drink in her perfectly manicured hands. Her face had been scratched out with a pen but her body remained untouched. Taliban. They were near, Tamanna could feel it.

As Yasmine looked out a window covered in thick plastic at the rocks and scrubby trees that pressed up against the back of the hut, Tamanna limped over to the stack of mattresses. They were paper-thin and very dirty. Yasmine turned and reared back in disgust.

"It is no safer in here than it is out there," said Tamanna.

Hesitant, but equally exhausted, Yasmine crawled between the mattresses and, as always, tucked the bag filled with Baba's and Mother's papers under her head. Tamanna clutched the other bag, although now it held only dregs of water in crinkled water bottles and crusts of bread. They were warm and, for the moment anyway, felt safe. Sleep was instant.

(⟨⟩)

Hours later, perhaps midday, they awoke to the sound of wings beating against the wind. Yasmine sat up. No, it wasn't birds, something was slapping against the wall. The plastic on the windows had come loose and snowflakes wafted in.

"What is it?" Tamanna whispered.

"Nothing. Sleep." Yasmine settled back down. They were warm, the air was fresh, and, despite the racket and their rumbling stomachs, they fell back into a deep sleep.

It was later, in the quiet time between day and night, that

the whining and pleading bray of a donkey jolted Yasmine awake for the second time. She squeezed Tamanna's arm. Both heard the *crunch-crunch* of feet on rocks coming towards the hut. They lay still, paralyzed with fear. The door opened. Tamanna and Yasmine lay buried under the mattresses in the darkened room.

The voice of a youth was yelling something. The girls strained to hear. "There is no one," repeated the boy. By the sound of his voice he was standing on the threshold. If the boy came in . . . *if* . . . *if* . . . *if*. The door slammed shut.

Neither spoke as they scrambled towards the window. Out went the bags, then both girls dropped over the side. Tamanna let out a muffled moan as a bolt of razor-sharp pain shot up her leg and into her hip. Thorn bushes scraped their hands and legs as they pressed their backs against the wall of the hut. Two hearts hammered. The door inside the hut banged open again. They could hear footsteps.

A head popped out the window directly above them. Tamanna looked up. The boy was peering off into the distance. It was growing dark. She could see his hands gripping the windowsill, his chest, his chin, the shape of his face— it was enough. She felt her heart thump, her body grow cold. How could this be? And then the boy pulled back and disappeared into the hut.

Wordlessly, Tamanna turned to Yasmine and mouthed the words, *Kabeer—my brother.*

Chapter 18

Star-Tipped Sandals

They waited with their backs to the wall and the *campal* covering their heads. Yasmine put her mouth close to Tamanna's ear. "Tell me, why did Kabeer join the Taliban?"

Tamanna hung her head and murmured, "My fault."

There were distant sounds. The girls tensed. Each held her breath and reached for the other's hand. The sounds became clearer—the *clop-clopping* of hooves and the repeated pounding of paws on the stony path. Dogs came bounding up and raced around the hut, sniffed under the blanket, and looked both girls in the eyes. Frantically Yasmine reached for the food bag. She tossed the dogs their last bit of bread. The dogs were young and poorly trained. A nibble was enough to make them happy and send them on their way. A horse whinnied. More staggered *clip-clops* followed, likely donkeys laden with supplies. Someone was yelling. The sounds of the small caravan were getting closer.

Sick rose in Tamanna's throat. She recognized a distinctive nasal voice. It was the Talib with the scarred face—the one who had wanted to kill Yasmine at the school. Then suddenly his voice grew faint, as if he had been swallowed up. He must have gone into the hut. With a thumping heart Tamanna peeked out from under the *campal* and crawled until she could peer around the corner of the hut. There was someone else with them, a boy with a yellow plastic flower tucked behind his ear. She inched back, throat dry, shaking.

"How many?" Yasmine whispered in Tamanna's ear. Tamanna squeezed Yasmine's hand four times.

There was no escape—the slightest movement would set the dogs barking. They sat with their arms circling their knees. The hut was quiet, and as far as they could tell no guards were posted. Tamanna's hip throbbed. Her leg and foot went numb. Sweat beaded on her forehead even as frost formed on the rocks around them.

Yasmine snuggled closer to Tamanna and thought of her parents. She could see her mother's dark eyes and long, shiny black hair, her father's smile, she could almost hear his laugh. *Mother, Baba, I do not want you to be alone in your old age. I love you. I think of you. I miss you.*

Large white flakes fluttered in the air and blanketed the ground. Baba's *campal* did little to keep out the cold. Only when Yasmine and Tamanna were sure that all were asleep did they push back the *campal* and feel the rush of cool night air. Tamanna, rubbing her leg, whispered in a barely audible voice, "Yasmine, I will go to Kabeer and ask for his help."

Yasmine could not believe her ears! "No, he is a Talib now."

"He is my twin. It is different. He would not betray me. And remember, he went to the commander and asked that your life be spared."

"We are so close to the border. We do not need his help," said Yasmine.

"And how do we cross without a *maharam*, a man?" snapped Tamanna. For the first time she could hear the anger in her own voice. How to explain the attachment of a twin to one who did not even have a brother or sister? "Yasmine, I cannot leave my country without saying goodbye to my brother. You must go on ahead. I will catch up to you."

Yasmine chewed the fringe of her scarf. "How will you talk to him?"

Tamanna had been thinking about this for hours now. "The sandals." She pointed to the star-tipped sandals on her feet. "It is many years since he has seen them, but he loved these sandals. I am sure he will recognize them. We can leave them out along the path. He will see them and know I am near."

This time Yasmine shook her head vehemently. "If the others see the sandals first they will steal them, and then what will you do? You cannot walk without shoes."

Tamanna thought for a moment. "Then I will leave one sandal. No one will take just one sandal. They will think it fell off a child riding in a cart." Tamanna was adamant. Even if it meant her life, she would talk to her brother one last time and tell him that he was loved, that he would always be loved, and that he was missed.

Defeated, Yasmine nodded, but she knew that if Kabeer betrayed his sister they would both pay the price.

Tamanna slipped off one sandal and left it on the path that led back down the mountain. Then she hobbled to a new hiding place. Yasmine, carrying the bags and the *campal*, hid farther down the path. They waited for the dawn. Finally, a smudge of a rose-colored sun rose in the east.

There was commotion inside the hut as the small caravan made ready to leave. The donkeys, burdened with packs twice their size, stumbled down the path. The little boy, still wearing a now wilted flower behind his ear, with bells around his ankles, wielding a big stick, came after the donkeys. The commander, on his horse, and the other young Talib followed. They walked carefully. One slip and they would all plummet into the ravine below.

Kabeer, dragging his feet in the dusting of snow, trailed behind. Tamanna's heart beat wildly. The sandal had been kicked by one of the lead donkeys and lay on the side of the path. No, no! He was walking past it. He'd missed it!

Tamanna bolted up and whispered, "Kabeer."

He turned, and with cold, dead eyes looked straight at her.

Kabeer scowled as he turned again to watch the small caravan move down the mountain path ahead of him. He did not ask his sister why she was in the mountains. He did not ask if she was well, if she was hungry.

Tamanna did not notice or did not care that he did not find her presence shocking. He looked different now, too. At the school he'd worn a poorly wrapped, fat, dirty turban. His clothes had been filthy, and hanks of greasy hair had hung down over his shoulders. Now he was dressed in a clean, pale robe, with a warm scarf around his neck and a cap on his head. His hair was trimmed, and there was not even the shadow of boy whiskers. Only an old Russian Kalashnikov rifle strapped across his back announced that he was Taliban. Tamanna ignored the gun. To her eyes he looked wonderful, like a student. She was remembering his sweetness and how they had played together.

"Our mother loves you," said Tamanna. "She waits for you always." Tamanna reached out her hand.

Kabeer reared back and cried, "Do not talk to me of my mother. You bring shame to our family." He spat out the words like dirt, like she was dirt, a fly on the wall, nothing.

Tamanna was confused. "I did not bring shame to our family."

"Where is your *maharam*? You walk outside the house without a male family member. Your face is uncovered. You embarrass me." He turned to leave.

"Please, do not go." Again Tamanna reached out, and again he shrugged her off.

"I am Taliban. We are pure Islam. Taliban apply Islamic rules and laws. Westerners are impure. They have nudity everywhere. Adam and Eve saw that they were naked and so they clothed themselves. We have the computers and DVDs of the infidels and we see their nakedness." His voice had a dead sound to it, as if he was speaking from memory. But what did all this matter? It was not the infidels she cared about, it was Kabeer, her brother.

Tamanna began to stutter. "But . . . but Mor sent you to live with Uncle in Kabul. How was it that you joined the Taliban?" She wanted to know, of course she did, but mostly she wanted to keep him talking.

"The man Mor hired to take me to Kabul took me to the commander instead. The commander is a warlord, a powerful man. Even the Westerners respect him." Kabeer's head flopped down and his chin rested on his chest. He hesitated, as if he was unused to talking about himself.

Tamanna remembered the night he was taken away by the man who owned the water cart. Kabeer, such a little boy, had cried out, "Mor, Mor, I do not want to go." She had hidden behind her mother. When Mor would not relent, Kabeer had reached out to his sister, "Tamanna, Tamanna, help me." The man had scooped Kabeer up in his arms. He'd been small for his age but strong, and he had fought fiercely. "Mor-jam, do not send me away. I do not want to go." His cries had been full of longing and fear. The stranger had raised his free hand and hit Kabeer hard across the face. Tamanna had felt the pain of the slap. It lit her body on fire. Shocked into silence, Kabeer had taken one long look at his mother, who remained stone-faced. And then they were gone.

Tamanna had run after him into the night, tears streaming down her face. "I love you. I will wait for you," she had cried.

Mor had grabbed her and pulled her back into the compound. "Stop your crying. We must keep him safe. This is the only way."

Tamanna had cried herself to sleep that night and many nights after. Behind the curtain that divided the room, Mor too had cried, but silently, afraid that any show of weakness would bring bad luck.

"The commander took care of me for many years. I became . . . I danced . . . I was a good boy. Last year, when I became too old for him, he sent me to training camp. There was little food, much prayer and exercise. My teachers did things . . . to make me worthy. Now I am strong. I can make *jihad* because I am a good Muslim. Islam will be victorious only if we are willing to die for it. Do you know that a foreigner's bombs make black smoke, but when a martyr commits *jihad* the explosions are white? White is a holy color. Proof that God is on our side."

"But Kabeer, suicide is against Islam. The Prophet, peace be upon Him, says—"

"Do not quote the Prophet's words to me, you stupid girl." Kabeer pulled a book from a pocket inside his robe. Its cover bore the image of two crossed swords and the Qur'an. "You see this?" He held up the little blue book. "It is the code of behavior for the Taliban. It will prove to all Afghans that we are good, that the Taliban care for the people. See?" Kabeer opened the book to a page. "It says that all fighters must do their best to avoid civilian deaths and injuries and damage to property. And it says that fighters should try not to cut off ears, noses, and lips as punishment for bad behavior."

Tamanna looked down at the book. It was written in Pashto. The words he was speaking were not on the page. He could not read.

"My brother, you cannot fight and win against the *kharijis*. They are too strong, too powerful. I have seen them. Their big convoys are filled with tanks and many weapons . . ." Tamanna stopped.

Kabeer's eyes darted down the path, then up into the mountains. "We do not have to win. We have to wait. The *kharijis* have no stomach for war and will soon leave our country and go back to the cesspool they call America."

Tamanna leaned forward. "Please, Kabeer, we will run away and begin a new life."

For a moment Kabeer looked confused, and then suddenly his black eyes narrowed and his nose flared as he pulled his mouth into a sneer. "Do you think I do not want to go to Heaven? Women do not have a full brain. If a woman takes one point of view, the other view is the right one. I am a Talib. I will always be with the Taliban, and I would never come with you. I will die for Allah, and my country. You will see. If you do not go home and do as you are told I will tell the commander and he will deal with you. He has four wives and so many daughters he does not count them, and he says that goats have more brains than women." His voice rising, his face flushed, Kabeer shook his clenched fist in the air.

Tamanna stared at him, bewildered. She looked down the path, then lifted her hands as if to say, *Hush, hush*, but there was no way to quiet him. Kabeer too seemed to be looking down the path.

Kabeer leaped up and stood over her. "The infidels pollute our country. They are filth. Look at how they urinate—standing up! They eat and wash with the same hand. They are dirty and Godless. It is *jihad* to fight the infidels. You bring shame to our family but I will restore honor." Twisting like a sapling in a great wind he turned and ran down the path.

"Kabeer, please, please. I am your sister. I love you!" She yelled as loudly as she dared. His shoulders were broad. He was tall and strong. He had been a kind child. He was a boy, just a boy, a lost boy. "Please, Brother." Five years had passed since the night he was taken and now he was leaving again, and the pain was just as searing.

He stopped a little way down the path and turned back. "The infidels will pass this way soon. They will come in their great convoy of tanks and armored cars and vehicles. You will see how little it takes to destroy them."

Tamanna watched him recede from view, growing smaller and smaller. This time he did not look back.

Yasmine had heard it all from her hiding place. She wanted to yell out, "You are an uneducated boy. They have brainwashed you. Your sister is your only hope and you have thrown her away." As he stomped by, his feet sprayed pebbles in all directions. Yasmine lifted her hands to cover her face but in that instant she saw that his feet were lined with brown burn marks, a sign of torture.

Yasmine waited until she was sure he was far away, then gathered the blanket and bags, picked up the sandal that lay along the path, and crept over to Tamanna. "Come, Tamanna, we must keep going." Yasmine reached down and touched her friend's shoulder.

Tamanna's head was in her hands, her shoulders heaving up and down. "I am not going with you." Her sobs were uncontrollable, her face wet with tears.

Shocked, confused, Yasmine stared at her friend. "Tamanna, you are not thinking straight. You will be killed if you return to the village." Yasmine could hardly believe the words she was uttering.

"I will go back to the old woman's house. Ariana is often away. I will take care of the old woman and the boy."

"Please, Tamanna, look at all that they have—boots, a stove, a horse! Ariana walks the hills like a man and is left alone. I think Ariana is a spy for the Taliban."

Tamanna shook her head. "You do not know such a thing, not for sure. And if she is Taliban, what does it matter? They do not hurt her. Why are the *kharijis* good and the Taliban bad? Haven't the *kharijis* killed our people just like the Taliban?" She paused to catch her breath, her voice low and edged in tears. "*Kharijis* do not help. They fight and innocents are killed. They pass by with their big trucks and tanks and then suicide bombers come out to destroy them. I do not know why the soldiers are here. Your father said that the Taliban attacked America. But *I* did not attack the great America. I do not know where this America is! Why are they in our country?" Her voice was ragged, and she drew in great gulps of air that sounded like sobs. Tears made tracks down her face.

"Tamanna, the Taliban have killed and murdered. They have gone against Islam. The foreign soldiers are here to stop them from regaining power. And was it not the Taliban that your mother was trying to protect your brother from?

Tamanna, please!" Yasmine reached down and tried to hold her friend, but again Tamanna snapped back.

"I know this. But I also know that whenever the foreign soldiers are near, bad things happen to us. The Taliban made my brother the way he is, and now he is the enemy of the soldiers. They would kill him if they could. Why can they not see that he is a boy who has been hurt by the Taliban? I was too young to save my brother years ago. It is my fault. I could not save him then, but right or wrong, I cannot betray him now."

Tamanna stood up and staggered down the path. They were on the crest of a precipice. Scrubby bushes were on one side and a sharp drop into a ravine was on the other.

"Please, stop. How can anything be your fault? You were a little girl. You could not protect him." Yasmine ran after her, calling, pleading.

"I could have tried! But I know now that I cannot leave my country. If I did I would bring shame to my family." Tamanna turned back. "The world you speak of scares me. Their clothes frighten me. What if a man in the West sits too close to me? What am I to do? In the bathhouse they say that the women in the West are divorced and live without family. I do not know how to live alone—without family."

"Please, Tamanna, just come with me. I am your family. You will feel differently later."

"I do not know what is right and what is wrong anymore. You do not understand what it is to be Afghan." Tamanna wiped her eyes with the back of her hand. She was resolute.

"I *am* Afghan, just like you, and I know that we cannot

fight the Taliban alone. We cannot fight men who would not let us go to school, who make us prisoners, who make people ignorant and then use ignorance to control us."

The tears stopped. Tamanna stood as tall as her bad hip allowed. "You are the sister of my heart. I love you. But I will not go with you." She turned and stumbled down the path.

Chapter 19

Pink Mist, White Smoke

Like buzzards, three small helicopters appeared suddenly from behind the hill. The first dipped. *Khariji* soldiers manning long, thin machine guns and wearing black helmets and menacing-looking masks bore down upon them. Tamanna looked up and shrieked. Sand particles were whipped into a frenzy, pierced the skin, blinded eyes, and blocked out the sun. Tamanna spun in a circle and instantly lost her bearings. Her arms flailed about. Rocks rolled under her feet. And then, a piercing shriek as she slipped and plummeted down into the gorge.

The helicopters veered up and disappeared into the sun.

"TAMANNA!" Yasmine, many yards down the path, screamed and lurched forward, running to the edge of the precipice. All she saw of Tamanna were flashes of gray, then white. Yasmine plunged down the embankment after her. Twigs, thorns, bushes scraped her face, legs, and arms as she slipped, righted, rolled, then snatched a branch. The haversack caught and uncaught on branches, both a hindrance and a help. Her *burka* was shredded into strips.

"TAMANNA?" Holding on to a branch Yasmine stood and peered down into the ravine. More than halfway down the slope Tamanna's body hung on a tree branch like a limp rag over a line. The strap of the food bag had prevented her from falling even farther—a small miracle. Again Yasmine slipped and slid down the mountain. Scratched and cut, she stopped at last and cupped Tamanna's face in her hand.

Tamanna lifted her head and moaned. Blood was everywhere—her nose, her head, her cheeks, arms, legs.

"I'm here. Hush. I'm here," whispered Yasmine. Softly, her hands barely touching skin, she felt Tamanna's arms and legs. They didn't appear to be broken, but it was hard to tell. An awful animal sound gurgled up from Tamanna's throat. Struggling, her arm circling Tamanna, Yasmine lifted her up and off the branch, then laid her on the steep, rocky slope. Tamanna's chest rattled as if filled with broken glass.

"We are not far from the road. Look, a walking stick, see?" She picked a stick up from the ground. It was too thick and too tall but there was nothing else within reach. "Can you stand? Please try. See, the road is not far. Lean on me. Please, Tamanna, don't give up."

"I will help."

Yasmine looked up and stifled a scream. Kabeer loomed over them both. His shadow was eerie and fearsome. Instinctively, Yasmine covered Tamanna with her body.

"Go away. You are Taliban. You would hurt your sister. I heard you," she hissed.

Kabeer look confused for a moment. "My commander was listening."

Was he telling the truth? How was she to judge? "Where is your commander now? Why has he let us go?" Yasmine stood up and looked him in the eyes. It was a challenge.

"You are not important to him. There is a *buzkashi* game, all the tribes are gathering. I will meet him there. He trusts me." He stared at her with glassy eyes.

Yasmine tried to sort it out. Ariana had talked about such a game. That at least was true, but . . .

"You cannot lift her alone." Without waiting, Kabeer reached down and pulled his sister to her feet. Tamanna cried out.

"Stop, you are hurting her."

Yasmine stood on the opposite side of Tamanna and pulled the girl's arm across her shoulder. Kabeer did the same. Tamanna's head lolled back and forth. She was neither asleep nor awake. Her toes dragged in the dust. Her scarf had fallen away revealing hair as black as ink. Kabeer and Yasmine did not speak. The only sounds coming from their lips were the huffing and puffing from the strain of carrying Tamanna's weight.

They came to the road. After the quiet of the hills, the sound and activity around them was bewildering at first.

Cars and multicolored trucks nudged bikes, women in *burkas,* and small children clutching jugs, all competing for space on the road. A water buffalo waddled along guided by small boys waving big sticks. The helicopters, like giant insects, flew directly towards them. And the dust rose up in the distance. A convoy was approaching. Women and children, men on bicycles, trucks and cars scattered in different directions. The vehicles pulled off the road. Within a minute the road was clear of all local traffic. Should she tell Kabeer that *kharijis* would help a person who had been injured by the war? That she herself was a *khariji*? She looked over at him. He had said he was Taliban but he did not *look* Taliban. He did not wear a fat turban or have *surma* circling his eyes. Nor did he carry a gun. Wait, where was his gun? He looked like a boy, any boy. She needed to think, she needed time to sort it all out.

Together, Kabeer and Yasmine lowered Tamanna to the ground. Yasmine tucked the haversack up close, winding the strap around Tamanna's hand. A woman in a *burka* clicked her tongue and hissed at Tamanna. Yasmine pulled off her *hijab* and tied it under Tamanna's chin. Kabeer looked away. Still, they did not speak. The lead tank was in sight. It appeared on the horizon as huge as a prehistoric, unstoppable monster. Yasmine fumbled for the catch on her necklace. Her hands were rough and the tips of her fingers cut. There, the necklace fell off in her hand. It flashed in the light. Yasmine knelt down and clipped the necklace around Tamanna's neck.

"Listen to me, Tamanna. If the soldiers speak to you, say nothing." Tamanna could only moan in response.

Yasmine looked over at Kabeer. He did not meet her gaze. She looked back down the road. The dust rose like smoke and caught the light of the sun, so that the trucks seemed to bend and shimmer as they barreled towards them. Time stilled. *In the Name of God, the Most Gracious, the Most Merciful. All Praise is due to God alone, the Sustainer of all the worlds, the Most Merciful, the Most Compassionate, Master of Judgment Day* . . . Yasmine's hair was uncovered and she was not ashamed. The roar around her was like thunder but inside there was silence. No fear. Nothing. Her fate was in the hands of Allah. Yasmine stepped out onto the road.

"Yasmine!" Suddenly waking, Tamanna looked up and cried out.

Yasmine did not respond. She stood between life and death and felt at peace. The encroaching convoy growled like a herd of beasts as it came hurling towards her.

"YASMINE!" Despite a pain that ricocheted in her chest, Tamanna lurched forward and screamed.

Yasmine closed her eyes. When next she opened them she was looking down the barrel of a large gun.

A soldier high up in the turret of the tank took aim. He was yelling but his words were lost in a cacophony of sound. Yasmine lifted her hands. Her sleeves fell back revealing bare arms. She was not holding a detonator. But that would not fully satisfy a soldier.

"Move off the road!" The soldier waved his hands. "Terp, where's the terp?" he screamed into a mouthpiece. Three soldiers scrambled out of a vehicle behind the tank and took up positions, pointing their guns in different directions. The soldier high up in the turret kept hollering, "Get me a terp. I need a terp. I got a kid up here blocking the road."

"Please," Yasmine called out. How to prove to them that she was not a threat? And then, "Babar the Elephant," she yelled as she clapped her hands together over her head and fell to her knees.

"Jeeze, say that again?" yelled the soldier.

"Please, sir," Yasmine screamed, "Babar the Elephant. His mother was killed by hunters. He went to Paris."

"Someone want to tell me what this kid is talking about?" The soldier was yelling at someone inside the tank.

"Hey, my kid has that book. Lieutenant, no Taliban kid knows about Babar the Elephant. I think she's trying to tell you that she's not Taliban." It was quieter now. The sound of the tank's engine seemed to ratchet down.

The Lieutenant hollered into a mouthpiece, "I've got a girl up here talking about an elephant and she speaks English like the Queen of England."

Yasmine turned. An Afghan man came running down the line of trucks towards her, his *shalwar kameez* flapping in the wind. He was waving his arms in the air. "Who are you? What do you want?" He spoke first in Dari and then in Pashto. Vehicle doors opened down the line. More soldiers scrambled out of their trucks and tanks. Two ran up a hill and stood under a tree, guns ready. The helicopters overhead were scanning the gullies and ravines.

A little white dog with short stubby legs leaped out from the back of a truck. "Miracle, check," a soldier called to the dog while slapping his hand against his leg. The dog trotted over to Yasmine and sniffed.

A female soldier wearing full battle gear with a large red cross sewn onto the shoulder of her uniform came running towards her. "Keep those hands up, kid."

Yasmine looked over at Tamanna. Kabeer was gone. She looked up towards the mountain, then to the desert. He had vanished. She had been wrong. He was a good brother after all.

While the dog sniffed her bag, the *khariji* soldier patted Yasmine down, just as Brenda had at the FOB. "She's clean," the soldier yelled over her shoulder.

Another soldier was bending down over Tamanna. "Clean here, too," he yelled.

The soldier in the turret, listening on his headset, looked confused for a moment, then yelled, "Are you the missing British kid?" As he climbed out of his turret he spoke first to Yasmine and, without waiting for a reply, spoke to the female soldier. "I just talked to KAF. It seems that there was a British citizen, a girl, sent in a rented car from a FOB to KAF more than two weeks ago. The kid never turned up. Bloody media got wind of it and now half the UN Forces are looking for her." He stopped, turned, and said, "Either of you girls named Yasmine?"

Yasmine stood still. The soldiers would care for a wounded girl, but what about *after* they treated her? Would they send Tamanna back to her uncle? "That is Yasmine. She is British. Here are the papers and her passport, too." Yasmine pointed to Tamanna.

"Yeah? Then why do *you* speak like a Brit?" The soldier put his hands on his hips.

Yasmine paused. "She taught me to speak English."

A young soldier holding a cell phone yelled, "Hey, Captain, HQ says to identify her by a gold necklace."

"Sir, this kid is wearing a gold necklace," said the soldier leaning down over Tamanna. He rooted around in the haversack, then held up papers. "Got papers, diplomas and stuff. Look, one is from Radcliffe. That's kinda like Harvard, right?"

"Yes, Private, nice little country school. Get that girl on a stretcher and let's get out of here, ladies and gentlemen," yelled the Captain.

Yasmine's throat constricted as she ran alongside the stretcher, bent down, and whispered in Tamanna's ear, "Tamanna, listen. I will try and cross the border alone, but if I do not make it, tell my parents I love them. Take care of them for me, Tamanna. Live for me."

"Moving on, Private," hollered one soldier to another.

Tamanna, lying on her back, between the world of awake and the world of asleep, struggled to look behind. "*Yasmine. Yasmine,*" Tamanna cried. "*Yasmine, Yasmine.*"

From a distance Yasmine watched as Tamanna's arms thrashed the air. She could even hear the medic say, "We know your name, honey. You are going to be fine now." The doors of a green military ambulance opened. Tamanna was slid inside as the soldiers climbed back into the tanks.

"Hey, Princess." Yasmine turned. Dan-Danny, almost indistinguishable from the other soldiers in his battle gear, jogged towards her. She recognized his grin and his giant wave. No, he must not see her. He would tell the soldiers who she was! Yasmine spun on her heels and made to run back across the sand and up into the hills. But something else caught her eye. No, not some*thing* else, some*one* else. Kabeer. He was walking across the sand into the middle of the convoy. He was smiling. No, not smiling, grinning—a grin so wide she could see his teeth even from a distance.

"My sister," he cried as he pointed to Yasmine. Yasmine turned back, half expecting to see Tamanna standing behind her. "My sister," Kabeer cried again.

"You know him?" yelled the terp.

Why was he calling her his sister? *You bring shame to our family but I will restore honor.* Information comes slowly, piece by piece, but revelations happen in an instant. *The infidels will pass this way soon. They will come in their great convoy of tanks and armored cars and vehicles. You will see how little it takes to destroy them.* She had led Kabeer right into the heart of the convoy. If Dan-Danny kept walking at that pace he would soon collide with Kabeer.

Yasmine ran. She felt her legs move, pumping, pumping. She stretched out her arms, screams tore at her throat, her chest heaved as she raced towards Kabeer.

"Bomber! Bomber!" she cried.

Kabeer's eyes were as big as eggs and just as white. He raised his hands up in the air—no detonator. Still running, she looked up to the mountains.

"Princess," she heard Dan-Danny call again. The interpreter was screaming too. He knew.

"Suicide bomber!" she cried in English.

"Get me an EOD, *now!*" bellowed a soldier. And then the ground shook.

She did not hear the sound of the explosion but she felt its mighty force. The first wave of air was warm, the second scalding hot. Yasmine was floating. There was pain as bits of debris embedded themselves in her skin. The explosion was white—bone white, ice white. And a voice called out from deep inside.

Run, run.

"Mother, I am running."

Hide. Hide. Hide.

"Mother, I am hiding."

"What the hell was that?" The soldier kicked the door open and jumped out of the ambulance, rolled, and took a position.

The medic grabbed her gun and yelled, "Eyes on the ground. What do you see?" Her eyes were focused directly ahead.

"Pink mist out there," yelled the soldier. "I can see that big red-headed guy, Dan—he's down, covered in blood, but I don't think it's his own."

"Wasn't there another kid out there? A girl?" shouted the medic.

"If there was, there isn't anymore."

"You sure?" The medic did not take her eyes off her visual search area.

"Not sure of anything . . . except that we're sitting ducks," shouted the soldier.

Tamanna, lying on the cot in the ambulance and more asleep than awake, lifted her head while crying softly, "Kabeer, no."

Chapter 20

Adrift in Clouds

Hide. Hide. The word reverberated in her head.

Hand over hand, Yasmine crawled behind rocks. Above, helicopters buzzed around like crazed birds. She crouched between rocks, then burrowed down into the ground. *Hide. Hide.* A wave of sand came over her. She closed her eyes, curled up tight, and fell into a deep sleep.

The stars came out.

Silence. She opened her eyes then slammed them shut against a piercing sun. Her head pulsed, each beat like a fist hammering inside her skull. She raised her hands to brush away the sand. Her hands! They were ugly, brown and bubbly. She moved one finger, then another. At least they worked. One foot looked fiery hot and smeared in black. Her *burka* was gone. Her skirt and shirt covered her. There was a stink of burning hair but, oddly, she felt little pain. It was quiet, so very still. Yasmine was wedged between two rocks. She looked up. Everything—the sky, the land, objects near and far—was blurry and smudged blue. She closed her eyes against the sun. Moments later she opened them. The stars came out. She dreamed about flying. Her arms dissolved into wings that beat back the air and lifted her up into the light towards Mother.

⟨～⟩

"*Dépêche-toi! Une couverture. Elle est en état de choc.*"[1]
Ribbons of pain shot up her spine. Her body was on fire. Her lips seemed to be stuck together. A damp cloth brushed her face and her mouth. There were whispers in her ear. A strange and foreign object was gently pushed between her teeth. Cool liquid drifted down her throat. Something cold was smeared on her face and mouth. She coughed.

"*Bon!*" said a voice.

Her eyes opened. Her lips parted.

"*Apportez-moi mon sac médical. Elle est gravement blessée.*"[2]

"*Bonjour.*" She heard the word come out of her mouth, but garbled, as if her mouth were filled with stones.

---

1 "Quickly! A blanket. She's in shock."
2 "Bring me my medical bag. She's badly hurt."

Astonished, the blue-eyed, barrel-chested man gasped. He peered down at her. "*Mon Dieu. Vous parlez français?*"[3]

"*Oui.*"

"*Bonjour, mademoiselle.*"[4]

"*Bonjour, monsieur.*"

"*N'ayez pas peur.*"[5] He turned and spoke to someone else.

What was he saying? She was not afraid. Why would she be afraid?

"*Votre mère est française, alors?*"[6]

"*Non, non.* But I speak, *je parle,* English, too."

"Unbelievable. Here, in this country, I practice my English." He waved his hand as someone, just out of sight, passed him a water bottle. The man unscrewed the lid and held the water up to her lips.

"Do not drink too much. I am a doctor. My name is André Latouche. One of your shoulders is dislocated, an arm is broken, and you have a very, very bad sunburn. I think, *mademoiselle,* that this is just the beginning. Nicolette!" he called over his shoulder. In a moment a tall, foreign woman was beside him. "She speaks a little French but better English," he explained in French.

"*Mon Dieu,*" said the woman.

"We speak English, no? Nicolette is a nurse. She will examine you." The man spoke, then receded into the sun.

---

3 "Good God, do you speak French?"
4 "Hello young woman/lady."
5 "Do not be afraid."
6 "Your mother is French?"

Nicolette covered Yasmine's chest with a crinkly silver blanket, then, running her hands underneath, removed what was left of her shirt and skirt. "Are you in pain?"

There was pain but it was muted, not searing, not sharp. Her neck was stiff, everything was stiff. But there was another feeling—something inside, as if she were filled with air.

"What is your name?" Nicolette asked gently.

Yasmine thought hard. "I do not know." She was empty and adrift.

"Doctor, look." Nicolette held up the blackened money-belt that had been tied around Yasmine's waist. The doctor again came into view. "There must be thousands in here, many different currencies. It's a good-quality belt—European, I think. It's amazing that the paper wasn't incinerated."

The doctor's eyebrows knitted together. "It might be drug money—she might be acting as a drug mule. Or she might have stolen it and been on the run, which would mean someone is after her. Given that she's been in an explosion and somehow crawled into a hiding place, whoever was with her is likely dead." The doctor shook his head as if to say that there could be many explanations and none of them were good.

"There was an attack on a UN convoy yesterday but it was a kilometer away. Could she have walked that far in this condition?" asked Nicolette.

"Unlikely, but in this country the unlikely is always possible. This explosion could have happened in a courtyard. Boys make homemade bombs that go off all the time. Lock the moneybelt up in the drug box." He peered down at Yasmine. Her eyes were heavy, so heavy. "*Mademoiselle*, try not to fall back to sleep. Can you remember how you got these injuries?"

Behind the doctor were ice-white clouds trailing across a light-blue sky. Yasmine fell into a dreamless sleep.

(꜀ᴄ꜀ᴄᴄꜰᴄ)

"*Mademoiselle,* wake up." The doctor spoke in a gentle but forceful voice. "Nicolette has been working on you for hours. We have given you a drug to dull the pain. You feel better, *non?*"

Hours? It seemed like minutes. She nodded, but in truth she felt nothing.

"Where is your family?" he asked.

"I am alone," was all she could think to say. Without moving her head she looked around as best she could. Donkeys tied to a hook that had been screwed into the dirt, Afghan men with flat hats and beads around their necks smoking nearby, and foreigners, some women, dressed in baggy pants and long Afghan shirts. Dogs. Tents beyond. Horses wearing bags on their faces. Yellow air. She looked back into the eyes of the doctor. Blue.

"Can you hear me? What is your name?" He was talking again. Nothing. She remembered nothing. Instead of memory, there was air.

The doctor slipped away and was immediately surrounded by others. They were talking about her, she could tell. Bobbing heads, nodding, shaking. The doctor was gesturing with his hands. Their clothes danced around them, pale and airy, and their shapes seem to twist in the air. He returned and bent down beside her.

"We are a medical caravan. We are a few kilometers away from Spin Boldak. We have many stops, and many clinics to set up. Then we leave Afghanistan for Pakistan through the town of Chaman and on to Quetta. It is a small city by Pakistan's standards, maybe half a million people, but there are good people there who will help you." The doctor stopped and looked around. Yasmine watched his eyes scan the horizon. Finally he turned back and sighed. "We cannot stay here, and we cannot leave you here. You will come with us, *non?*"

Yasmine closed her eyes. What was he saying? She felt no pain. And then she thought, *I understand. I am dead. But what a funny thing that God and his angels speak French.*

The Border

*"Listen to the reed, how it complains
of separation . . ."*   —Rumi

She was not dead. As the medication wore off she felt less and less dead. Everything hurt—it was as if pins were pushing though her skin. Nevertheless, the pills staved off the worst of the pain.

"Opium?" She looked up at Nicolette.

"*Non, ma petite.* Do you know the drug?" Nicolette looked concerned.

Opium was bad, addictive, she knew that, but she did not know how or why she knew it. She shook her head and

206

then looked down. Her left arm had been put in a white plaster cast.

"Move your fingers, one at a time," said Nicolette. "Good. But without a proper X-ray machine, it is impossible to see if the arm was set correctly."

For travel, they had placed her on a portable cot to which she was secured with ropes wrapped in cloth. The cot had been slipped into the back of a cart. The same crinkly silver blanket covered her. It kept her warm, but it was not comfortable. When they stopped she was lifted off the cart and slid into a tent that Nicolette called a *pop-up*. "See how it pops?" she laughed. True to her word, out of a disk tossed on the ground appeared a shiny blue tent.

Everyone, even the Afghan guides, rode horses, although along the mountain paths they all walked. Land mines were a worry. Sometimes guides walked ahead, their eyes glued to the ground.

"There are roads nearby, but we work in the hills," said Nicolette. "To reach the people in small villages, horses, pack donkeys, and carts are of more use than trucks. We have a half dozen horses, thirty donkeys, fifteen escorts with guns, three nurses, and one doctor."

The trip through the mountains took longer than it needed to because of the fear of land mines, but they also stopped often, treating sick children and men who wanted attention. Women seldom stood in line, and if they did it was to get help for a child. All patients—farmers, children, tribesmen—were treated equally, even Taliban. Within minutes of stopping, small crowds would gather. Infected sores, dog bites, tooth abscesses, boils, burns—there was no end to the complaints. Yasmine pointed to a woman in a *burka* who was big with child.

"That woman, there," she whispered to Nicolette. She could see just a little through the opening in the tent.

"Who?"

"Over there. She is holding the hand of the little girl. I think something is wrong with her baby . . . inside."

Nicolette gazed over and nodded. The woman was wavering as if pushed and pulled by a wind. Even from a distance they could hear her sobbing under her veil. "The husband will not allow us to examine her. I fear she will lose the infant, if not her own life. Many women here die in childbirth. The doctor is talking to her husband again."

Nicolette spoke while taking Yasmine's temperature. The number on the white stick seemed to satisfy Nicolette because she smiled as she unscrewed a jar and smeared a cream on Yasmine's burned face and hands, legs, and feet. It was cooling. Soon it was time to pack up and move on.

"You need a name. If you cannot remember your given name we must think up a new one," said Nicolette as they stopped for the third and final time that day. They were alone in the shiny tent. Instead of wearing a *hijab*, Nicolette wore her hair tucked up into a flat hat. She yanked it off and threw it in a corner. Dark curls bobbed around her face; her lips were red and full and her cheekbones were high. Her clothes were baggy and drab, but still she was beautiful.

Nicolette bent down over her work, gently pulling away the bandages that covered Yasmine's sores. The pain was sharp, instant. Tears circled her eyes as she clenched her teeth.

"Does this hurt?" Nicolette looked at her intently as she peeled back the bandages.

She shook her head. To admit pain would be to compound her embarrassment.

"You are very brave, *ma chérie*. *Bon*, what name do you like?" Nicolette applied a new bandage to her left leg, then moved over to her right.

What name *did* she like? Who was she? Where did she come from? Was she loved? "I do not know."

"I shall tell you what my papa used to say, 'It does not matter what name you are called, what matters is the name that you answer to.'" Nicolette laughed. "I have a cousin named Famia in Kabul. You remind me of her. She is small and lovely like you, and you both have wise, old eyes. Shall we call you Famia?"

Famia. Famia. She tested the name out in her mouth. It felt like blowing a kiss. She nodded. From now on her name would be Famia.

"What does it mean that I have *wise, old eyes*?" she asked.

"It means that you have seen too much for someone your age," Nicolette answered. "And do you remember my name?"

"Nicolette," said Famia.

"Good. And do you remember the doctor's name?" Nicolette looked up from her work and stared at her intently.

Famia remembered that he was French, that he was beardless, that he had blue eyes, a big stomach, and a gentle manner. "No," she said.

"His name is André Latouche. What else can you remember?" asked Nicolette.

"I remember nothing." The past was a wall, the future was a blank, and the present was empty.

"No matter. It will come slowly." Nicolette pulled off a long bandage. Famia winced. "I shall tell you about myself, yes? My mother was born in Kabul but emigrated to France when she was very young. My mama loves France. She loves clothes, you see. In her heart she is French. French women dress beautifully. Look at my poor clothes. Maybe I am more Afghan than French!" Nicolette's words were punctuated with laughter, and her whole face smiled. "What is wrong? Are you all right, *ma chérie?*"

"French women dress beautifully?" she whispered.

"*Bien sûr*, but what is it? Why are you so pale?"

"I do not know. I . . ." Those words, they *felt* familiar. How was that possible?

"Take deep breaths. *Bon*, lie back." Famia did as she was told and Nicolette continued telling her story. The more Nicolette talked, the less pain Famia felt.

"I was raised in Paris, but a small part of me is drawn to this—how do you say?—arid, parched land. Arid—it means scorched, barren, *n'est-ce pas?*" At the end of her English sentences Nicolette almost always said, "*n'est-ce pas?*"

The job was soon finished. The tent flap went up and a small tray of food was passed inside. Nicolette lifted a metal spoon to Famia's mouth and tipped in a spoonful of foreign mush. "It's porridge," said Nicolette. The metal spoon clinked against her teeth. "Sip," said Nicolette as she slipped a plastic straw between Famia's lips.

Dinner done, Nicolette flipped back the wings of the tent so that Famia had a view of her surroundings. All she could really see was Paul McCartney's big backside and long tail. "Your horse has a funny name," said Famia.

Nicolette came around the horse and laughed her wonderful, deep laugh. "Paul McCartney is my favourite Beatle."

Nicolette took a big sponge from a bucket and sprinkled the horse with enough water to make his skin gleam.

"A beetle is a bug?" Famia said quietly.

"*Excusez-moi*, a Beatle is a British group, and Paul McCartney was one of the singers. And now also a horse!" Nicolette was laughing as she threw an old blanket over the horse.

"Like Babar is an elephant, but not an elephant," replied Famia.

"What did you say?" Nicolette stopped, spun around, and stared.

"I . . . I am not sure," Famia stuttered.

"You know about Babar the Elephant?" Nicolette's eyes widened. "You are remembering something. Think, Famia. What about Babar? Think."

Famia shook her head. "I am sorry, that is all I know, except that he wears a green suit."

"A green suit!" Nicolette clapped her hands. "You see, it is beginning. Maybe soon it will all come back, suddenly, *n'est-ce pas?*"

But nothing came after that, nothing.

The sky darkened, and with the night came the stars, and with the stars came the promise of a new day.

Chapter 22

How Tall the Mountain

*"However tall the mountain, there is
always a road."* —Afghan proverb

"See ahead, that's Spin Boldak," called Nicolette over
the clatter of the donkey-cart and the jingle of her horse's
harness. Famia nudged her head out from under the blanket.
Each bump on the road was painful, but the pain was muted
by the pills Nicolette carefully doled out.

Nicolette pulled on Paul McCartney's reins and drew up
alongside the cart. "Paul McCartney, behave." As if answer-
ing her, the horse snorted. Nicolette, a good horsewoman,
reeled him around in circles until he settled. Eyes wide,

Famia watched. In that moment there was a flash—horses jumping over fences, riders wearing tall boots, a manicured lawn. And then it was gone.

The town of Spin Boldak was ugly, flat, and filled with garbage. Tents, held up with spindly wooden beams, lined the main street. Fires flared in large steel drums. Bags of rotten apples and potatoes sat unattended on top of rubbish. Famia was sore and her stomach felt queasy. After being up in the mountain air for so long the stink of the village made her feel faint.

Nicolette and Paul McCartney pulled up alongside the cart again. "Famia, look, the crossing into Pakistan is up ahead. We will stop here. Dr. Latouche wants to talk to you."

Mostly hidden under the blanket, Famia waited. She could see the colors, the shops, smell the food cooking on makeshift grills, see the children playing—it was all exciting, and in those moments of wonder she forgot the pain, and forgot what she had forgotten. Hundreds of people, from many different tribes, were milling around. Despite being a woman and uncovered except for her flat hat, Nicolette moved about freely, as did the other two nurses in their caravan. They were treated as neither men nor women but as oddities in between. Dr. Latouche's status brought further protection to the women and guides in the medical caravan—everyone wanted the attention of the foreign doctor.

"See the Tajik with their long robes and flat wool hats? They are the light-skinned people with blue eyes and blond hair," said Nicolette, who was holding on to Paul McCartney's reins with one hand and pointing with the other. "Those men wearing the *chapan*, a silk coat with a sash, they are Uzbeks. It is said that they are great horsemen and skilled *buzkashi* players. Do you know *buzkashi*?"

Famia nodded. She knew but was not sure how or why. It was a dangerous, fast game played on horseback.

"And see the women over there?" Nicolette pointed to a group of women walking in flowing clothes of bright red, yellow, and blue. "They are Pashtoon nomads and belong to the Kuchi tribe. Look, over there—those men who look Chinese are from the Hazara tribe. They are Shiites and the descendants of Genghis Khan. Many play beautiful music."

"Yes, I know about Genghis Khan," said Famia. "He founded the Mongolian Empire. He . . ." She stopped.

Nicolette gave a smart tug on Paul McCartney's reins then came up beside the cart and stared down hard at Famia. "What else?"

"It was in the thirteenth century . . ." Famia's voice petered out.

"How do you know that? *Think*, Famia."

Famia looked up at Nicolette. Didn't she know that if she could remember she would? There were images—a beach, a bed, a man under a tree, a beautiful woman lying in a bed, a girl limping on a road—but how was she to connect it all?

Nicolette sighed. "We will camp here. Tomorrow you will cross the border with an Afghan guide."

Famia lurched forward. Was she going alone?

"Dr. Latouche will explain. You must rest. Tomorrow will be an important day." Nicolette gave Paul McCartney a gentle kick with her heels and galloped to the back of the caravan.

Later, Famia sat on a blanket with Nicolette beside her. Dr. Latouche, having checked her cast, measured her blood pressure, and felt her forehead, said, "You will go ahead without us. Foreigners are detained at the border."

Her heart started to race. Nicolette put her arm around her and whispered, "It is safer this way. We could not explain your presence in our caravan. Do not be afraid. Just listen very carefully."

"The border has changed," continued Dr. Latouche. His brow was furrowed and his voice rumbled. "Once, Afghans and Pakistanis passed back and forth across the border without checks, but now the Pakistani police are doing random searches, and some will ask for passports. There is a building, security towers, armed guards and gates, but do not look around. Our most trusted guide will lead you across the border. You will pretend to be his wife. He has the money to pay a bribe if need be. Do not speak to him as you cross the border. Do not speak at all. You will be ahead of us, but if we pass you, do not acknowledge us in any way.

"All animals must be left behind. You must get off the donkey and walk as best you can. Once you have crossed the border the guide will get a car. It will take four hours to get to the city of Quetta—the Afghans call this city by their own name, Soba Baluchistan. Many Afghans feel that the city rightfully belongs to their country. It is the capital city of Baluchistan and is 1,600 meters above sea level. There is an orphanage in Quetta, a small hospital, and a school. The city is a good place for many, but it can be dangerous, too. It is

believed that Quetta is where the Taliban have their headquarters. The Taliban pass back and forth over the border.
Use caution. Do you understand?"

Famia nodded, but in truth it was all very confusing.

"The driver will take you to a safe house. It is owned
by good people from Kabul." Dr. Latouche patted her hand
as if to reassure her, but Famia thought it might be to reassure himself.

"I have put new bandages and cream in this bag."
Nicolette held up a small sack. In her other hand she held a
small pill bottle. "Once you have crossed the border I want
you to take one of these pills. The pills will help with the
pain. Do not take one before the border crossing. Your mind
must be clear. You may take another one once you are in the
safe house. There are extras in case we get detained, but no
more than two pills a day." She placed the pill bottle in
Famia's open palm. She stared at it. It looked familiar.

"Be brave," said Nicolette.

Startled, Famia looked up. She wasn't brave, not even a
little. "Nicolette, please don't leave me," she whispered. Her
words came out in a sudden gush. Never mind the burns,
never mind the pain, she threw her arms around Nicolette's
neck and hung on tight. Her behavior was unseemly, childish
even, and she knew it was, but she had no one, she was
no one.

"Take a deep breath. No more tears, *n'est-ce pas?* Now, I
want to explain the money that you have in your moneybelt."
Nicolette spread the bills on the ground. "These are British
pounds, American dollars, Pakistan rupees, and of course
you know the Afghani banknotes." Nicolette explained the

value of each foreign currency. "Do not take the moneybelt off until you are in the safe house." The tears started again. "*Ma petite*, we will not be far behind. We will join you soon. It has to be this way. And wait until you see the city of Quetta. Quetta is Pashto for *fort*. It is surrounded by snow-capped mountains. Their names are Chiltan, Takatoo, Mordar, and Zarglum," said Nicolette with a smile as she tucked the bills into the moneybelt. "Now let me put this around your waist." Tears welled in Nicolette's eyes.

She is afraid for me, thought Famia. "You love this part of the world," she said to Nicolette.

Nicolette nodded. "It is possible to love a country, even one that I was not born in, but hate its politics. In this part of the world it is not only possible, it is probable."

Famia stood very still. It was as if a breath of warm air had brushed her face.

"Famia, what's wrong? Do you feel sick?"

Famia shook her head. "Nothing, nothing." But there was something. She had heard those words before.

With a new *burka* flowing around her, Famia, with help from Nicolette, climbed onto the gentlest donkey in their small herd. Propped up on the donkey and from a short distance, she looked like a tiny, expectant mother. The trusted Afghan guide held the reins of her donkey and, walking well ahead of the medical convoy, trudged on. Panic seemed to rise up and wash over Famia. "Nicolette, do not leave me alone," she whispered, although the nurse was much too far away to hear. The veil of the *burka* hid her tears.

Dr. Latouche was right. The actual crossing was confusing. With the fingers of one hand entwined in the donkey's mane, and the other hand pulling the grille of the *burka* close to her face, she looked at her surroundings. People and animals were everywhere. The sounds of barking dogs, braying donkeys, angry goats and spitting camels, children yelling and men shouting was muffled by the sand underfoot. She could smell meat cooking over grills. Bread was baking somewhere. To the side of the road a tailor, stooped over a brown sewing machine painted with colorful flowers, guided yards of yellow and blue material under the needle. Near the tailor, a tooth-puller sat cross-legged on the ground. The tools of his trade—pliers, small hammer, and cloth to catch the blood—were displayed on a tattered rug in front of him. Raggedy lines led up to the actual border.

They waited their turn in line. Finally they reached the crossing. The guide held the donkey still as she climbed off. The animal was led to a corral. Scabby-kneed boys with matted hair were sitting on the top of a fence and poking the animals with sticks. What about Paul McCartney?

Famia hobbled on her two bandaged feet. Large sandals, meant for men, were roped overtop of the bandages and around her ankles. Famia shuffled behind her pretend husband. He was old, his beard long, a grandfather perhaps, but he muttered words of encouragement under his breath as they walked. She was grateful for his kindness but said nothing.

The border guards ignored them. They were paying attention to rich-looking Afghans who carried many boxes and bundles. With guns dangling off their shoulders, the guards punctuated the air with indignant, shrill screams. From the little she could see, those from Persian tribes—the Hazras and Uzbeks—were getting the more brutal attention.

Across the border, in Pakistan, different vehicles lined the road—automobiles, vans, buses. The guide walked up to a small Toyota. "We want to go to Quetta," he said. He and the driver argued about the price. Negotiations settled, Famia sat in the back of the car while her "husband" sat beside the driver.

Fear washed over Famia. Her pretend husband could take her anywhere, he could drop her at the side of the road. He could sell her and no one would know. The mountain air was cool, but the heat under the *burka* was stifling. She couldn't catch her breath.

"Please," she leaned forward and whispered, "where are we going?"

The guide ignored her. The driver turned just a little, his eyebrows arched in surprise. Famia slumped back into the seat. Her body ached, her mind traveled. Her fate was in the hands of a stranger. This, too, was a familiar feeling. Famia reached into the bag Nicolette had prepared for her. She pulled out the small vial of pills and a water bottle. With her hand under her veil she lifted the pill to her mouth and swallowed. She tried to sleep.

Twice the car was stopped by police. The guide pulled out little packets of cigarettes from under his robe and passed them to the driver, who gave them to the police.

The driver turned a sharp corner, sharp enough for Famia to fall sideways and wake suddenly as her head slammed against the door. Four hours had passed. She had slept most of the way. They were in the city of Quetta. Groggy and confused, she looked out the window at pale-yellow walls close enough to touch. Ahead there was a small, neat house.

The car came to a stop. The guide paid the driver, climbed out of the car, and yanked on a bell-cord outside the door. What should she do? What was expected of her? Trembling, she waited. A man appeared at the door. He and the guide spoke. Finally the guide turned and motioned to Famia to come. She climbed out of the car and tried to coax her feet to move. *Walk, walk,* she willed her feet to move. She took one step, two, three, crossed the threshold, and entered a courtyard.

Pots of flowers and herbs lined the passageway through the courtyard to the front door. When the door opened, a woman, her face exposed, stood in the doorway. Behind her the upper walls and much of the ceiling of the house inside were decorated with blue mosaic stones, while the lower part of the walls were painted a startling pink. It was sparkling clean. It was a welcoming room. The woman opened her arms in greeting.

Famia fainted.

Chapter 23

Prayers on a Breeze

Lying on a thick, soft mat, with an even softer blanket tucked around her, Famia was coaxed out of sleep by the sound of the call to prayer echoing from a speaker on the top of a nearby minaret. *Allahu Akbar, Allahu Akbar.* Another prayer from another minaret joined in, and then another and another, as if the mosques were singing in chorus. The prayers were carried on a wafting breeze that billowed the curtains and seemed to penetrate her bones, until she could hear the call from within. She looked up at the walls, at the ceiling decorated in blue and pink tiles, and the peace she felt dissipated.

She took in a breath, and then another, and then another. *Where? Where?* Panic rose up as the sting of sores on her skin and the pain of bones not yet mended hit her with the force of a fist. *Get up. Get away.* A small cry, more a yelp then a scream, rushed up her throat. And then a hand reached from behind and a cool cloth dabbed her forehead.

"Do not be afraid. You are safe."

Famia turned and looked into clear, gray eyes. The woman was older than Famia, but young all the same, maybe nineteen or twenty.

"My name is Mina. I live in this house with my husband, Babrak. You have been asleep for a long time. You are in Quetta, Pakistan. Do you remember coming by car?"

She thought for a moment. Like a wave on a beach being pulled back into the sea, the panic she had felt receded. She nodded, and gradually she remembered that she could not remember.

"Nicolette? Dr. Latouche?" Famia struggled to sit up.

Mina shook her head as she placed her hand against Famia's back, then adjusted a small pillow so that she could sit up. "They will arrive soon." Mina placed a bowl of fruit in front of Famia. "Eat slowly. Will you tell me your name?"

"I do not know my name but I am called Famia."

Mina looked perplexed but did not demand answers. Famia ate, sipped green tea sprinkled with sugar, and chewed naan.

Later in the day, and a bit at a time, Famia told her story. It was a short story. There had been an explosion, one that she could not recall, but the evidence of the bomb was on her body. By Allah's blessing, her face and eyes had been spared. She told Mina about Nicolette, about Dr. Latouche, about Paul McCartney.

"What if they don't arrive? What if something has happened?" She looked into Mina's eyes, which seemed to grow lighter or darker, depending on the light of the room.

"You are welcome in this house for as long as you want," said Mina.

Famia turned and looked to the wall. How was it that strangers were so kind? Again she slept, and again awoke in the care of good people.

Mina's food was nourishing, and she cared for Famia as though she were her little sister. Carefully she unwrapped the bandages around Famia's hands and feet. "Look, see your hands? I do not know what the original injuries looked like, but I think that they are much improved. I attended nursing school in Kabul before I married, but I did not get very far in my training."

Babrak, Mina's husband, was shy and did not talk to Famia directly. He brought fresh fruits and even helped his wife with the household duties. Perhaps it was because Mina was expecting a baby. "Our first," she said with delight. By nods and small smiles it was clear that Babrak was just as excited.

Another day passed. "Might we not go back to the border and see if they are still there?" Famia asked tentatively.

"Babrak is out in the market every day. He will tell us the news. Come, walk a bit," said Mina. With Mina's help Famia stood.

They were in the family room at the back of the house. The room was divided into two. On one side, and behind a curtain, was the sleeping area. That area too was divided between Famia's area and Mina and Babrak's. It looked as though they had tacked the curtain up in haste. On the other side of the curtain was the kitchen.

Leaning lightly against Mina, Famia hobbled through the next room and out the door until they both stood in the courtyard. She had seen the pots of flowers and herbs when she arrived, but now she noticed a garden of vegetables on one side of the passage and fruit trees on the other side. The air smelled of mint. But most beautiful of all was a tree, and under the tree a bench, and beside the bench a pillow.

"What is it?" Mina asked. Famia just shook her head. "Come, sit on the bench. The pillow is too low. I think that you with your injuries and me with the baby, neither of us would get up!" When Mina laughed her eyes sparkled.

"How did you come to live here?" asked Famia.

Mina told her that she and Babrak had married a year ago. It was an arranged marriage, of course. Both were from educated families. Their fathers and mothers were old friends, and when they were little they had even taken car trips together.

"My father came under attack for sending my older brothers and sisters to America. The *mullahs* pointed fingers," said Mina. "My father supported the president and the foreign soldiers. But in the end it was not the Taliban who killed my parents, it was a roadside bomb. Babrak's parents, too, are dead. He sends money back to Kabul to support his sister and brother-in-law, who lost his leg when he stepped on a land mine. He was playing soccer with his little girl when it happened. Babrak has a younger brother too. His name is Atal. He studies hard and is a good boy." Mina paused and looked around. "We left Kabul to find peace, if only for a little while."

"But you can leave this place forever, can you not? You have family in America," said Famia.

"I miss my family. It is hard to be so alone in this place. At home in Kabul I would have had many hands to help with our baby. Soon we will return to Afghanistan." For a moment there was sadness in her voice.

"But if your family is not there, and you miss them, why return?" asked Famia. It was a very personal question, but Famia felt so comfortable in her company.

Mina leaned in close. She smelled of flowers and mountain air. "We wait until it is safe for us to return. We are young, we are educated, we are strong. If we too run away, what hope is there for our country? It is not the West that the old *mullahs* fear. It is modernity. Anything modern or new is a challenge to their way of thinking. Education is our only hope. Meanwhile, Babrak and I support the medical efforts of Dr. Latouche and others who would help our people—all our people, not one tribe over another. We are all Afghans first."

"Famia!"

Famia looked up to see someone coming into the courtyard—it was Nicolette! A huge smile lit up her face. Babrak stood smiling, too, in the doorway.

"*Bonjour, ma petite.* We are here at last!" cried Nicolette.

Famia began to shake with relief, and she saw Nicolette's smile replaced by a look of tender concern.

"Oh, *ma petite*, were you worried? It was just a delay. A boy who had stepped on a land mine required surgery. His father is chief of police. The doctor could not say no. The horrible man locked us up in a room until he was sure the boy would live! Can you imagine?"

Famia, pale as ice, leaned against the tree. She had thought she was getting stronger, but she realized then just how much the fear of losing her new friends, the only people she felt any connection to, had hurt her.

Mina pulled herself up. "Come, sit here," she said to Nicolette. "I will get you tea."

"*Excusez-moi*, Mina. I have forgotten my manners. How are you feeling? How is the baby?" Nicolette smiled at the young woman.

"We are well and will talk later. Sit with your friend. She has missed you."

"*Merci*, Mina." Nicolette sat and put her arm around Famia. No matter how she tried, Famia could not stop shaking, or stop the tears from trickling down her cheeks. "Hush, hush. I am so sorry we worried you. But now it is good. We are here, *n'est-ce pas?*" Famia nodded, but the tears ran down her face and onto Nicolette's shoulder. "Hush, I am here."

There was a commotion outside the front door. The door opened and in spilled Dr. Latouche and the nurses. Mina, her faced flushed with excitement, was rushing around preparing tea and a plate of fresh fruit and sweets. Nicolette offered to help, but Mina brushed her aside. "It is better that you two talk. Perhaps Famia should rest?" suggested Mina.

"Yes, that seems wise." Nicolette's voice was suddenly serious. "Come, Famia. You rest, and I will tell you what I've been thinking about," she said.

Nicolette helped Famia into the cool quiet of the sleeping area, where she settled back down on a mat, facing the wall. She was ashamed of her obvious weakness, her tears. Nicolette held her hands.

"Famia, *regardez-moi*. For three days I have thought of you, and I think I know what might be best, for both of us. Come home with me, to France. Begin your life again." Nicolette looked at her with equal parts love and concern.

Famia caught her breath. It was so touching, but confusing, too, that these foreigners—these strangers, really—cared for her so much. She felt so . . . grateful.

"You are young. You can go to school. There is nothing for you here. Come home to France." Nicolette put her arm around Famia's shoulder and kissed the top of her head.

A shiver went down Famia's spine. Was her home really France? She looked up at Nicolette's face, and words seemed to stick in her throat.

"Famia, say something."

"I was afraid I would be alone. How does one live without family?" She spoke while choking on tears.

"You will never have to be alone again. I promise, Famia."

"I love you. I love you like my sister and my mother and my friend." Famia looked back at the wall.

"Then say yes. Come with me and begin again, no?"

What to say? She turned and again looked into Nicolette's eyes. "Is it true that in France there is much chocolate?" asked Famia.

Nicolette's eyes widened in surprise. "Yes, of course. Why do you ask?"

"Because your eyes are dark like chocolate." It was Famia's turn to smile.

"How do you know about chocolate?" asked Nicolette.

"I just do," whispered Famia.

"Then come to France and we will drink *chocolat* with *croissants* every morning."

"Before, I was afraid. I am not afraid now. But . . . I cannot go with you. Not now, not . . . not like this," she stammered.

"Why not?" Nicolette pulled back in surprise. "Famia, you must listen to me. You may be in danger. You must have been running from something or someone before the bomb went off. And your memory should have returned by now. You may never entirely remember your past. *Ma petite*, the money you carry, perhaps it is drug money. What if someone comes after you? Please, Famia, come home with me. You will be safe, and happy. You will have an education. You will have a life."

"But I do not *feel* afraid of anyone. Is it possible that memory lives on the skin? To whom do I owe my life? I cannot go forward without looking back to say thank you." The words, filled with anguish, came out in a rush. Famia struggled to sit up. "What you offer is so kind, so good. It is more than I deserve. But the answers to my life are here, I feel it. I must wait for my life to find me. And I think perhaps I can be of use here. If Mina and Babrak will have me, I can help with the new baby. Forgive me."

Nicolette's own chocolate-brown eyes filled with tears. "If I ever have a daughter, I hope she is just like you."

Famia sniffed. "What happened to Paul McCartney?"

"I left him behind," Nicolette whispered.

"That is what you must do with me."

"Famia, you are not a horse."

"No, I am not as useful." Famia laughed. It was an unfamiliar sensation, but it felt good.

Nicolette held Famia in her arms for a long time. "Dr. Latouche and I were afraid that if we investigated your past we might have attracted the attention of those who mean you harm." Nicolette sat back and ran her fingers through her hair. "You are educated, you speak many languages, and yet you were running from something. It is a mystery. But perhaps now there is no choice. When I return to France I will contact the Red Cross. They have a long history of reuniting families. We have to be careful. Do you understand? If your family is angry, and if they find you, we will have no way of protecting you."

Famia nodded. "Forgive me?"

"My dear, yes, of course. This stony land has a strange hold on people. I feel it, too. *Bonne chance, ma petite.*" Nicolette hugged her tight.

Chapter 24

One Year Later

"Look what I have!" With a great sweep of her arm, Mina pulled off her *burka*, hung it on a hook, then dug deep into the pocket of her skirt. Smiling, she held a white, almost egg-shaped object in the palm of her hand.

"What is it?" Famia looked up from her embroidery.

"It's soap. It is made in Kandahar from the oil of wild almonds. Smell. The father of a patient gave it to me. We will share it." Mina held it up as Famia took a deep breath.

"Lovely." Famia laughed.

Baby Toran was crying, but before Mina could reach him Famia scooped him up and rocked him in her arms.

"You fuss over that baby too much!" Smiling, Mina pushed aside the embroidery that Famia had been working on and plunked down a bag of mulberries and pomegranates.

"I love him as if he were mine, but I hope the next one is a girl. *Kalaq kalaq kalaa*," sang Famia. Toran let out a great baby chuckle as Famia tickled him under the chin. The announcement that a second baby was on the way had been cause for great celebration.

"What shall I call the next one if it is a girl? Famia?" Mina laughed.

"No, call her Tamanna," said Famia as she plopped Toran onto a puffy *toshak* and began sorting the fruit.

"Tamanna, why that name?"

Famia looked up. "I'm not sure. It's just a nice name, don't you think?" she said.

Mina and Babrak had gone to great lengths to keep her safe. Mina had told everyone in the bathhouse and in her sewing circle that Famia was her little sister from Kabul. In that way, her husband Babrak could be seen walking with his "sister-in-law" without inciting gossip. The only time Famia walked alone was on her way to the school, but there were many women out in the morning in their *burkas*, most shopping, some visiting the bathhouse.

Famia had tried to repay Mina and Babrak with money, but they would not allow it. Miraculously, though, a new brass tray and a set of hand-painted teacups in tin holders had appeared. A comfy daybed arrived. It was lovely to lie on it and hold little Toran as he drifted off to sleep. After that came a stove, and then a small television, and a DVD player. Babrak came home with a movie called *The Wedding Crashers*. They watched it twice and laughed even louder the second time.

Months ago they had turned the back shed into a new room. Now Famia had a place all her own to put her books. Sahdi, Rumi, Khalili, Khayam, Wafaqi, Jami, Tolstoy, Twain, and many more authors and poets sat on a shelf. There were history books, too, and a much-thumbed book on the stars. Already she was teaching baby Toran to find the North Star in a night sky.

They had worked out a schedule that accommodated Toran's care. Mina worked half-days in the hospital. Babrak taught at a school for boys full time but took care of the baby at night so Mina could study for the entrance exams to a midwifery school the foreigners were running. Famia worked as a teacher at a boarding school for girls. At sixteen, Famia was the youngest teacher in the school. She had taken a test and achieved the highest marks of a teacher applicant in the memory of the examiner. Children attended school six days a week, but Famia had arranged a five-day week so that she could care for Toran while Mina worked at the hospital.

Her memory had not completely returned, although she did have some recollections. She could not remember specific events, names, or places, but she could sometimes *feel* a memory. And sometimes she could almost *hear* a memory, like an echo. She told herself that she was an orphan. It was better to believe that her parents were not on this earth than to think that they had deserted her. Mina, Babrak, and Toran were her family, she was loved, that was enough. The gnawing emptiness that had plagued her a year ago was slowly ebbing. The hole in her heart was being filled with new memories, new plans, and a vision of her life's purpose.

Mina scooped the baby out of Famia's arms. "You must hurry. You will be late for school. Babrak will pick you up. Do not walk home alone. And do not give me that look," laughed Mina as Famia rolled her eyes. "You must stay safe if you are to educate the world." Mina often teased Famia about her plans to start her own school in Afghanistan. But really, Babrak and Mina believed in her, and that made it easy to believe in herself.

Famia kissed baby Toran goodbye, pulled on her *burka*, and, hugging her books close to her chest, raced through the house. They had a good life in Quetta as long they adhered to the rules, although what those rules were was often hard to fathom. The Taliban were near, warlords controlled the hills, and gangs roamed the streets, but in the light of day they felt safe.

Head down, Famia walked quickly through the streets. There were the familiar smells from the food-sellers— kebabs and baked bread. A waft of garlic blew over a wall. In the distance she heard the hum of the generator that kept an ice-cream freezer going. Ice cream was their favourite treat. Chocolate was her favorite flavor.

The sounds of fruit-sellers calling out the names of their freshest fruits and the voices of ragtag children playing in the streets were sweet to her ears. Sadly, many of the children were parentless—orphans were everywhere. They were hungry, and easy prey for the Taliban and their training camps, which populated the mountainous regions between

Pakistan and Afghanistan. Child soldiers were as easily picked up as pomegranates at a fruit stall. If only she could teach each one of these street children to read the Qur'an for themselves, then those who would distort the word of the Prophet would have less power.

Bubbly voices of little girls greeted Famia as she entered the school. She loved all the children, but one little girl in particular had stolen her heart. Her name was Roshina and she walked with a limp. Weeks before, Famia had caught other girls teasing her. Famia, a gentle, understanding, and loving teacher, discovered an anger inside her that day that she had not known existed. From that day to this, Roshina would wait for her at the school entrance and the two would walk into class together.

All the children welcomed her as she entered the classroom. Famia clapped her hands until the children quieted. Together they recited the class motto: *May God protect us. May God bring us peace. May God give us strength to continue our education.* "We will begin with arithmetic," she shouted over the din. Silence was immediate. And so the day began.

The children worked hard, and Famia often rewarded them at the end of the day by reading a story out loud—the tale of "The Little Black Fish" was a favorite. Today, though, they would sing.

"Simi, will you play your *dambura* for us?" Famia smiled at the tiny girl from the Hazara tribe. With her shoulders back and her head held high, Simi smiled and picked up her lute. The neck on the instrument was almost as big as she was.

"Now, remember the words?" Famia said to the class. "*I'm a friend of children. I am beautiful and eloquent. I have lots of words hidden in my heart . . ."* The children sang out, their faces bright with expectation.

༺❀༻

Babrak was late that day, but that was to be expected. His school was many streets away and he was often asked to supervise soccer games after class. Famia stood on the school steps and waited. There really was no rush to get home. It was Mina's turn to cook. They took turns making the meals. To her surprise, Famia enjoyed cooking. Even Babrak took a turn in the kitchen. His specialty was *mantoo*, a delicious mixture of beef and garlic, coriander and mint, layered with yogurt. The kitchen area was a disaster by the time his creation was completed, but no one complained.

After the evening meal Famia would prepare her lessons for the next day. Mina often chastised her for worrying that her students did not have enough playtime while she herself took none.

Now Famia poked her nose out the school door and looked up and down the street for Babrak. Tall yellow walls crowded the road. The sun was setting. There was a telephone at the school but none at home. There was no way to find out about Babrak's delay, but if she waited much longer it would be dark. She had no choice. Famia set off for home. The streets were narrow and poorly lit but still Famia walked on, faster and faster. Twice she tripped over the hem of her *burka*.

Breathless, she reached for the door and tumbled inside. Mina stood in the passageway, her face chalk-white. Toran, cranky and ready for bed, was in her arms.

"Mina, what is wrong?" Famia let the door swing shut. She pulled off her *burka* and lurched towards Mina. "Are you ill? The baby. . . ?"

"Babrak was called out of class. Someone is looking for you."

Before Mina could say more the door opened behind her. Famia turned. Standing beside Babrak was a tall, elegant man, dressed in a long-sleeved shirt and Western-style pants, wearing a white, trimmed beard. He was old, his face wrinkled, his color faded, but he was handsome all the same. He carried a box in one hand and a package in the other. Babrak, his face normally so open and trouble-free, looked worried, almost pensive.

Babrak spoke first. "This is my wife, Mina, and this . . . is Famia."

The man nodded his head towards Mina but stared hard at Famia. Normally she would have considered him rude, but instead her heart began to bang in her chest. What did her heart know that her eyes did not?

"Come, we will have tea." Babrak stood to one side as the tall man walked into the front guest room. Babrak motioned to Famia to follow. Famia looked at Mina.

"Go, see what he wants. I will get the tea," Mina whispered in Famia's ear.

The old man, so refined and well dressed, sat easily and comfortably on the *toshak*. Babrak sat across from him. Only with Babrak's encouragement did Famia sit.

"Are you well?" the old man asked Famia. She nodded. "A young woman in Paris asked me to give you this," he said while passing over the box.

Nicolette! Famia tried not to leap for joy. Who else would send her a package from France?

"The young woman, Nicolette, asked many questions before she would reveal your location. She was worried that I meant you harm. I mean you no harm."

"I know that," said Famia. She had no reason to say that, no proof, just a sure knowledge that sprang from somewhere deep within her.

"I have carried that box a long way. I, too, would like to see what is inside." The man chuckled. It was a pleasant sound. The box was well sealed with tape and paper.

"Let me help." Babrak removed the tape with a pocket knife. "You do the rest," he said.

Tentatively, Famia peeled back the paper and opened the box. The cardboard wings flopped to the sides. She reached in and pulled out a stubby cylinder. "What is it?"

The old man smiled. "It is a telescope, a very expensive and powerful one, too."

Nicolette, how did you know? With all my heart I thank you. It had been a long time since she had felt tears well up in her throat, in her eyes, and in her heart.

"Do you know the story of Ulugh Beg?" asked the old man.

Famia nodded. She had told his story many times to her students. "Prince Ulugh Beg built the world's greatest observatory and catalogued thousands of stars."

"That is correct. What else did he do?" asked the man

"He founded schools for both girls and boys. I remember . . . inscribed on the wall of the Ulugh Beg Madrassa were the words of the Prophet Muhammad: *The seeking of knowledge is incumbent upon all Muslim men and Muslim women.*" Famia looked into the old man's eyes and smiled. "Peace be upon Him."

"Do you remember the person who told you this story?" The man leaned forward.

"No," she whispered.

"I was told that this might help you remember more." The man placed a large, colorful book before her. Famia stared down at it. "Your name is Yasmine," said the man gently. She heard a sharp intake of breath. In the corner of her eye she saw Mina reach out for Babrak's hand.

Yasmine, my name is Yasmine. Yes, that sounds right.

Slowly, as if each page were precious, Famia thumbed the pages of the book. She laughed at the funny fellow in a green suit. "Babar," she whispered. She felt a rush of confusion and then a feeling of complete calm. Doors in her mind began to open, some with a startling bang, others as if a mild wind were pushing against them.

"My family . . ." In her mind's eye they stood before her: Mother, Baba, Tamanna.

"They are safe in England."

There was a picture in her head—a beautiful woman lying in a bed. Mother. "Is my mother free of pain?"

"Yes. She walks with a cane, but she walks tall."

"Is my father alive?"

"He is not well enough to travel, but he has taken up his old position as a professor at Oxford University."

"Tamanna?" The name rolled off her tongue as if it were there always, waiting to be spoken out loud.

"She wants to be a doctor. She is a very quick student.

Yasmine, your parents were told that you had been killed in an explosion. They took the news of your death very hard. I think your father almost lost the will to live, and your mother—she blamed herself for bringing you to Afghanistan in the first place. Now they wait for you to come home." The man's eyes were filled with love.

She looked up into his eyes and saw her own. Mother, Baba, Tamanna, her family. There was so much that she could not recall, but the love she had for them, and they for her, engulfed her, surrounded her, and brought a peace she had not known for a long, long time.

"Thank you, Grandfather. I look forward to seeing my parents and Tamanna. But Grandfather, my home is Afghanistan."

When the Future Comes to Pass

Mother, Baba, and Tamanna left Afghanistan for Dubai, and then England, a month after they arrived at Kandahar Airfield (KAF). They were told that the suicide bomber had killed not only an interpreter and three soldiers but a young girl too, likely *Yasmine's* traveling companion.

Fearful that Tamanna might be sent back into the care of her uncle, and therefore certain death, Baba and Mother did not tell anyone that Tamanna was not their daughter. The birth certificate and the gold necklace around Tamanna's neck convinced the authorities that she was indeed the missing British citizen. Yasmine's eyes were reported to be green in her passport and Tamanna's eyes were ebony brown, but no one said a word. Perhaps the authorities knew, perhaps not. Mother, Baba, and Tamanna mourned the death of Yasmine in silence.

Mother underwent a grueling operation at KAF, followed by two more operations in England. After months of physical therapy, she was able to walk with a cane. In England she works tirelessly for an organization involved in building schools in Afghanistan. She completed a Ph.D. in Persian Literature, and is currently teaching at the university level. She plays bridge regularly with her friend Audrey Ashberry, and with her husband's probing, has recently taken up the cello.

Yasmine's father lost the use of his left arm. The bullet that perforated his lung left him physically diminished. Nevertheless, he became a tenured professor at Oxford University in England and a visiting lecturer at Yale in the United States. His book, titled *Interaction Between Islam and the Bible*, is currently on the non-fiction bestseller list. He is also a published poet.

Tamanna received the best medical care available at KAF. However, she had to wait until reaching England for her hip replacement operation.

Before leaving Afghanistan, efforts were made to get a coded message to Tamanna's mother that her daughter was alive and well. They do not know if the message was received. Later they heard that her mother died shortly after Tamanna left Afghanistan. The source of this information is suspect and the cause of her death remains unknown.

With a great deal of tutoring, Tamanna completed an undergraduate degree in science and immediately enrolled in medicine. She hopes to become a pediatrician.

Tamanna struggled for many years with guilt. She continues to mourn the death of her brother Kabeer, not the young man he became, but the boy who was stolen and so badly abused.

One night, fellow Oxford University students took her out to hear a stand-up comic who was a woman and a Muslim. "That was the night I learned to laugh," she later said. She has not yet married and says proudly that she may yet end up as what the British call *an old maid*. Tamanna shares a small cottage with two other graduate students a few doors down from Yasmine's parents' home in Oxford. She hopes to spend part of her medical training in a clinic in Kandahar City. She is happy and unafraid.

⊱✦⊰

After her meeting with Grandfather in Quetta, Yasmine returned with him to England for an extended stay. She sat in on Baba's lectures at the university and nearly burst with pride. She spent days with her mother in some of England's finest gardens. She and Tamanna attended plays by Mr. Shakespeare, and sat up night after night and wondered at the miracle of it all. "Did it all really happen? Is this us? Are we really here?" they asked each other over and over.

Yasmine took advanced teaching courses and received her degree and teaching diploma in a record three years.

In an English rose garden, on a warm summer evening, Yasmine told her parents of her plans to return home, to Afghanistan. They were alarmed.

"Baba, did you not feel the call to return to our home?" Yasmine placed her hand over his. "If we who have the most to offer leave, what hope is there for our country?" In truth, Baba felt pride in his daughter's love of their country.

Mother tried to reason with Yasmine. "It is too dangerous," she said.

"But Mother, did you not once return? Am I doing anything different?"

"Understand, Daughter, we lost you once. It was a pain I will never forget or fully recover from. And your life here, in

England or in any part of the West, will be free. You may choose your destiny." Mother's voice dissolved into a faint sigh.

"But Mother, that is exactly what I *am* doing," whispered Yasmine.

With tears in her eyes, Mother nodded and said a prayer: "*Du'a, du'a, du'a. Everything begins and ends with du'a. It is only by His Generosity that I have been blessed with such a wonderful daughter. Go with the blessing of Allah.*"

⟨══⟩

Nicolette married in Paris and became the mother of twin girls named Famia and Yasmine. She plans to return to nursing when the girls are in school.

Before returning to Afghanistan, Yasmine visited Paris and drank *chocolat* with Nicolette and played with the twins. She and Nicolette toured the Louvre and the Musée d'Orsay, cruised the Seine, ate crème brûlée in a sidewalk café, and stood at the top of the Eiffel Tower.

Yasmine has never entirely regained her memory. To this day she remembers nothing of Tamanna's fall down the mountain or the explosion. Oddly, she does remember Dan-Danny and the women soldiers in the FOB. With Nicolette's help, Yasmine found the e-mail address of Dan-Danny on the Internet.

⟨══⟩

Directly after the explosion, Dan-Danny suffered blindness and an acute loss of hearing. Both afflictions were temporary, although he was out of action for six months. It would be months before he realized that Yasmine had changed places with Tamanna. Seeing no breach in security, he kept the realization to himself. Dan-Danny signed up for a second tour of duty and, upon request, was reassigned to the same FOB. He sought out the driver who had been given the task of driving Yasmine to KAF. The driver suffered a broken nose. Tamanna's Uncle Zaman was also the recipient of Dan-Danny's flying fists. Called upon to explain his actions to his superiors, Dan-Danny apologized for losing his temper but smiled as he left HQ. Dan-Danny also told Yasmine that all the soldiers who had been so kind to her and her parents had returned home safely.

༺❀༻

After receiving her undergraduate degree and teaching diploma in England, Yasmine returned first to Quetta, Pakistan. She met and married Atal, Babrak's younger brother, also a teacher. Like his brother, he is kind and smart, can cook, and is a teacher. Yasmine and Atal now run a school in Kandahar City. They are in constant danger, not from the Taliban, but from those afraid of change.

Yasmine and Atal have three children. Their oldest daughter, Mina, now eight years old, lives with her Aunt Tamanna in Oxford, England, and visits her grandparents on her way home from school almost every day. She will take her Common Entrance exams next year, with plans to go to a local prep school the following year. During summer break she stays with her Aunt Nicolette in France. She is brave, smart, and funny. She hopes to return to Afghanistan one day and build bridges. She says that her two little brothers are pests.

◦❧◦

The strangest story, and one that cannot entirely be explained, belongs to Noor. During the period when both Yasmine and Tamanna were studying in England, Noor suddenly appeared at Babrak and Mina's door in Quetta. How did he find them? How did he know that Yasmine lived there, when much of the time Yasmine did not even know her true name? These questions have never been answered, but there are many such mysteries in Afghanistan.

Obedient to the very old tribal codes of *Pashtunwali*, which require one to give shelter to a traveler, Babrak invited the young man in. Tall, broad-shouldered, now with a short beard, Noor handed Babrak a large, carefully wrapped package. "The people of my village thought that Yasmine's parents were spies. They raided the house and took all they could. I rescued the Qur'an," he said.

With his hands cupped around a glass of green tea, Noor said that the *kharijis* had rebuilt the school in his village of Bazaar-E-Panjwayi. There he had learned to read. He had read the very Qur'an that he was just now returning. "I did not understand that it is Allah's own command that both men and women receive an education," Noor said simply and humbly.

"And so you did not rescue the Qur'an, the Qur'an rescued you." Babrak smiled.

Sheepishly, Noor grinned and nodded.

"I shall see that Yasmine and her family receive this."
Carefully and respectfully, Babrak took the covered Qur'an
in both hands and put it high on a shelf.

A polite young man would never ask about the welfare
of a girl, and so when Noor, stumbling and sputtering, men-
tioned Tamanna's name, Babrak was surprised but offered
Tamanna's news freely. "We know of Tamanna only through
Yasmine, but we hear that she does well in her studies and
wants to be a doctor who cares for children."

Noor nodded. "That is as it should be." He left the
next day in the direction of India. No one has heard from
him since.

⟨❧⟩

As for the country of Afghanistan, it is Baba's and Mother's
conviction, and remains Tamanna's and Yasmine's hope, that
with new insight into the workings of the society, the United
Nations will begin to listen to the people. Only then will
it be understood that this culture has served many well for
thousands of years, has often flourished, and will not change
on the timetable imposed by the West.

With Allah's blessing, peace will come to Afghanistan.

⟨❧⟩

There came a day when Yasmine and Tamanna sat in the
courtyard of Yasmine and Atal's home in Kandahar. Yasmine
had spent the day teaching in her new school and Tamanna

working as a visiting physician in a medical clinic. Exhausted but content, the two friends looked up at stars as bright as twinkling jewels. They sat together in the comfort that sisters share, sure of their love and loyalty for each other, their shared history, and trust in the future. Floating in the air was the murmur of Atal's voice as he read sleepy children a bedtime story.

"Do you remember the first English word you learned?" asked Yasmine.

"Ketchup," said Tamanna. They both burst into laughter, and in that moment they were girls again, kicking a ball between the two posts Baba had hammered into the hard ground of the courtyard, eyes filling with tears as Mother told stores of bravery and heroism, and giggling behind open palms as Baba recited poetry. The hard times, the fear, the heartbreak and loss would never be forgotten, but love for each other, family, and their country would triumph.

This is not a glossary, but it provides some brief definitions to help with the text. In many instances there is more than one possible definition and spelling for the given words.

Afghan—a person of/from Afghanistan.

Afghani—the currency of Afghanistan.

ahmaq—a fool.

Allah—God.

Al-Qaeda (also spelled **Al-Qaida**)—an Islamic movement founded by, among others, Osama bin Laden some time in 1988–89. This fundamentalist movement calls for a complete break between Islamic nations and what are considered "foreign influences." Al-Qaeda has claimed responsibility for many attacks, including the September 11, 2001, attacks on New York City and Washington, D.C.

ANA—Afghan National Army.

Baba—father, grandfather, elder.

Babar the Elephant—character introduced in a French children's fictional book, *Histoire de Babar,* written by Jean de Brunhoff and published in 1931. The English version is called *The Story of Babar* and was published in 1933.

bacha bazi—is a boy, fourteen to eighteen years old, who is dressed in women's clothing with bells tied to his feet and paraded out to dance at parties and weddings. This tradition is condemned by human rights activists and Muslim clerics.

Beg—*see* **Ulugh Beg**.

bride-price (*sher baha*)—the money negotiated between the bride's family and the groom.

burka—head-to-toe fabric that covers the body and face. A lattice or grille covers the eyes, allowing minimal direct vision and no peripheral vision.

248

buzkashi—popular Afghan game played by men, sometimes compared to polo as both are played on horseback. However, polo is played with a ball, while *buzkashi* is played with a dead animal. Games often last for several days.

campal—a blanket.

chapan—a silk coat with a sash.

chars—marijuana.

dambura—a musical instrument, similar to a long-necked lute.

Dari—one of two official and national languages of Afghanistan.

dastarkhoan—a cloth spread on the floor before a meal.

du'a—tends to mean personal prayer. The name is derived from an Arabic word meaning to "call out" or to "summon." This prayer is regarded as a profound act of worship.

ETA—estimated time of arrival.

FOB—a military's forward operation (operating) base, any secured position away from the main base. (In Afghanistan the main UN base is called KAF, or Kandahar Airfield.) A FOB may contain an airfield, hospital, or other facilities and is usually used for an extended period of time.

Genghis Khan—founder of the Mongol Empire who began the Mongol invasions of eastern Europe in the thirteenth century. By the time of his death, in 1227, the Mongol Empire occupied a substantial portion of Central Asia and China. He promoted religious tolerance in the Mongol Empire and created a unified empire from the nomadic tribes of northeast Asia.

Habibullah Khan (1872–1919)—Emir of Afghanistan from 1901 to 1919. He attempted to modernize his country and worked to bring Western medicine and other technology to Afghanistan. Habibullah was assassinated on February 20, 1919.

***Hajji* (*Haji*)**—title of respect given to anyone who has made the pilgrimage (Hajj or Haj) to Mecca, Saudi Arabia, the holiest meeting site in Islam. It is believed that those who have gone to Mecca and touched the cube-shaped building known as the Kabah have had all their sins removed from "the book of record." The Kabah is the most sacred site in Islam. Every capable Muslim is expected to perform the pilgrimage once in their lifetime.

Hajji Zeynalabdin Taghiyev (1823–1924)—philanthropist oil baron who built the first boarding school for Azeri (Muslim) girls in Russia. It opened in 1901.

halal—lawful or permissible according to Islamic law.

haraam—bad behavior, or actions forbidden by Islamic law.

haversack (British)—knapsack, backpack.

Hazara—ethnic group who mainly inhabit the Hazarajat region of Afghanistan, although there are significant populations in Pakistan and Iran because of the refugees fleeing the conflict in Afghanistan. There are dozens of tribes within the Hazara grouping.

hijab—type of head covering traditionally worn by Muslim women, but this can also refer to modest Muslim styles of dress in general. The literal translation, in Arabic, means to "cover," to "veil," or to "shelter."

imam—the leader of prayer in a mosque (place of worship).

International Security Assistance Force (ISAF)—in Afghanistan, troop contributors include the United States, Canada, the United Kingdom, Italy, France, Germany, the Netherlands, Belgium, Spain, Turkey, Poland, and most members of the European Union and NATO, including Australia, New Zealand, Azerbaijan, and Singapore. The American, British, and Canadian forces have sustained substantial casualties in combat.

Islam—based on the Qur'an (Koran), a record of the teachings received by the Prophet Muhammad. Islam literally means "submission to God."

Jada-e welayat—*jada* means street and *welayat* means governance. Together they mean the street where the court, and possibly government building, are located.

jihad—an Islamic holy war against non-believers or infidels (literally "one without faith"). The literal meaning of *jihad* is "struggle."

Kabul—the capital of Afghanistan, located in Kabul Province. It is over three thousand years old. Since the Soviet invasion of Afghanistan in the 1980s, the city has been a constant target of destruction by rebels or militants. It is currently in the early phases of reconstruction.

Kandahar Airfield (KAF)—also known as Kandahar International Airport and located ten miles southeast of Kandahar City. Built by the United States in 1960, it was occupied by the Soviets in 1979. The airfield has been maintained by the Canadian Armed Forces since 2006 and includes the International Security Assistance Force (ISAF).

Kandahar City—the second-largest city in Afghanistan, located in Kandahar Province. It is over three thousand years old. It is often called the birthplace and spiritual home of the Taliban.

karakul (QaraQul)—a breed of long-eared domestic sheep, which originated in Central Asia and have been raised continually since 1400 BCE. They thrive under extremely harsh living conditions.

khak—soil, grave, tomb, ground. There is no exact translation.

Khalili, Khalilullah—Afghanistan's foremost twentieth-century poet (1907–1987), as well as a noted historian, university professor, diplomat, and royal confidant. He lived in many countries, including Saudi Arabia, Iraq, Germany, the United States, and Pakistan. He was buried in Peshawar, Pakistan.

khariji—foreigner.

khoda-hafez—means literally "God look after you," and is a formal way to say "goodbye."

lagaan—a large pot.

madrassa—an Islamic religious school.

maharam—a male family member who may accompany a woman outside the home. Also in Islam, *maharam* are people to whom a woman, or man, may communicate freely, such as a mother, sister, brother, husband, and so on.

martyr—in Arabic, a martyr is termed *"shahid,"* which literally means "witness." Typically a martyr is thought of as somebody who suffers persecution, and dies, for a belief.

Mecca (or **Makkah**)—located in Saudi Arabia, this is the center of the Islamic world and the birthplace of the Prophet Muhammad and the religion he founded.

millie **buses**—brightly decorated public buses, most are donated by India or Pakistan.

Mor—the word for "mother" in the Pashto language.

Mora, Mora—words for "Mummy" or "Mom"; a term of affection, in the Pashto language.

muezzin—one who calls the faithful to prayer, usually from the minaret of a mosque.

mujahideen—a person who fights a holy war to protect Islam. This name is often used by Afghans to refer to those who fought against the Russians and then the Taliban.

mullah—a term generally used to refer to a Muslim man who is educated in Islamic theology. It is derived from the Arabic word meaning "vicar" or "guardian." This man is highly respected in the community.

Muslim—devotee of the Islamic faith.

naan (**nan**)—unleavened bread baked in a tandoor, which is a clay or mud oven.

naswar (also *nass* or *niswar*)—a type of dipping or chewing tobacco mixed with calcium oxide (*chuna*) and wood ash.

NATO—North Atlantic Treaty Organization. A military alliance based on the North Atlantic Treaty, which was signed in 1949. Headquarters are in Brussels, Belgium. Members of NATO agree on a defense as a response to an attack. In July 2006, a NATO-led force, made up mostly of troops from Canada, the United Kingdom, the Netherlands, and Turkey, took over a military operation in Afghanistan from a U.S.-led anti-terrorism coalition.

Nekahnama **certificate**—this document, more than the actual vows, is what makes a marriage legal in Afghanistan.

NGO—non-governmental organization. For example, Doctors Without Borders, UNICEF, and Save the Children would all fit into this category.

noor—means "light." It can also be a proper name, or used to mean "the light of someone's heart."

Northern Alliance—coalition of non-Pashtuns who succeeded, with U.S. assistance, in overthrowing the Taliban in 2001.

opium—the raw ingredient used to make heroin.

Parwan (or **Parvan**)—a province in northern Afghanistan, north of Kabul Province. Its capital is Charikar.

Pashto (also **Pakhto, Pushto, Pukhto, Pashtu, Pathani,** or **Pushtu**)—language spoken primarily in Afghanistan and western Pakistan. The number of Pashto speakers is estimated to be 60 to 70 million. Pashto is written using the Arabic script.

Pashtuns—the largest ethnic group in Afghanistan, making up approximately 35 percent of the nation. Most speak Pashto, although some speak Dari. Pashtuns are governed by *trabgani*, a code of behavior that stresses loyalty to family.

Pashtunwali—the Pashtun tribal code. Pashtuns are thought of as the most hospitable people in the world.

patoo—a type of shawl.

pediatrician—doctor who specializes in childhood illness.

Qur'an (Koran)—the central religious text of Islam. Muslims believe the Qur'an to be the book of divine guidance for mankind, the teachings of God as revealed to Muhammad by the angel Jibril (Gabriel) over a period of approximately twenty-three years.

rickshaw—two-wheeled vehicle, sometimes motorized.

rupees—this is the common name for the currencies used in India, Sri Lanka, Burma, Nepal, Pakistan, Mauritius, and Seychelles, and near the Afghanistan–Pakistan border.

"Shadow of the Sky"—description of an overcast day cited by the ancient writer Curtius, who recorded the travels of Alexander the Great.

shalwar kameez—also called *pirahan wa tonban,* this is a set of clothing that consists of a tunic over wide-legged pants.

Soviet-Afghan War—a ten-year conflict beginning in December 1979 and ending in May 1989. The Soviet Union supported the Marxist government of the Democratic Republic of Afghanistan against the Islamist Mujahideen Resistance. They controlled cities but not the countryside. Nevertheless, those in villages did not escape Soviet aircraft raids from above.

surma—also known as *kajal* or *kohl*, this is a mixture of soot and other ingredients to make an oily black paste that is smeared around eyes. It is thought to prevent eye disease and to provide protection from the sun.

Tajik—a group ethnically related to the people of Tajikistan in the northeast. There are about 6 million Tajiks in Afghanistan, making up approximately 25 percent of the population.

Taliban—Afghan fundamentalist Muslims (the name literally means "seekers of religious knowledge" or "students") led by Mullah Mohammed Omar. Most are Pashtuns who have spent their youth in religious schools or camps in Pakistan. They support al-Qaeda, whose leader is Osama bin Laden. The Taliban imposed strict codes of behavior and dress based on literal translations from the Qur'an. They prevented girls from attending school and women from working outside the house. All women were ordered to wear the *burka* and leave the house only in the company of a male relative. Men were ordered to grow beards. Kite flying, dancing, television, and keeping pet birds were just a few of the activities prohibited to the population.

Note: The term *Taliban* is often used to describe all the insurgents in Afghanistan, but there are additional players in Afghanistan that are operating against the NATO coalition forces.

tandoor—a cylindrical clay oven used in cooking and baking.

***tasbih* beads**—comparable to a Roman Catholic rosary, these beads are traditionally used to keep track of how many times one has recited Islam's prayerful recitations.

taweez—a talisman or a charm. One kind of *taweez* is simply a written *du'a*, or prayer from the Qur'an. They are used only for good.

toshak (also *tooshak*)—a large, often long, pillow made with heavy cloth and carpet backing. It is used to sit on and sometimes to sleep on.

Ulugh Beg (1394–1449)—built one of the earliest Islamic astronomical observatories, in the fifteenth century. It is considered to have been one of the finest observatories in the Islamic world at the time. It was destroyed by religious fanatics in 1449. It was only rediscovered in 1908.

United Nations—an international organization established in 1945 after World War II to promote cooperation among nations.

Uzbeks—minority ethnic group (approximately 6.3 percent of the population) mostly found in the northwest. Most are farmers or herders. Besides growing crops they produce high-quality *karakul* fleece and rugs.

330 BCE: Alexander the Great conquers Afghanistan and incorporates it into the Persian Empire.

50 CE: Afghanistan becomes part of the central Sassanian Empire.

652: Arab armies invade and bring with them Islam.

1220: Genghis Khan invades the north and west of Afghanistan.

1839–42: First Afghan war against the British.

1878–81: Second Afghan war against the British.

1901: Habibullah becomes king (assassinated in 1919).

1919: Third Afghan war against the British ends with bombing of Kabul and Jalalabad. British recognize Afghan independence.

1946: Afghanistan joins the United Nations (UN).

1979: The Soviets are "invited" into the country to keep order.

1980: The *mujahideen* fight the Soviets.

1982: The United States start to fund the *mujahideen*.

1989: Soviet withdrawal.

1992: Civil war.

1994: The Taliban capture Kandahar and Osama bin Laden sets up al-Qaeda bases.

1995: The Taliban capture Herat.

1996: The Taliban capture Kabul and rule most of the country. The Northern Alliance fight back.

1998: The U.S. launch missile strikes on al-Qaeda bases in retaliation for bombings of U.S. embassies in eastern Africa.

2000: United Nations imposes sanctions on Afghanistan.

2001: The September 11 attacks on the World Trade Center in New York City and the Pentagon in Washington, D.C., claim the lives of over three thousand innocent people. Al-Qaeda claims responsibility.

2001: The United States begins attacks on Afghanistan. Canada's military mission to Afghanistan begins soon after the attacks on the United States on September 11, 2001.

2001: Anti-Taliban groups sign the Bonn Agreement (a series of agreements intended to re-create the State of Afghanistan following the U.S. invasion). The Taliban government fails and Hamid Karzai is declared president of an interim government.

2002: Loya Jirga (Pashto term meaning "grand council") agrees to a new constitution. An election keeps Hamid Karzai in power.

2007: One hundred and forty more suicide bombings in this year—more than in the previous five years combined—kill more than three hundred people, many civilians.

2009: Taliban regain control over the countryside in several Afghan provinces.

Peace remains . . . beyond reach . . .

Acknowledgments

❦

It all began with the Canadian Forces Artists Program (CFAP). With gratitude to: Dr. John MacFarlane, program manager; Dr. Serge Bernier, president of the CFAP; and the entire CFAP committee. Also, to Ken Steacy, military artist, author/illustrator, and graphic novelist; and to my traveling companion to Afghanistan, the beautiful, astonishing, incomparable Althea Thauberger, filmmaker, photographer, and military artist.

Every book has it challenges, but along the way I met some amazing people, and most, if not all, are friends for life. High on the list of keepers is my publisher at Annick Press, Rick Wilks, along with staff Katie Hearn, Brigitte Waisberg, Susan Shipton, and Kong Njo. Such patience!

My relationships with Barbara Berson, editor, and Catherine Marjoribanks, copy-editor, go back longer than any of us want to admit. As always, thank you.

Most amazing of all were the new people who came into my life during this project. The women of Canadians in Support of Afghan Women, cited in the dedication, continue to be inspiring.

Famia Haidary read every word ten times over. Famia, I will remember your contribution and dedication forever. Roya Rahmani, human rights activist, and A. Rahim Parwani, author and journalist, came late to the project but offered insightful comments, suggestions, and corrections with unparalleled generosity. Mojo, your name is disguised but I thank you. I hope that in a future edition I can name others, now in Afghanistan, who generously offered their support.

Thank you Lauryn Oates, project director of Canadians in Support of Afghan Women and education specialist and human rights advocate. Lauryn leads a fearless life of integrity and adventure that leaves me breathless.

My thanks to those posted at Kandahar Airfield (KAF) and Masum Ghar (Forward Operation Base) in northern Afghanistan who took such good care of Althea and me—Captain Gail Sullivan, Corporal Greg Van Sevenant, Captain R.L. Hackett, Lieutenant Brenda Andrews, Master Corporal Stephanie Emond, Master Corporal Michelle Neilson, and Major Diane Kirby.

Thanks to the best e-mail friend I have ever had, Gail Latouche, deputy director of the Correctional Service of Canada, Kandahar Provincial Reconstruction Team.

And then there are my dear friends who read, commented, and told me the truth (you can stop that now): Dr. David Parsons, Linda Bronfman, Kim Zarzour, Christina Dockrill, Jennifer Kerr Hlusko, Kathy Kacer, Ann Ball, Linda Holeman, Donna Patton, Shelley Grieves, Linda Bellm, Nancy Sermon, Joan Viaene, Carole Dixon, Meg Masters, Eva Salinas, and, in Northern Ireland, Roberta Daniel.

As with every book I write for young adults, this manuscript was vetted by young readers. My thanks to Zohra Bhimani, John McNally, Holly Caldwell, Jack Caldwell, and Alaina Podmorow, the founder of Little Women for Little Women in Afghanistan.

Author's Note

My sincere thanks to the Canada Council for the Arts and the Ontario Arts Council Writers' Reserve Program.

The photographs, by Rafal Gerszak, were taken in Kabul, northern Afghanistan (Panjshir Province), and eastern Afghanistan along the Pakistan border, in 2008 and 2009.

With all due diligence, the material in this book has been vetted, pondered, and discussed by Muslims (both in Afghanistan and in the West), young adults, teachers and adults of different faiths, and editors. That said, if there are errors, as the author I take full responsibility.

Sharon E. McKay